The
CHARLATAN

The
CHARLATAN

William Hamilton

WEIDENFELD AND NICOLSON
LONDON

In memory of Connie

One

he austere, antique civility preserved in Edgar's London tailor's rooms made a new suit seem more like a dignified responsibility than an indulgence. A pendulum clock ticked imperial hours in air that seemed restfully faded, like the old sepia photographs of high-ranking Edwardian patrons embellishing the place. Septuagenarian Mr. Pollifax himself insisted on waiting on Edgar, even going down on one knee in the tailor's curtsy when his measuring tape demanded it.

"A black suit," directed Edgar.

"Would you like to have a bit of a stripe in it, sir?" queried the venerable tailor as Edgar sorted through black swatches with the hopeful, judicious air of a bridge player.

"No, just black," replied Edgar, exhaling a sigh, an effect not lost on a man as expert in subtle weaves as Mr. Pollifax.

("It was a mourner's sigh," he would much later tell his cutter, Mr. Nelson, "as if he knew all along.")

When the black cloth was chosen (a superfine mohair Pollifax seized up and cracked open like a fan with shiny old fists to demonstrate the stuff's tensile capabilities—this fabric could obviously withstand the most demanding funeral, the most rigorous mourning, the most violent, even acrobatic exhibitions of loss), Edgar, as if in need of relief from the dour duty of buying black, looked up and immediately spotted a bolt of gay checks lying on a high shelf like a sunning jaguar.

"Let's have a look at that," he enthused in the more British speech pattern London inspired in him.

"Yes, that's very nice," agreed Pollifax.

"I'll have a jacket of that," Edgar proclaimed with more pleasure than he'd displayed placing his black order.

Edgar's ideas about details for his check jacket were in recreational contrast to his serious attitude toward the black suit, which he left entirely up to Mr. Pollifax. On the check jacket he wanted the pockets at raked angles, gaily speckled horn buttons and a lining that Mr. Pollifax pronounced "roguish."

"Edgar, what does 'bespoke' mean?" Betty had once asked. Edgar was surprised by the question. He looked up from a handful of swatches Pollifax had mailed him and saw her puzzling over the word in Pollifax's letterhead.

"Pollifax & Pollifax. Bespoke Tailors."

"I don't know," he'd answered. After she left he saw why she'd asked: the wet ring left when she set down her Bloody Mary had circled the word.

"It's because you speak the clothing into being," Pollifax later explained to Edgar. "You speak, sir, and we make up whatever it was you spoke."

By the time Edgar had the explanation, Betty was no long interested in the subject.

"Poor Betty," intoned their acquaintances as Betty retired early, failed to show up or had to be escorted away. They gave Edgar expressions of sympathy and reassurance that came eventually to suggest approval to him. He'd earned what Betty's decline would leave behind, the Bishop fortune, one of the truly great wads of American dough. His stoical escort throughout twenty years of her ever-increasing disintegration gave his inheritance the dignity of succession. For the last couple of years Edgar had detected avariciously bright eyes in the doleful faces comforting him. When they sympathetically patted his arm after some fresh example of Betty's increasingly fatal-looking disinclination to go on, some of them felt as if they were copping a feel.

The fact that she'd come over with him to London surprised Edgar, even though he'd solicitously urged her to make the trip:

"Betty, the queen is coming to the thing," he had, for instance, told her.

"What thing?" she answered, her head bobbing on its stalk like a flower ruffled by a breeze. She was almost always in the same place now, sandwiched in soft white sheets and creamy counterpanes, floating in the lacy, billowing flounces of her already heavenly bedroom.

"The garden thing. The gardens the foundation restored (he didn't call it "your foundation" anymore) at Bridalbin Castle. The queen is coming to the opening."

"Neat," Betty had vaguely enthused.

That certainly hadn't sounded like she was actually going to go, so Edgar had said to that marvelous-looking young woman, all rounded and sticking it out, tongue like a lipstick:

"How would you like to come over to London for a week?" And she'd growled back her enthusiasm like a cat in heat.

Two more enticements, neither from Edgar, finally did inspire Betty to travel over: her trainer, Tommy Smithers, said there were a couple of good prospects—two yearlings and an unraced three-year-old for sale privately at Mr. David Small-Granger's stud—and then there was the Chelsea Flower Show. Horses and flowers could still bring Betty out, but what really convinced her to make the trip was a bit of mathematical calculation: it was five hours later in London than it was in New York, and if they took the Concorde, she might go to bed at Claridge's at a decent hour that was actually four in the morning and get a real night's sleep at real night for a change.

That's why his wife was back at Claridge's Hotel reluctantly blinking at an unfamiliar ceiling even as her husband was ordering a suit for her funeral at his venerable London tailor's rooms just off Savile Row.

*　　*

There she sat, grim as the queen of spades, in her bed with the waxworks of an untouched breakfast on her lap. She looked at Edgar as if he were a handyman fetched for an unpleasant duty. Edgar dropped the morning paper next to her like a suggested activity, but she just stared at him, or perhaps through him in that imploring way.

"You're all dressed up," she observed.

"Well, I had some business."

"I feel rotten."

"Can't you eat?"

The mention of food brought forth a flatulent mouth noise, one of several examples of behavior she'd preserved from her professionally tended childhood.

Her face looked so fine in magazine and newspaper photographs at charity events and far away places. That remove of photography made her look beautiful, rich, out of reach and better off than readers. They, of course, weren't, like Edgar, married to her.

This present imploring look didn't photograph. There she sat, a depressing reminder of present reality, lodged between Edgar and his happy plans like an orphan with an empty rice bowl looking at a jolly diner through a restaurant window. It was so illogical on her face, that pleading look. Her fortune was so big it disappeared up into mists and clouds. How could she look so bereft? Edgar, an avid materialist, found it at least unseemly and maybe even blasphemous, this yearning on the part of someone who had everything.

How could he know what Betty knew too well: that the more money you have, the more things you have to buy from those without it—dubious merchandise, often, like their opinions and their love.

"I think if you just take it easy today . . ."

"But then I won't sleep tonight."

"How about a Bloody Mary?"

"Yes."

"Hello? This is Edgar Barnes in seventeen-seven. Send up a bottle of Möet and a couple of Bloody Marys. Spicy. There we are."

"I just don't want day and night all mixed up. I always slept so well at this hotel, and in England, it's day when it's night and the Concorde gets you here so fast I thought that's how I could do it."

"What's that?"

"Get day into the time when I'm awake and night when I'm asleep. I've *always* slept at Claridge's, ever since I was a little girl. What can we do? I want to do something."

"Aren't you going to the hairdresser and all that?"

"I want to go on a boat."

"Now there's an idea!" Edgar was furious. It was hard enough juggling Camilla into his schedule when Betty was horizontal. With her up and about it would be harder still. He sighed so hard he had to turn it into a fake sneeze so she wouldn't notice. Edgar's attention switched to a more pleasant consideration: the soft authority of the fine linen and laundered fragrance into which he plunged his profile.

"The hairdresser takes all day," complained Betty with no "God bless you."

Betty didn't say it, but she didn't want to go to a hairdresser because the environment was too medical: the sheets, the sinks, the bright, sharp little tools. Was it last year she had that nightmare at her New York hairdresser? And was it a nightmare? Can it be called a nightmare if you're awake at the time? Couldn't she just have a river breeze in her hair instead of silver scissors?

"Maybe Tessa could come and Alexander and the Heskeths."

"I can't face them looking like this."

"You look fine, dear. I'll get a picnic and charter a boat and call Aeneus and Lolly and the MacKays . . ."

Heaping more on Betty's plate, Edgar knew, was how to ruin her appetite.

"Couldn't we just get a sight-seeing boat? I just want a little ride."

Her tone had become girl to governess, her request a weakling's plea. With a nod and a patronizing glance at her and his suit (which wasn't suited for a public sight-seeing boat), he conveyed the notion that while he would do this for her, it would cost him unpleasantness. Nanny's angry sigh informed the girl that what she wanted to do would be done, but that doing it would be a trial.

"Oh, never mind."

"Ah, yes. Put those down here. There you are. Thank you. Well, here's looking!"

What a grim beginning to a trip, thought Betty, holding the red glass glob. There was some peppery stimulation in her mouth and a pleasant entrance by the first dancer carrying alcohol to her brain.

"Forget about it. I'll just go to the hairdresser."

"You don't want to take the boat?"

She shook her head and had another soul kiss with Bloody Mary.

"Oh, well, now you'll be all set for the flower show thing."

Betty nodded. He kissed her and he was gone. One thing Betty always marveled about was what fun Edgar seemed to have with that damn money of hers.

Two

o die, as a rose, in aromatic pain," said Betty to a bloom at the Chelsea Flower Show.

"I think that's a tulip you're talking to," advised Edgar, edgy even though pleased by his quip.

The flowers were so spectacular to Betty she felt she could almost hear as well as see and smell them. She sensed two ethereal orchestras, one divine and the other damned, playing symphonies all around her in the silent sound of dreams. Whatever state she was getting herself into these days often had the not-always-unpleasant effect of making reality seem dubious and arbitrary. She was so moved it was hard to walk. She shuddered at the ecstatic rush of sensation the flowers ran through her. She swayed. She was, Edgar judged, just this side of falling-down drunk.

He grimaced and glanced at his watch. In another half hour he'd take her back to the hotel, knock her out with a couple of stiff highballs and take Camilla somewhere expensive. Tonight Edgar planned to make love to Camilla, real love, not the little she'd let him do in Newport. Tits were teen temptations, not good enough to keep the attentions of a man of his age and station. It was ludicrous, giving him just a little more each time, holding out. How could a mature rake like Edgar be falling for it? They were fine tits though, big, strong, opaque, tender tits. Edgar shuddered.

"Better not touch them," Edgar warned Betty, bringing her hand back from a bloom. She crumpled her hand and tucked it timidly at her throat. She looked at Edgar. He was impatient again. He was always leaving now. Or was it Betty herself leaving? Which was moving and which was still, Betty or the rest of the world? There was Edgar, sliding off, like her houses and horses and gardens—all of it slipping by as the great ship of her being disembarked, or was she the one left and all of it the thing sailing away?

Then, in a moment, the whole world seemed like a little thing she held in her hand, a sugared Easter egg into which she peeped through a tiny porthole. She held it to her eye. There, inside its sugared walls, stood Edgar, natty and impatient.

Either way, great or tiny, disembarking or left behind. Betty and existence seemed to be separating. She watched Edgar passing a regiment of African violets. What a clever, self-conscious dresser he was, thought Betty, but, then, he hadn't much else to do.

She looked at the bloom above his collar, Edgar's handsome, not entirely fine, head. A hundred lilies behind him nodded, urging her to continue her examination of the configuration of her husband's head.

What was wrong with those looks of his? The bones were all set for handsome. Was the color of his eyes too flat? What were the nuances that ruined the possibility of a heroic head? The cut of the mouth? That sheen of the skin? Maybe if he'd done something those looks could have focused around some sort of authority. He was an enthusiastic and handsome man. His effect in a room still stayed there with him a moment after greetings. But he didn't do anything except shopping, parties, and trips and this had left him just hanging there in his clothes. Edgar, Betty judged at the Chelsea Flower Show, was a bad example of a handsome man.

Completely blasted, Edgar was thinking about the same time as Betty tottered through the tulips. If she weren't got up in one of her "best dressed" rigs, people would probably step away from her.

Sighing and chattering away at the vegetation, she was getting to be a regular bag lady.

Accompanying Betty in this state was the grimmest part of Edgar's work. Glances comprehending Betty's condition were quickly taken back by discreet strangers noticing Edgar had seen them. Should he smile and nod at the double takes she caused, "Had a little too much sherry" unspoken, implied, or should he pay attention only to Betty, picking her drunkard's way through an invisible obstacle course, so they might whisper among themselves, "Oh, that poor man. His wife's tight, but isn't he good about it?" Or should he just pretend he wasn't with her and didn't know her?

Be patient, Edgar almost growled aloud at himself. A man who's waited twenty years should easily discount a mere afternoon. But he hadn't been waiting all those twenty years. It was only when he perceived the fact that she was nearing the end that his impatience had set in. The last grains falling through the waist of an hourglass look the most turbulent. After a heavy ignorance, not knowing the bottom is falling out, those last grains of sand suddenly seem to rush and tumble rudely past each other.

A consideration of the grandeur in which he and Betty lived admonished Edgar's impatience. He drew himself up and smiled in a wan and superior way, looking around for other visitors of quality at the flower show. Betty's wasn't the only limousine waiting for lovers of the lurid knobs poking out of the green all around them.

Edgar posed with a self-conscious intelligence, scrutinizing the bed of tulips. Like horses, they all looked alike to him. Edgar smiled when it struck him he'd spent much of his life with Betty like a visiting dignitary making military inspections of identical-looking platoons of horses and flowers presented at their best.

Betty did a fast little minuet with a pillar. Edgar caught her just before she tripped and went down.

"Maybe we better head back," he muttered ominously.

"Look at the horsies," she enjoined, oblivious. Nearby orchids bobbed in a draft. They were, it's true, like galloping horses. Betty probably wasn't sure which she was looking at, considered Edgar.

"Yes, horsies," he enthused, mocking her in a child's voice.

This exchange caused a nearby English matron to rise up from her study of a label and regard Betty curiously. Edgar gave her the grin that depicted his good-humored patience with an intolerable situation.

"Mrs. Barnes?" asked the stranger (calling it "Bonze").

"Yes?" chirped Betty with the eager, apologetic tone of a person whose millions fated her to be known by many more people than she would remember.

"I thought that was you, Mrs. Barnes. I am Rowena Wigmore."

"Are you running in this race?" asked Betty politely. Edgar took his wife's arm in a brace on his hip, a bar for the boozer to lean on, and gave a laugh meant to signal his wife's apparent confusion—thinking for a moment she was at the races—was a little joke.

"I'm Edgar Barnes," he offered.

"How do you do. Aren't they beautiful?"

"To die, as a rose, in aromatic pain," Edgar winced, hearing Betty say this again.

"That's enough," he was about to say, but before he could, the Englishwoman said, "That's Pope."

"Yes," said Betty sweetly to the stranger, " 'An Essay on Man.' " Betty's education was something that made Edgar nervous. There was probably nothing there, he often assured himself, but he, having no education, couldn't be sure. Edgar stretched his neck and cleared his throat in an overall gesture of thoughtfulness, as if literary allusions were bubbling through his head.

"I am Robin Bridalbin's sister, Mrs. Barnes. You know, the gardens you so graciously restored at Bridalbin Castle."

"Oh, yes," identified Edgar. "We're here for the opening."

"I shall see you there, then," fluted the lady, stepping away from them.

"Good luck," Betty suddenly nearly shouted, bringing up both her forearms bearing crossed fingers.

"This isn't the races, Betty, it's the Chelsea Flower Show," prompted Edgar sarcastically.

"Look at the crunchy little cymbidiums," Betty said next.

"Don't you want to just nibble them all up?" Her hands hadn't descended from her gesture to Lady Wigmore. Now they were two fists held up as if she were resting barbells. Edgar grabbed one arm, bent it down, turned it like a tiller to sail out of the public place.

"Let's get back."

"But I want to see everything."

She was unusually adamant. Her next flower show, Edgar considered cynically, would probably be invisible to her. He looked at his watch and decided to be generous.

"Another half an hour," he said.

"Look at *these*," she exulted.

*   *

Camilla knew Edgar was a handsome man, twenty years older than she, with a seriously rich and seriously ailing wife. Camilla had been through enough romances at thirty-two to value these qualities. Furious, as she was when the London fling turned out to be a dull matter of enthralling postponements no amount of apologies, florists and promises could dismiss, she even considered how someday she might herself be playing a vivacious Edgar to Edgar's wilting Betty.

She winced through smoke from the cigarette between her lips as she splayed his latest volley of roses in a vase: a dozen roses, one for each hour he'd kept her waiting today? They rose in glum and proper splendor on the mantelpiece. Yes, it was a nice hotel, but what a bore. Why hadn't he planned better? Someday, it would serve him right to be an old and helpless man, shiny and sagging and brittle—with teeth as easy to pull as peach pits—watching Camilla displaying the very same impatient indifference Betty must be experiencing from Edgar now.

Camilla had seen Betty, a handsome woman, all any man could ask for (unless, like Edgar, he thought he could have everything). "Shit," sighed Camilla, sibilantly exhaling smoke. Camilla was beautiful. Men like Edgar were the fate of a beautiful woman, an unlucky one anyway. Did she look thirty-two? Camilla inhaled dignity and studied herself in a mirror. She sighed it out and turned away. If only Peter hadn't turned out to be a genuine mental case or the baron less tied to the apron strings of his snooty old bat of a mother or Tim had met her the year before he did, she wouldn't be fuming and running up enormous phone bills killing time with friends in New York while both she and Edgar waited for Betty to pass out. How sick was Betty, really? Could a terminal case go to the Chelsea Flower Show one day and down to the country the next?

Even though it had been overanticipated, Edgar's arrival was somehow a surprise. It was much more fun than Camilla expected.

Pretty in a smile she was resisting, Camilla was pleased by admiring glances from men in the restaurant. At the nightclub they were taken up by Lord Somebody or Other, an old friend of Edgar's, who told flattering stories about Edgar as he worked his knee between Camilla's knees and sent his hand right after it until she dug her nails into his fat palm.

"Damn," he said to her, pulling the injured hand up.

"First the pound goes to hell and now it's rats at Annabel's."

"I'll say," she'd brightly replied.

It was fun, the night with Edgar, even though it had been so tediously delayed. His manners were better than she expected. He liked everything and everyone. He did things surprisingly well. He really did make love. Sometimes they just talked about it.

"Just try to tell me everything, darling," she said with real fondness when he got up at the crack of dawn to return to Claridge's, "so I can plan and not get stuck, ok?"

Three

 young man squeezed Edgar's foot through the leather, checking Edgar's new jodhpur boots with the dedicated intensity of a surgeon judging the extent of a tumor. Amazing, the nineteenth-century sparks you could still find in the gray socialist ashes of modern times. This youngster with his Dickensian London pallor, his obsequious manners and craft pride appeared to reactionary Edgar as wonderful as the dove bearing the olive branch must have appeared to Noah.

Edgar paid and tipped what he thought of as the "lad" and privately exulted in the way the creature backed away from him at a bow, carrying tissue and shoe box like an eighteenth-century courtier's plumed hat and gloves as he reversed out of Edgar's suite.

The boots, shiny and eager as hunting dogs' tongues in the field, flashed on his feet as Edgar donned a jacket that fit and felt as perfect as a lovers' embrace. He looked at infinities of his effect from three angles in the dressing mirror. He felt damn good, "smashing," as the old warrior race of Britons liked to tag their high spirits (a term probably kept from battle-ax days).

He'd had Camilla! Taxiing back through gray dawn he had chortled to himself in admiring congratulations. In the hotel corridor a white-haired functionary was returning shined shoes from a Santa Claus bag to the doors they'd been left outside the night before.

"Morning, sir," said the merry old night worker with a smile Edgar was certain bespoke an admiring deduction of Edgar's roguish escapade.

"Can you find me some tea at this hour?" asked Edgar, who drank an English breakfast in England. The shoeshine man went off to find tea. Edgar called him back and gave him a five-pound note. The old flunky gleamed his appreciation. Edgar felt genteel and magnanimous.

In his bath Edgar thought about Camilla. She really was a fine-looking young woman. He'd seen other men watch her everywhere they went. Should he marry her? She did seem to adore him. They'd made substantial love. Claridge's really was a superb hotel. The bathtubs were big as imperial mummy cases. But, then again, why marry Camilla? After Betty died, women as beautiful as Camilla—even more beautiful—would probably appear, arrive from hiding like wild African animals at a water hole, the huge water hole of wealth, the Bishop fortune. Edgar raised and lowered his groin, sending a tide down the tub.

It was odd how tea tasted fine for breakfast in London, but in America, inadequate.

"I love you," Edgar had snarled when he and Camilla were bucking in the rodeo of love, and she'd replied, "I love you too," in a cry that sounded just as false, just as enthusiastic and just as hopeful as Edgar's. Clearly, Edgar had found himself a real romance.

*   *

Betty did dress superbly, Edgar was reminded in the hotel lobby. No matter how cloudy her brain got, enough light broke through to keep her beautifully groomed and dressed. What a pair they made, crossing Claridge's lobby to the waiting, dignified old Rolls. Edgar felt he and Betty, at least to look at, were the flowering of wealth's possibilities, the point of it all—service, privilege, craftsmanship. He believed it was reassuring to bystanders to see him and Betty exiting Claridge's that morning, beautiful people, living beautifully.

"Hello, Pulmer," said Betty brightly to the driver who'd sailed her about England in titanic limousines since her childhood. She was clear as blue sky today. Edgar had forgotten there was a regular Betty behind the irregular one.

"I slept," she said exultantly, even giving Edgar a pat.

* *

If Edgar's outfitters preserved a bit of nineteenth-century London, Betty's horse-racing interests brought them to what was left of the eighteenth century. The cars parked in the courtyard of David Small-Granger's stud looked out of place before the rosy old stone walls, like seeing a digital watch or a cigarette and eyeglasses on an actor in a powdered wig and silk breeches awaiting his cue.

"Do you know you can't get it in England anymore?" David Small-Granger was speaking, to Edgar's delight, of a piece of ribbon looped over the gold signet ring on his little finger. The ribbon, repeating the worn armorial bearings on the ring, was new piping for the livery of Small-Granger's servants.

"Have to go to Italy for it now." To be where such a particularly exquisite proof of how the world has gone to hell was being aired sent a happy shiver through Edgar.

Lucky Small-Granger, he thought, shuddering from the goosing pinch of a shot of whiskey as they headed out by old battlements to the stableyard. Edgar glanced again at the man's armorial ring. Even though Small-Granger wasn't a lord, he was right where his genes had done their trading for twelve hundred years. Edgar decided it was even grander to be a mister in such circumstances than a milord, more subtle, like a man appearing in a dark suit instead of a dinner jacket who seems above instead of beneath it all.

The barnyard was a beautiful Palladian structure of roast beef brick and silvery stone. It was built in a world where gentlemen thought more of their relationship to the divine order of things than to the working classes. This was the glorious landscape of that top surface up through which Edgar had broken after a long, secret tunneling. Once here, he'd changed behind a tree and approached the others. Nobody but Edgar knew he hadn't been here all along.

Betty sat on an ancient stone mounting stoop, her elbow cocked back, her legs crossed and her fashionable clothes as correctly and naturally displayed as plumage.

Grinning functionaries responded to this stately visit of high strangers in a way that further gratified Edgar. "They're so much happier this way," he would later tell Betty in the car.

The groom produced a chestnut colt and led him around the courtyard of this elegant barn.

"By Rumpelstiltskin out of Filoli by Muckross," said Small-Granger, identifying the pedigree to Edgar who considered this information as pretty and useless as a magician's invocation. Betty's inheritance of the Bishop Stables ("The See," as old-timers called it) hadn't made a horseman of Edgar Barnes. Even though he patted an occasional neck in the winner's circle and nodded sagely in horsey conversations, Betty's horses meant no more to Edgar than her jewels and houses. They were merely beautifully valuable and high-ranking possessions among which he moved (he thought, rather handsomely).

Edgar squinted an inspection of the creature, remembering some of the things which had so often been explained to him to look for, and forgetting others: the shoulder was supposed to be a forty-five-degree angle, generous enough so the foreleg could stretch out front for a big stride. The legs were supposed to be straight from both side and front—what else? And who could tell what angle anything was as a nervous yearling pranced around just the stable-yard Edgar wished had been his own birthright? He looked at Small-Granger's hand cupped next to his whipcord breeches, the signet ring glowing in the breeder's palm like the seed of his ancient family tree.

A family and an education—could any of the people among whom Betty and Edgar moved imagine being there without either of these taken-for-granted advantages?

A second colt was halfway around the walking path when, with a crack that brought Betty to her feet, a door blew out of a stall and fell flat, followed by the hindquarters of a dark chocolate, almost black colt whose shoes actually struck sparks on the cobblestones of the little plaza now separated from Edgar's feet by his startled jump in the air. It was so surprising: a sudden, total pandemonium in a landscape one moment past as calm as a willow reflected in a still pond.

Small-Granger managed to grab the colt's halter and the animal froze a moment, testing this impediment before deciding how to escape it. The groom ran up and got a lead rope attached to the prancing creature's halter. The wild-eyed colt laid his head on its side as if to unscrew the rope.

"This is a devil!" said Small-Granger, once some order was restored. The colt threw his head over on its other side, eyeballing the groom's head as he worked the ivory shears of his mouth as close to the groom's ear as he could.

"Look out, man," shouted Small-Granger, and the groom did, thereby saving his ear.

"I don't want you winding up like Vincent Van Gogh," joked Small-Granger to the groom, who laughed ignorantly, Edgar observed, of what the master meant specifically, but aware it was a witticism. Edgar had never heard Van Gogh pronounced this Dutch way. He knew when to include something new in his own behavior and he resolved he also would henceforth use this guttural pronunciation of the famous painter's name.

"By an unraced Native Dancer colt called Wendyboy. I think he'll have to be gelded."

Small-Granger was talking instinctively to Edgar as the man of the couple. How could he know Edgar neither knew nor cared much about Betty's horse world?

"Oh, no," said Betty to Small-Granger, "you mustn't do that." She made a snipping motion with her long fingers.

"He's terrible rank, miss," confirmed the groom. Betty was petting the colt. It was a situation the squire found worrisome. This was a dangerous animal. Small-Granger was prudently considering his insurance policies—was he covered if his colt broke this American woman into kindling wood before their eyes? Edgar, meanwhile, was making up his mind to buy an old gold signet ring he'd looked at in an antique store on the Brompton Road the afternoon before.

The groom leaned his shoulder into the colt's to keep the American lady in the safe zone of the pivot in case the colt started up again.

"Get him on the path, Crawley," instructed Small-Granger, "before there's damage. I expect you'd like to see him at a better distance," he joked to his customers.

As far as Betty was concerned, this colt was bought.

Four

s easily as his costume had come to him for the trip to Small-Granger's stud, dismaying sartorial failure arrived for the much more socially important display Edgar was trying to arrange for his appearance at the party formally opening the gardens fertilized by Betty's foundation at Bridalbin Castle. Rejected neckties lay like vipers about his feet as he held further possibilities to his boldly striped shirt.

Why are there days when one's dress is an inspiration, when, reaching for the perfect tie, you get an even better idea, when you suddenly realize shoes you could never understand why you ever bought would be perfect, and then days like this where nothing works, where rejections mount around you as every combination proves to be worse than the last? Today, it seemed, Edgar's clothes would stand between him and the human race like a bad report card. He hissed through his even, stacked teeth at the last ungodly effect he'd arranged.

It had something to do with that little bitch Camilla going suddenly back to New York. "I'll see you there, where we have more time together." She'd promised, but it affected his internal compass, leaving him lost in his own wardrobe.

"I'm sorry, darling, but I'll see you in New York. Darling, it's got to be right for both of us, don't you think?" So many "darlings." Too many canceled any sincere meaning. Edgar pulled a tie out of his collar so fast it left a hot necklace. The phone tinkled.

"Hello?" said Betty, asking what was taking him so long by the way she said that one word.

"Be right there, darling," replied Edgar.

When uninspired, Edgar usually trusted good sense and wore the simplest, basic, classic formulations. But Camilla's departure reminded him he had nothing to expect from her. She could do anything she wanted in New York. She probably was, at that. Were there already a pair of drawers on the floor next to her bed? What did her bed look like? Edgar had never even seen her apartment. He snorted. He shouldn't be so wrought up over something that had only barely started. Edgar got as far as a gray suit and a white shirt toward discretion, then he revenged himself on such reason with cream-colored socks and a pink tie that called for attention, but had nothing further to impart.

Betty was startled by Edgar's creamy shanks crossed before him in the limousine on the way to Bridalbin Castle.

"Glowworms," she offered. Edgar's tiny spark of hope for the bold effect of these unusual stockings hissed and disappeared in a braid of smoke. His ankles switched places, as if that might diminish his mistake. "It will be mainly standing and walking, won't it?" he asked, signaling his own lack of faith in his ankle flash.

"You're all bright and pink," she said, now moving her condemnation, Edgar thought, up to his necktie. How could he have worn such ridiculous clothes? Royalty was expected. Edgar sighed often on the drive to Bridalbin Castle.

He felt his socks flicker each step up a stairway wide enough for a marching band. The earl, a limp, skinny bohemian, was dressed much worse than Edgar, which relieved Edgar considerably.

The earl was in green tweed, the hue of overcooked vegetables. Stooped and skinny, he looked like last night's asparagus spear.

"Dear lady," said the earl, "how do you do, Mr. Barnes." Braying platitudes, he conducted them through the first old hall, lined in the tin shells of departed knights, to a sherry with himself before a general introduction to the guests in the gardens.

"Or would you rather," he hesitated, "have some American. Yes?" He opened a cabinet glittering with bottles. "Here's Kentucky bourbon. And it really ought to be in larger glasses, don't you agree? Jumbos, jumbo jets don't you think? Yes, we'll fly our American whiskey in jumbo jets over our gardens. Do you know my great-uncle saw your original Jumbo the elephant at the J.P. Barnum circus? He said it was by no means the world's largest elephant. I don't know, of course. Before my time. But he said it was merely a large elephant, far, far from the largest. Uncle was in India, you see, so he knew the things, elephants. That's uncle."

Rows of ancestors sat in golden windows sightlessly watching the room.

"Now she's an interesting one," he said of another picture. "You see what was happening all along there, don't you? Degeneration —you can see it—aren't they an insipid lot, and then great-great-grandfather—that's him—married her, Irish, and things improved markedly. There's David, who, of course, wrote, and our prime minister—it's all from her. There was precious little and then the right cross and the family's right back up! She drank and gambled and died in a fire that took out the east wing—but she was worth every penny."

When he talked directly at Edgar, the earl's breath seemed to be blowing over the carnage of a ripe battlefield. Edgar could see in Betty's face the same fluctuations of suffering when the aristocrat directed his monologue her way. Betty and Edgar exchanged a glance, following their host down ancient halls. The man's malodorous breath had made a sort of naughty, giggling bond between them.

The earl had begun to show Betty and Edgar his own uninspired and repetitive watercolors in his library.

"Oh, it just makes me want to be outdoors," said Betty of a stiff rendition of green trees on brown dirt. Edgar checked himself from laughing out loud and patted Betty's arm, signaling he recognized the motive of her effort to get that breath outdoors where it could dissipate. She gave Edgar a conspiratorial smile.

"Yes, let's go outside and see what inspired all this," enthused

Edgar. The earl complied. He didn't stop talking as he guided them outside. Edgar squeezed Betty's hand. Sharing the adversity of the exhalations of the earl of Bridalbin was the closest Betty and Edgar had felt to one another in years.

* *

The fast and expensive airplane called the Concorde is like a small church. Passengers in two rows face the hymn board digitally informing them of their speed like well-dressed worshipers in the chapel of a very exclusive resort. They size each other up appreciatively and puzzle over the luncheon service laid out for them in luxurious, red-tasseled menus. Canapés, exquisite as rare stamps, are presented to wash down with crystal columns of lambent champagne. Raising this beverage, Edgar flexed his little finger, saddled with the unaccustomed weight of a small, worn, ancient gold signet ring.

"What's that?" asked Betty. Edgar's hand closed with the reflex of a sea anemone, disappearing the ring into his fist.

"What?"

"Your ring?"

Edgar's hand splayed like an asterisk a moment, then curled up again.

"Family thing."

"I've never seen that."

"You haven't?"

"No, let me see."

Betty rubbed the worn face of the ring with her thumb.

"Mayfield. My maternal grandfather," Edgar said in a voice close to a grumble he often used when making things up.

"You can barely see it. What is it, a flower?"

"Cinquefoil quartered on sable," slurred Edgar, "the Mayfield crest."

"But, Edgar, I never saw you wear that."

"You didn't notice. I just usually wear it sometimes when I fly, for luck."

"Then I hope you keep it on Saturday."

"Why?"

"Because that's when our new colt is running in his maiden race."

"What colt?"

"I bought him."

"Who?"

"That bay colt we saw. He's already at Aqueduct."

"Small-Granger's colt?"

"Yes."

"I didn't know you bought that colt."

"I bought him yesterday morning."

"You did?"

"While you were out buying that ring."

Edgar's ears burned in a blush. His thumb rubbed his ring rapidly. "Betty, this ring came down to me from my grandfather Mayfield. I always wear it when we fly. If you weren't so goddamn drunk every time we fly, you might have noticed it."

Betty was stunned by Edgar's rebuke. Once Bounce, her favorite dog, had been loose in the fields and come back with burrs so thickly entangled and matted in his silky fur she'd decided to cut away what wouldn't comb out with scissors. When she'd started shearing off the burred hair packs near dear old Bounce's faintly shining balls, the animal had begun a fierce warning growl, quivering his lips back over his suddenly cruel and dangerous-looking white hooks of tooth. She was shocked. Bounce, her intimate, bosom-close doggy, who put up with anything from her and gave back only love, had become a werewolf. This is how Edgar's slapping retort struck Betty. She looked at him, puffing wide-eyed, high up in his airplane seat. He looked like an escaped gorilla pinned against the wall by fire hoses.

"I'm sorry, Edgar," offered Betty. He squatted his head defensively down on his collar and continued to flick his ring with his thumb.

"Huggins Mayfield was ruined by the Civil War." He spoke ominously, staring straight ahead under thick, writhing eyebrows. "Lost everything, one of the oldest families in the South. They were planters since the seventeenth century and the boy was left with nothing; there was nothing left for Huggins Mayfield except his gentility. He became a courtier in the court of Maximilian of Mexico. He went up on the Alaska gold rush, but nothing worked. All he had to give my father was this ring, all that was left of five leagues of land in Tennessee, three hundred slaves and the ancestral silver." Edgar looked at Betty, but his glassy gaze went through her, to his vision. "The Mayfields only came to America because their properties were seized when they stood beside the bastard duke of Monmouth in the Battle of Bosworth Field."

When Edgar lied, it was perversely thrilling, a mysterious adventure for both of them. Where would the lie go? And where would it leave him once he'd spoken it? Did it fit among previous lies? Would this one parse with the rest? They were both moved by this colorful story arriving from the clouds, intact and detailed as a dream, while the numerals of the Concorde speed indicator jerkily danced higher.

Betty, embarrassed and worried she might smile, bobbed down to her glass like a toy drinking bird. Edgar, fidgeting with the family pride of his own hoax, did the same. They both grazed on their champagne in the supersonic silence.

"Edgar?"

"Yes."

"That's what I'll call the colt."

"What?"

"Family Ring."

Edgar stretched his neck and nodded an acceptance of this suggestion, which somehow successfully finished the Mayfield moment.

But the Jockey Club rejected the name Family Ring. It was already taken. Betty, sitting at her desk, made a face hearing this. She picked up a postcard sent from China while they were in England, looked at it and said to the man on the phone at the Jockey Club, "How about Shanghai Pagoda?"

Five

elmont Park," said Edgar. Something about the driver's reaction made him add, "Do you know how to get there?" Uncertainty belied the increasingly vigorous nod the chauffeur returned. "Go Midtown Tunnel," ordered Edgar in the remedial pidgin he employed for communication with foreign servants.

"Goddamn it," Edgar bellowed in his normal accent as the limousine went right by the sign for the Midtown Tunnel.

"It's back there, for Christ's sake," shouted Edgar at the thick, reddening male neck before him. "Go around the block. It's back there."

With more vigorous nods the driver, used to crude Soviet tractors in the Ukraine, suddenly muscled the unexpectedly compliant power steering and the big Cadillac lurched up on a corner of sidewalk, causing shocked pedestrians to jump back.

"What's up?" asked Betty, cheerful from breakfast drinks. Edgar was lipreading the obscenities hurled at them through the limousine's tinted glass.

"Stop the car," Edgar shouted. The driver only nodded and accelerated.

"Stop the car," repeated Edgar.

The driver did stop, in the middle of the avenue, causing cars behind to begin barking hysterically.

"I can, please, mister," offered the driver in a Slavic accent heavy as boots. Now horns were braying uninterruptedly.

"Go there," pointed Edgar, realizing any more complex command would leave them where they were. The chauffeur seemed past his crisis. He got them into the Midtown Tunnel. Like many breakdowns that seem about to unravel everything, this one passed into a mere snag.

"Why didn't you get Ozzie?" asked Betty in the frowzy Midtown Tunnel.

"He's at his daughter's for the weekend."

"You didn't even ask for him."

"I did too."

"No you didn't."

The kindergarten debate depressed Edgar. Why didn't she just take another pill or have another drink and leave him alone? He hadn't specified Ozzie, it's true, because Ozzie had an annoying way of deferring to Betty for final approval even after Edgar had given him a direct order.

Edgar heard first Betty's handbag, then her pillbox click open. She shook out a little beetle of a capsule, cocked her head like a communicant and tossed it back. Soon she was stretched horizontal, feet on a jump seat, head staring at the tabid gray felt of the ceiling.

They were passing the populous cemeteries of Queens. Edgar began to fantasize. Horizontal Betty in the long black car, the cemeteries—everything finally his.

He'd keep the horses, of course, in her memory, even though he'd never cared for the creatures: shiny, long-necked, rubbery dinosaurs. They had always appeared to Edgar as strangely nude and sinister things—almost erotic when you added the flashy racetrack lingerie of belts and silks, dwarf Latino pimps humped up on their backs. Somehow they were related to the cheap black hooker department of Edgar's imagination.

But she loved the horses and there had been so many wonderful parties connected with their racing friends. Of course he would keep her horses! He owed her that much. Besides, the Bishop Stables was one of the oldest still racing in America. Edgar's wealth gave him the responsibility of preserving such class and dignity. Edgar smiled at Betty's still remaining remains sweetly. This long black car was so much like a hearse. There she was, all laid out. He spread his mourning smile.

He'd keep the house in Florida and the apartment in New York, but he'd sell the rest: the house in Maine, the house in Saratoga and especially the farm in Virginia. Edgar loathed Bothwell, Betty's Virginia farm, more than anywhere else because it offered nothing for the mind, the spirit and the senses that hadn't to do with horses. Not only were there horses to be seen out every window in the fields, representations of them infested most indoor surfaces as well. There were horses on the glasses Edgar loaded with whiskey to forget about horses. He even found them crawling on neckties hanging in his closet. All right, he'd keep the horses, but farmed out somewhere he didn't have to watch them eat, which is all the species ever did unless they were harnessed and beaten.

Edgar regarded his recumbent wife. Betty was so sentimental about animals. Edgar decided he would give a million to something in her name: the Elizabeth Bishop Barnes Pavilion, Dormitory, Chair in Animal Sciences—something with her sweet, generous dignified name preserved to focus the gratitude of the future's beneficiaries.

Abruptly, Lazarus sat up.

"Penny for your thoughts," she said.

*　　*

"Oh, I was just wondering if we had a chance," said Edgar. Picking up the *Daily Racing Form* beside him, he stuck out his lower lip and squinted at the page.

"Of course we're going to win. Shang Shang," purred Betty. Shanghai Pagoda had won his first start at Aqueduct by eleven lengths, just a tick off the record time for seven furlongs, but today's race was the Wood Memorial, a very fancy race with the best three-year-olds in the East all entered. Edgar considered Shanghai Pagoda's entry in this race something Tommy Smithers, the trainer, was doing more to keep Betty happy than because he had any notion of winning. Having a colt in the Wood enabled Betty and Edgar to be actively connected to a highly important racing occasion, an entertainment trainers had to provide rich owners as often as they could, especially when their horses were faring as poorly as Betty's were this year under Tommy's training.

Edgar turned the pages to the section where various handicappers' advice is printed. Pep Talk was the universal choice. Of Shanghai Pagoda an analyst called Tricky Dick noted "too far up in class" which caused Edgar to chuckle.

"Pep Talk looks awfully good," sighed Edgar, as if he cared.

"I had a dream about Shanghai Pagoda—just now," said Betty with sudden fervor to Edgar. "There was a hearse too—a hearse in there somewhere."

Edgar gave his wife a felon's glance.

"Shang Shang was running against hearses," she continued excitedly—"and he won!"

"A hearse race," said Edgar weakly.

Six

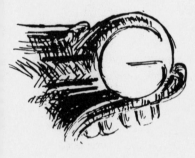

ood luck can be very demanding. Nineteenth-century impresarios discovered it can come as a prima donna, filling your opera house but driving you crazy. Tommy Smithers' first really "good one" was a plainly crazed, rank, eccentric colt the owner refused to let him geld. Shanghai Pagoda was particularly insane the morning he was to run in the Wood Memorial. Harold, the sparky little wino who was now on Tommy's payroll as Shanghai Pagoda's groom because the colt had formed a profound, aberrant infatuation for him, was missing. Harold didn't have the brains, sense, purpose or dependability to be any more than the hot-walker he was when Shanghai Pagoda first got the sweet, rank, alcoholic wind of him that led to the unnatural infatuation Tommy now had to patronize at a rate of two hundred fifty dollars a week. The whole day and night before Shanghai Pagoda's most important race, Harold was nowhere to be found. Typically, the born loser, Harold the hot-walker, dropped out when he was finally needed, when something had come his way. The horse was so crazed with lovelorn loss, he'd taken a nip out of his own shoulder.

Tommy'd spent much of the night searching for Harold in every bar and ditch in Queens without success.

When there was no Harold in the morning with his breakfast bucket, Shanghai Pagoda had ignited in his stall like a string of Chinese firecrackers. Tommy had restored calm for a while by putting Harold's bedroll, reeking of wine and bachelorhood, in the stall.

The big devil had immediately come down off the ceiling, dropped his nose to the bundle and nickered. But an hour later when the bedroll didn't arise, fart, rant paranoid advice and nip at a little, flat pocket bottle of fortified wine, the colt started getting crazy again.

Inevitably, the owners' limousine appeared, nosing its way toward Tommy's barn right at this difficult juncture. Betty and Edgar Barnes disembarked to a strange, violent bow from their stocky chauffeur, and ambled in the expensive, glossy, alien way of owners appearing in the barnyard atmosphere of the backstretch to Tommy's barn. Betty Bishop Barnes put up her arms when she saw Tommy, smiled and to Edgar's horror, kissed him.

This trainer has to go, considered Edgar. Tommy Smithers was a drawling Virginia dandy in Edgar's eye, from some bred-out old family. Lanky and tweedy, an infuriating inch or two taller than Edgar, the bastard belonged at point-to-point races, married to a trust fund, not in the tough, larcenous, real world of big-time American racing.

"Shanghai's fractious as the dickens today," said Tommy, giving Edgar the urge to kick him in the pants. "Fractious as the dickens." What the hell did he think this was, *Black Beauty*? Chippendale talk. It gave Edgar such a pain, especially as he watched Betty light up and play little princess when she heard it.

*   *

With the Barneses at Shanghai Pagoda's stall, Tommy Smithers was particularly aware of the glints of raw-wood wounds kicked into the wall by the colt, and of the dark patch of disinfectant on his shoulder where he'd bit himself.

"Shang Shang," sang Betty sweetly. Apparently oblivious to the shuddering, wild-eyed state of the animal, she was letting herself into the stall.

"What's that on his shoulder?"

"This isn't a good time, Mrs. Barnes," urged Tommy, his hand, like a riding aid, signaling to her upper arm, turning her back.

"He's hurt," she worried, moving again to step into his stall. Once again, Tommy gently brought the hen back from the chopping block.

"Wait, I'll bring him out on the lead."

There was no lead rope where it should be (had Harold, the hot-walker, taken it to go hang himself somewhere?). Tommy paused before he went around the corner to fetch another one. He signaled Edgar not to let Betty in the stall. Edgar nodded.

Betty, confident as Saint Francis of her rapport with the animal kingdom, reached for the latch on the half door. Edgar, fascinated by the coming accident, only watched until he saw Tommy returning with a lead rope. At this point the tranquilized heiress was stepping into the pounding zone. Edgar's facial expression changed to grave concern and he stepped after her to stop her in front of this witness.

"Wait, don't go in there, darling," said Edgar, his arm rushing in after her to save her. Quick as a black mamba, Shanghai Pagoda struck Edgar's arm, coming away with a croissant of cashmere and cotton in his mouth as Edgar screamed, causing every horse in the shedrow to lean out for a look, guilty cats to land from leaps all over the barn and run like minnows, and a pickup truck filled with the most expensive oats in the world to jam on the brakes.

"Jesus Christ," howled appalled, wounded Edgar. Shanghai Pagoda nodded, slashed his tail and pranced backward. Betty laughed as if Edgar were the fat boy at dancing school who just sat on a tack.

"Hey, get back," shouted Tommy furiously. He directed this command to Shanghai Pagoda, but he meant it for Edgar and Betty. What the hell were they doing in that stall? Are any of the other entries in the Wood being subjected to prerace circuses like this? he wondered. It was a question with a long footnote, pointing out the one time Tommy Smithers got a chance at winning a race like the Wood (a) his essential hot-walker (it galled him to consider Harold a groom) disappears, (b) the owners decide to picnic in his racer's stall, with fireworks.

Shanghai Pagoda, like a boxer between rounds, retired to a neutral corner and looked mean. Edgar was examining ruined tailoring and a small flesh wound. Tommy saw it wasn't serious.

Suddenly he noticed that Betty, like Little Red Riding-Hood entering her fateful forest, was back in the stall. She was still more concerned about Shanghai Pagoda's old wound than Edgar's new one. The colt was quivering like a rattler about to strike. Tommy got to her just before Shanghai Pagoda kicked her to confetti.

"Oh, Tommy," she chuckled coquettishly in his arms. Shanghai Pagoda kicked an ax stroke into the wall where Betty's head had been a moment before.

"Boom!" she said, and laughed. Betty was the only creature within twenty square yards of the stall uncharged by the bolt of panic the horse had cut loose.

"Honestly, I just want to pet my horse," she said, holding out her hand which Tommy retrieved before the colt severed it at the wrist.

When Betty felt Tommy's hand on hers, she gave it a little squeeze. The whole dangerous drama occurred to Betty as a school dance at which, somehow, Tommy'd cut in on Edgar.

When Shanghai Pagoda reared up, Betty looked at his underside as if it were something she was being shown to admire culturally. Tommy froze for a moment as the colt's forelegs swam in the air over Betty's head. Then he got between her and the horse and waited for the avalanche of doom, for sparkling dandelions of pain to appear as his skull was crushed. But instead of coming down on them, the colt somehow harmlessly rewound into a quadruped, totally, instantaneously calmed.

His ears, which had been laying back, mean as a pair of switchblades, pricked up like a sweet bunny rabbit's. He nickered and pawed the floor like an ambassador going down to kiss a hand. Magically, Harold the hot-walker had appeared among them.

"Good boy," said Betty, oblivious to what had almost happened. She spoke like a parent encouraging a new swimmer, "I knew you were a good boy."

Shanghai Pagoda stepped away from the lot of them and smothered Harold with kisses.

Seven

rom the barns at Belmont Park where Shanghai Pagoda was quartered, on the way over to Aqueduct Race Track for the Wood Memorial, Edgar wanted to stop somewhere for a more attractive sling for his arm, but there wasn't time. Even more disconcerting was the way they were stopped in the parking lot at Aqueduct by a young woman smiling at them like a Moonie in an airport.

"Mr. and Mrs. Barnes?"

"Yes?" said Edgar, stepping protectively in front of Betty's vast wealth.

"We'd love to do a prerace interview with you for television."

"Oh," cooed Betty enthusiastically.

Edgar's first reaction to any stranger's intrusion was negative. He didn't give quarters to bums, directions to strangers, opinions to surveys or purchase anything from anyone without a store around them. Moreover, he did not want to appear on television with his arm wrapped, as it was, in a scarf he would not have chosen.

"What do you mean?" he demanded.

"About Shanghai Pagoda, for the prerace interviews."

"Oh," Betty cooed again, at a higher and more enthusiastic pitch.

"I don't think so," said Edgar, in an admonishing tone that

meant to refer Betty to her wealth and its invitation to kidnapping, harassment and importuning strangers. This warning had been instilled in Betty all her life and could be signaled Pavlovian style by a mere tone of voice. Only Betty wasn't responding. She wasn't backing behind Edgar's protective wall.

"Great," she enthused.

"I don't know," continued Edgar.

"Where?" asked Betty.

Soon a camera was looking down on Edgar's wife from a man's shoulder like a pet vulture, while a dapper man wearing Pan-Cake makeup held a little microphone her way like a sugar cube offered to a pony. She was, Edgar noticed with surprise, gobbling it up. Even her pill and booze fuddle was gone. She spoke with enthusiasm, in a clear, precise voice Edgar was shocked to realize he hadn't heard in years.

"He's a competitor," Betty said, focused, poised, even standing in a way her dress designer must be applauding.

"I don't take any credit for picking him. He picked me. Honestly, Shanghai Pagoda just told me to buy him, so I did. When he broke his maiden—oh, I'm sorry—is that all right to say? That's what it's still called in the horse business when they win their first race—anyway, he did it with real style so when Tommy Smithers asked me about the Wood, I said you bet!"

The news parasites were smiling with delight at Betty's answers. Edgar was as disturbed as they seemed amused—what the hell was going on here?

"I know there're lots of wonderful colts in this race, but we're kind of special."

Everyone grinned and nodded at Betty's performance.

On the way to the saddling paddock after the television interview, Edgar was deeply disturbed. Beside him, Betty's radiant smile and lightened step suggested a change in the order of the world as he knew it. How could someone he knew so intimately suddenly appear in a guise unknown? Edgar was having trouble adjusting to his newfound perception of what the existentialists called the "otherness" of his wife. Where was the declining Betty, the near corpse whose memory he was already strewing with flowers and monuments? The goddamned glass eye of the tin idol, that Aztec gargoyle of a TV camera, had transmogrified her.

* *

The saddling paddock at Aqueduct is a little tropical green island surrounded by a walking ring. On it stand millionaires with their trainers and their friends. The tremendous mob searching for more clues than they've found in their racing forms gaze down on the lucky inhabitants of the little kingdom. The colts circle the elect like big leather ladders. Suddenly, magically, into this garden party stride tiny men in brilliant motley. After an elfin moment chatting with the magnificoes, these pretty little creatures are boosted aboard the animals.

It's probably as near as America gets to a truly ancient, corrupt, imperial Roman spectacle. The little green island of the rich surrounded by a parade of mounted dwarves in clown suits stared down upon by the masses from iron and concrete pens.

Whenever Edgar didn't bet on Betty's horses, the damn things won, and when he did, they didn't. This one had bit him, should he bet him? Any horse that had been through such folly just before a race probably had shot his wad, Edgar decided. Besides, Pep Talk had won the Flamingo, a real race. All this mean brute of Betty's had won was a little maiden race. No wonder Shanghai Pagoda was fifteen to one in the betting. But what a nice payoff fifteen to one could make—enough for a bauble for Camilla—if the romance continued, of course. No, it was a bad bet, Edgar ultimately decided. A thousand from Edgar on Pep Talk would bring back at least enough for a bracelet. On his way to the betting window he pictured Camilla, wearing nothing but her new bracelet. Girls— they were like primitive tribes in the good old days, reflected Edgar, easily bought off with trinkets and mirrors so you could begin to pound away in their rich mines.

Her breasts really were superb.

The gates opened and seven horses with bright-colored little stings on their backs ran down the fenced fatality of their illusory escape. Pep Talk and Shanghai Pagoda got right to the front. The first quarter was run fast, according to the clock—too fast? Down the backstretch, far away on the other side of the racing oval, the horses became a puppet show: only their silk, jockey-topped, pumping upper halves were visible; the bottom halves were obscured by the rail. Far away, these horses running down that distant rail looked like a long, strung-out, multicolored, slow drip. By the end of their passage down the backstretch, Pep Talk and Shanghai Pagoda had got far enough from the bunch behind to suggest an important couple fleeing from a pursuing band of paparazzi. Their distance ahead increased around the turn. They appeared at the top of the home stretch together while the rest were still deep in the turn.

The Roman roar of the many-mouthed populace got that note it hits when something special is up. Pep Talk and Shanghai Pagoda were in the last furlong, side by side more than a dozen lengths in front of the rest. Then, as if the clasp on Camilla's new bracelet suddenly gave way and it slithered off and went away down some hole forever lost, Pep Talk fell back into the pack running up on them. Shanghai Pagoda, still a dozen lengths in front, started slashing his tail with terrible relish, as he had when he'd got some mayhem under way in his stall. He was all alone, plunging along in big smooth stitches, sewing up the Wood Memorial.

*   *

Eyes and nostrils glittering red, all the complex wiring of his circulatory system embossed on the surface of his shining coat, a Honduran jockey looking like a grinning Aztec priest in Betty's black and tan silks on his back, Ebullient Tommy Smithers and (mortified with stage fright) Harold the hot-walker at his head, Shanghai Pagoda was annoyed that the metal in his mouth made it impossible to get another bite of Edgar's jacket. There were more people than air around him, many of them pointing glittering tools, whacking his retinas with flashes of light too bright to behold.

People they knew and didn't know congratulated Betty and Edgar. Edgar found himself resenting them.

"What happened to your arm?" people who hadn't seemed to have noticed it before asked Edgar, increasing his regret about the dumb scarf Tommy Smithers had produced wound around it (sky blue, sailboats, not even silk—where was paisley when you needed it?).

"Oh, nothing, little accident at the barn. . . ."

In the Trustees Room, golden fuzz in glasses, congratulations and enthusiasm on everyone's lips, Edgar wasn't feeling like the happy winner everyone seemed to see standing in his shoes. Stiff and unhappy, he had a grin lashed onto his face with barbed wire. This manic enthusiasm of everyone around depressed him because he couldn't feel further from it; he'd lost a wad of money, his wife had changed in a way he found ominous and the hero of it all was a horse that had bit him.

Betty was on the other side of the room. She'd let go the handle Edgar'd provided for her with his elbow and gone sailing about smartly on her own. Every time he checked, her head was thrown back laughing, or forward, listening intently.

At social functions she usually sat unhappy, often in dark glasses, and whispered please to go home if Edgar fell within range.

How could Edgar not be enjoying a celebration to which he was so intimately connected?

"Great job, Smithers," boomed Edgar in a voice he seemed to hear from another source.

"Thank you, sir."

"For Christ's sakes, Tommy, don't call me 'sir'—it's Edgar."

"Great, Edgar."

Edgar was immediately annoyed to hear Tommy use his Christian name.

"We're going to the barn, Edgar," announced Betty.

"I've got to get back. Why don't I just get a cab and you come back with the car?"

"Fine," said Betty easily, as if it didn't bother her a bit, as if it really were fine.

Alone in a tinny taxi, its upholstery rubbed shiny by butts and necks and shoes where it wasn't dirty shadows, Edgar found himself immobilized, clapped in the irons of gridlocked traffic. He looked into the adjoining vehicle, a station wagon, and found three children, one of them female, staring at him. They stuck their tongues out and tumbled over one another laughing when they saw how they'd got the angry, shiny old red face of Edgar even angrier, like the bulldog chained up in animated cartoons, outraged and outwitted by cats, little birds and mice.

Eight

rinning at the attention shown to Shanghai Pagoda on the "backstretch," the pleasant little tree-lined village of barns and cabins next to Belmont Park Race Track where the racehorses and their attendants were quartered, Harold rubbed the gleaming, fanning equine muscles off which he'd scraped and hosed the creamy surf of sweat after the race. He could still feel eyes on them, glances at the winner. He felt self-conscious until he had Shanghai Pagoda back in the privacy of his stall.

"You devil," he kept saying admiringly to the horse. "You big black devil. I knewed you was one. I knewed you was the champ, you big son of a bitch."

Back in his stall Shanghai Pagoda gave a happy shake. He was thrilled to have let go in that race and glad to be home alone here with his love, whom he was beginning to wonder how to bugger.

"Looky that." Harold showed Shanghai Pagoda three hundred and twenty-seven dollars he'd collected from laying twenty on the colt's nose. Harold cackled when Shanghai's lips peeled back and the colt kissed at the money.

"You big goddamn, crazy, fuckin' . . ." Harold cut off his accolade when he saw Tommy Smithers and the rich owner lady coming into the stall. Ever since the race, every person Harold had looked at was looking at him and smiling. Now Mr. Smithers and the rich lady were doing it too. Winning turns the world to smiles.

"Oh, Shang Shang," said Betty.

Shanghai Pagoda was spent and happy enough to fondle the lady's jewel-throned hands with his soft, prehistoric muzzle.

"Yes, Shang Shang," she kept saying to the great beast.

"Harold, have you met Mrs. Barnes?" asked Tommy Smithers. Harold's sharp odor, beloved of Shanghai Pagoda (perhaps because the groom smelled something like the Yangtze River carrying corpses of baby girls out to sea in imperial times), startled Betty who, by a turn of the horse, found herself suddenly standing over the little man she had barely noticed.

"How do?" said taciturn Harold, whose urge to interact with the human race had been—by a childhood of blank brutality, an adolescence in reform schools and an adulthood with his irregularly shaven cheeks often pressed to floors and streets—refined down to an occasional blow job in public toilets.

"How do you do, Harold?" said the lady in a voice as refined and inestimably high above his condition as her queen's clothes and genuine jewels.

Harold bet she had on pure silk underwear and ate caviar. He liked things this way. The feudal hierarchy of racing, one of the few intact class-laminated, undemocratic social structures left outside the military and prison systems (and they were corrupted in Harold's view by integration) suited him fine. Harold was a rat who liked to hide in the woodwork of corrupt, antique institutions.

"Wonderful," Betty kept saying, not only of the race, her horse and winning, but more—the backstretch itself, this little secret Arcadia hidden behind bushes, gates and guards right in the middle of prosaic Queens—and still more—a wonderful feeling she had that her life was changing.

This last reason for her exaltation was too wonderful to dare to reveal. She was afraid just by noticing it she might jinx or cancel it. It would be the best thing that could possibly come her way—

a change from the dull, unsatisfactory torment from which her only escape had come down to anesthesia. How nice it was to be here, how quiet and peaceful—barbecues beginning in the barn-sweet evening shadows, walking with Tommy, a handsome horseman in a hacking jacket.

She was afraid to admit to herself how well she felt, neither drunk nor hung over, neither drugged nor hurting. It was as though something that seemed as if it had been there all along had sent away a roomful of rascals and was standing with strong arms crossed in a doorjamb, watching them flee.

She couldn't stop herself from investigating her satisfaction, even though she feared doing so might finish it. What caused it? Winning? Yes, but she'd won before, all her life. Shanghai Pagoda? She did love the way this colt won his race, slashing his tail and stretching his stride when the rest had nothing left. Tommy Smithers? Yes, but not romantically. There was something else. She was glad to be with Tommy here and now because—she had it! Part of Betty's satisfaction came because Edgar wasn't there.

*   *

"Buy you a drink?" offered Tommy.

"I'd love it," said Betty, "but I don't want to leave. It's so lovely here."

Tommy had a bottle of Scotch in the little office and sleeping quarters he kept at the end of his barn. Betty loved her drink there, in the undecorated makeshift of papers, tack, horse medicines and minimal, unconsidered furniture. One of the problems of great wealth is the setting doesn't change much. It modulates between good and bad taste, between public and private luxury, but, like poverty, it's always around. Only out a tinted window or at the occasional breakdown of itinerary does it allow people like Betty to feel, as she did now in Tommy's office, "behind the scenes."

They toasted Shanghai Pagoda with unmatching tumblers and discussed the surge in the cost of insuring him.

"I don't really like insurance," said Betty.

"It's damn expensive," agreed Tommy.

"That's not why. I just don't like betting against yourself—that's all it is. They take your bet you're going to die or burn up or crash. You bet you will and they bet you won't. It just never seemed very nice to me."

Tommy was particularly baffled by Betty's complaint because it was well known a large piece of her fortune came from a gigantic insurance company.

"I know I'm not supposed to complain about it because Grandfather Williams started that insurance thing but" (here Betty made her startling little Bronx cheer). Tommy laughed.

"He was such a grouch," she reminisced. "No one was particularly fond of him. That's why he made all that money I think, because nobody liked him. If you have lots of cash it sort of makes people decide that's why they don't like you, because of the money, so they have to feel a little bit bad about not liking you just because you have lots of money, and they don't notice they might not have liked you anyway."

Betty had never expressed these thoughts before, not even to herself. It was coming from that stern, clean, prairie wife she'd found in herself, standing firm in that doorway, scattering the hooligans.

Now it was dark, and the acidic burn of the whiskey turned her thoughts to her inevitable return. The sudden, unpleasant sight of the big, morose limousine reminded her of the unhappiness she'd somehow left behind.

Betty gave Tommy a kiss, Shanghai Pagoda a pat, Harold a twenty and, with lights igniting in the windows of that pleasant place, she rolled out in the limo at a funereal pace.

Nine

n the apartment in New York, as in the rest of their residences, Betty and Edgar didn't sleep together. His suite, although luxurious, was a touch smaller than Betty's and lacked her view. Were their apartment in Pearl Harbor, December 7, 1941, Betty would have known of the Japanese attack way before Edgar. She would have seen the Zeros back when they were dots over the Pacific. Edgar wouldn't have found out until the concussion and flames.

She was the queen bee. Edgar could dart and menace, buzz about and undulate his stinger, but without Betty there was no honeycomb, no home and no life at all. Passive, she reigned.

Reduced to the grandeur of mere luxury, Edgar was extremely picky about his clothes and his wine and his food. How he was served, how it tasted and what was wrong with other people was all he really had dominion over, so it was where he exercised his masculine authority. Cooks, house servants, waiters, restaurateurs, drivers, sommeliers, valets and merchants were passed on the tyranny Edgar felt from what he scornfully called "Betty's bucks." He didn't particularly go after the gardeners, decorators, florists, artists, curators and scholars impinging on their life together because he considered them part of Betty's suite. He'd never bothered much about horse trainers on the same grounds. Edgar knew roses from daisies and roans from bays, but he left further scholarship in these matters to Betty and her appropriate attendants.

With a glittering brown fistful of whiskey, Edgar found himself glaring at the Degas. It showed a horse race forming up in Brittany a hundred years ago. Edgar had always liked this picture for a variety of specific reasons: it was extremely valuable, it was pretty and it had been painted by a man named Edgar.

But this particular evening, it only turned his thoughts back to the unhappy day at the races from which she *still* hadn't returned. Edgar was extremely annoyed. In the picture, jockeys, bowed over horses that floated up like flowers as they rode away from the viewer, gave their asses to Edgar. It was damn near ten o'clock at night! Smithers, the trainer, would have to go. Edgar's masculinity was growling like a watchdog.

All right, maybe he did bully too much in restaurants. Maybe he fell asleep too soon in theaters and snapped out certitudes too early in dinner conversations—but goddamn it he was and had been for twenty years the goddamn man of the house. "Goddamn it," he shouted aloud at the picture. He wasn't one of those homosexual walkers women like Betty so often wound up with, or one of those backbiting miserable bisexual bastards who fuck anything to live in pretty places.

Maybe their sex life had fallen all but off, but not because Edgar was carrying on with her goddamn flower boys, interior decorators and art experts. Edgar went to the phone, punched out Camilla's number again and listened to her insipid recording.

"Hi, I'm not in right now, but . . ."

Sexy voiced so anyone calling could hope for a piece—Edgar threw the receiver in its cradle and stormed out to the bar.

Why did he keep holding his breath? He was in the largest room in the apartment now, where they had cocktail parties. He was there because his anger was getting operatic. It needed a big room. He found he was listening for her—how stupid. She should be listening for him. He should be the one coming back late from fluffing Camilla's feathers in the henyard. Where did horse trainers do it, in the goddamn stalls?

Edgar shook himself like an appliance that needs a jiggle to be restored to function. He gave a snort of a laugh to cheer himself up and looked around the big formal reception room like a U-boat captain circling his periscope to discover what's making him feel afraid.

At last he heard the clicks of arrival. Should he go out and find her? Of course not, how awkward that would be! He could step into the archway right over there and boom "Hello, you're back" across the hallway to the vestibule where he could picture her lowering her purse and the collections of little picked-up things she always managed to acquire.

Let the bitch find him. Edgar sat down and opened a big book of modern painting. He snorted a laugh at the preciously repro-duced crap in the book, a laugh loud enough to reveal his position in the apartment. What madness had produced a market for this meaningless painting?

"Oh, you're in here," or "Oh, what are you doing in here?" was what he was waiting for. Maybe she wouldn't sound elated or delighted or even particularly glad to see him, but it would sound like a reaffirmation of their twenty years together. She was married to a real man and that must please her and protect her and . . . These pictures were just puddles of color; couldn't anybody draw any-more?

He heard her footsteps on the hard floor of the vestibule. Edgar cleared his throat and cracked his glass down on the malachite tabletop and held his breath again, expecting an increasing volume of her mincing footsteps. Instead, the steps went away.

"Is that you?" he called loud as a cannonade. He heard a door close. Edgar had the humiliating sensation of being a stranger there, in what he had never before doubted was his own house.

*   *

Betty phoned the kitchen for supper, flicked on her TV and prepared for bed.

"Here, madame," said cheerful Pilar with her tray. On the TV was just what Betty wanted: an old movie about nice people who didn't realize they were in love.

Of course she thought about Edgar, but elliptically. She thought how nice it was not to be thinking about him. The movie was excellent. What nice accents American actresses used to have! Her wand vanished the TV picture and she tucked in, like a child after a birthday party, her head filled with images from her happy day: Shanghai Pagoda in the stretch not pushed like ordinary horses, but pulled by destiny in a pure, graceful, glorious speed; her pretty new shoes on the escalator; the tumbler of whiskey in nice Tommy's nice office, faces, faces, faces, all smiling, all happy, all congratulating her; Shanghai's soft, supple muzzle on her hand . . . Lovely thoughts mixed gently into dreams as consciousness faded away.

A sharp rectangle of harsh light punctured her sleep. It was the doorway to her bedroom framing the silhouette of Edgar. Conscious again, she perceived aggression.

"Why did you just sneak right by?"

"What?"

He glared at her, her hand shading her dilated eyes from the light he'd unleashed on her. She saw him as the sharp, threatening black hole in the square of light. Then he moved in and dropped on the corner of her bed, sluggishly from booze, just after she managed to pull her foot away under the covers.

"I thought you might say 'hello' on the way by."

"What are you talking about?"

"You sneaking in after you spend the whole night fucking National Velvet out there."

"Edgar, go away."

"Well, did you fuck that preppie Chippendale Black Beauty trainer of yours? Could he get it up?"

"Get out of here."

Pulling back under covers anchored to the bed corner by Edgar's weight popped up Betty's breasts, toaster style, from her nightgown. Edgar saw them as two more big eyes staring shocked at him. He began to crawl toward her over the big bed like a baby across the playpen floor, happy to feel a charge run through his groin. He would have something to show her this time.

"Stop it," she said, batting at his head with weak little fists which felt to emboldened Edgar like the concussion of roses on the bared head of a young hero marching through the streets of a town just liberated by his regiment.

Her tension and defense excited Edgar. He dropped his hand to be sure what he hoped was happening between his legs in fact obtained. On many unhappy occasions over the last couple of years Betty had spent hours playing the flute to raise this cobra, and here it was all ready!

Why was she yelling at him to stop and get out? Was that what was making it finally work? What an ingenious device! Good for Betty! He got it at the right place and spiked in. To his surprise, instead of gliding in like a gurney into the operating chamber, it had to wedge through tight, dry resistance. She was screaming. Edgar screamed back like a rodeo rider and kept her pinned until he was delighted to feel it release.

Betty was weeping. When he sat up she turned away and curled up in a fetal position, weeping and weeping. Now what? He'd given it to her, hadn't he?

"Get out of here," she whispered with terrible fierceness. "Get the hell out of here."

*   *

Baffled, unbuckled, askew and poorly balanced, Edgar went through the box of light to his room. He heard a servant's door close in the distance when he got to his own.

In bed, nightmares, or a nightcolt anyway, that Shanghai Pagoda toppled down on him. How horrible horses are! Their legs end in axes.

Ten

here is a cruel moment between sleep and waking when you realize a hangover is about to pounce like a puma and you can't get out of the way. Dreams may cause fear, but they can't inflict physical pain, so you try to hide in ever shallower sleep only to be wrestled out again and again by the muscular monster you know plans to spend the day with its claws in every nerve of your body.

Too weak to fight, ravaged and murdered, Edgar couldn't even stay standing to pee. He slumped on the john, his cold sweated palm filled with a cheek that felt like a hot, greasy bag of nettles. An acidic rapier of poison piss stabbed through his chaffed member into the darkness beneath.

It was the sort of time when poverty has a certain greater appropriateness than wealth, because lying all day unshaven on an unmade bed, alone and groaning in a wretched room littered like a vacant lot, is the correct setting and circumstance for such misery as Edgar felt the morning after his fiasco with Betty.

He sensed some repressed manic state when the maid set the breakfast tray and newspapers before him. Edgar replayed the click of the servant's door closing in the unfortunate scene last night. They were always amused by trouble between him and Betty.

Edgar consumed every liquid on his breakfast tray and gruffly asked for a second orange juice. This time he could almost see Pilar gripping back giggles as she carried out her task. Servants spirits had probably soared when pharaohs fell down.

Sunlight brightened the pretty surfaces of the rather feminine library Betty had worked out with her decorator. Originally it was to be a sort of male reserve for Edgar lined with such masculine symbols as glossy leather books, vertical as erections, drawings of stallions, racing cups and nudes chosen by a decorator, but Betty and the decorator had gotten so charmed by their work it quickly became her room for days she made it out of bed. There were picture books of houses and horses and great families, including a couple of unauthorized renditions of her own.

It was too pretty for Edgar's grim mood. He shut out the sight of it with the morning newspaper.

Much more like it. Evil was reported on local, national, international and solar system levels. Humanity had again, for another twenty-four hours, been vile to itself, right down to its cells, and vile as well to everything around it, earth, ocean, sky—and space —every physical thing within reach. Edgar rooted for the calamities and calumnies bricked between the ludicrous advertisements showing smiling, physically perfect beings in brand-new duds strolling in elegant and exotic scenes. What a nice dichotomy the newspaper laid out on every page! Stories of utter evil mortared to lavish commercial visions of human paradise!

SHANGHAI PAGODA STUNS IN RECORD WOOD. Well, reflected Edgar over this item on the sports page, that ought to cheer her up.

ADD SHANGHAI PAGODA TO DERBY PICTURE read the marquee over a sports columnist's performance.

"Even though the Wood was only the British-bred colt's second race, it had Triple Crown written all over it."

"Triple Crown" was the mantra chanted all around them now. What if the colt did win the Kentucky Derby, the Preakness and the Belmont? wondered Edgar. What more would that do to Betty if the Wood alone could already change her so much?

Edgar took his second glass of orange juice to the bar and flushed it over the ice and vodka he'd loaded into a highball glass. It was ominously quiet in the apartment, as if sound had fallen off the edge of the world. Edgar sensed a huge conflict focusing on him. He drank and shuddered.

A tray with a delicious breakfast drinky and the sports page opened to the success story of Shanghai Pagoda occurred to Edgar as a good way to set things right with Betty again. Orange juice and champagne, a dash of bitters and a charge of rum. Perfect! He put the small vase of flowers from her desk on the tray. Would his reentry into her room remind her of his performance of last night? The chance had to be taken.

Past servants' peeps Edgar carried toward Betty the tray bearing cocktail and sports page which he hoped she would accept as a trophy proclaiming his apology and love. Why was it so wrong anyway? Edgar considered, a man making love to his wife? Why the screams and sobs? Why did she act as if he were hurting so? Maybe even, he considered as he reached for her doorknob, she was sore from the damn trainer.

She wasn't in her room. Gone. The place was tidied to the point of utter anonymity. It looked like the rooms behind velvet ropes in museums. Edgar drank the cocktail himself and considered where to go to hide from this painful and dangerous day.

*   *

Occasionally Edgar went to an office maintained for him in the executive headquarters of the Bishop Bank. In this office, Edgar reflected, bravely dressing back in his own room, was a sofa and a bar. He could lie there through the working day without eyes on him, without giggles after him, without feeling like a bad guest in Bettyland.

When he and Betty were first married, Edgar had regularly reported to this office and worked on a little experimental patch of Betty's money, but it hadn't flourished under his husbandry. No more money was released for Edgar's speculation. The piece he'd shrunk to a third its original worth (and this in a great bull market) was still under his control, but he left it in municipal bonds out of sight and out of mind. A certain amount of commissions on stock

sales plotted by the bank were paid to Edgar at this office, as if he'd
placed the orders, but these were really just tips clapped discreetly
into his palm by the bored, wealthy bank rushing by the factotum
called Betty's husband. In fact Edgar was an authentically poor
man, but what passerby would believe that, watching Edgar in
purposeful passage from limousine to skyscraper, an important-
looking scowl laminated between his perfectly cut and laundered
collar and his handsome hat?

*   *

The reception area of the executive headquarters of the Bishop
Bank had been redecorated since Edgar's last journey to his office.
Instead of evoking men's clubs and suburban estates the way he
remembered it, a place of paneling and leather with engravings of
English fox hunts and secretaries undoubtedly chosen for the per-
fection of their cute bottoms stooping to water ferns, he found
himself the subject of armored scrutiny in a mean, bleak antecham-
ber. International terrorism had apparently changed the image of
banking while Edgar was away. The space was half what it was,
the paneling and pictures gone, the receptionist who was formerly
installed at a desk floating in the middle of a pond of masculine
luxury was now a guard in a glassed-in box whose voice reached
Edgar through a loudspeaker which could apparently hear his.

"Yes," asked the broadcast voice twice as Edgar headed straight
to the door he presumed admitted him to the offices. The knob
didn't turn and the big door didn't even wiggle at Edgar's sally.
"Yes?" the voice had got a notch more peremptory. The plain
young woman under glass was glaring at him, hostile as a machine
gunner in a North Korean bunker.

"I am Edgar Barnes," retorted Edgar.

"Do you have an appointment with someone?"

"I have an office here." Edgar's attempt to bully the woman
sounded hollow to him.

"Just a minute." She spoke like a bored minor god from a cloud.

He observed her talking into some device with her sound
switched off. Something in this visible but unhearable communica-

tion caused her to laugh. Edgar suspected it was a joke at his expense.

"You have to wait a minute, sir." She didn't even look at him as her brightly painted lips synchronized perfectly with this announcement.

"What is going on in there?" boomed Edgar with a burst of black powder that made the glassed-in woman look up from her beauty magazine. Edgar slammed her glass with a fist. It was thick, silent, sullen glass, probably bulletproof. It didn't even thud.

"Stop that," commanded the receptionist.

"You get John J. Walker out here this minute," ordered Edgar, so thoroughly furious hairs rose on his wrists and at the nape of his neck. John J. Walker, chairman of the whole bank, was a name that could scare even through bulletproof glass. Now the receptionist reconsidered her reception. This guy might be big.

"He's not here either, sir. See—it's lunch."

Now at least she sounded vulnerable.

"Open that door," said Don Quixote to the windmill.

"What's your name again, sir?"

"Edgar Barnes."

She was scared when she found his name on a list. Had she made an employment-terminating error?

The door buzzed and Edgar pushed the vibrating knob. The great wood slab caved away. The receptionist stood in the flesh, smaller than she'd seemed behind glass, worried she'd done this all wrong.

"See they got somebody using your office whose like at lunch," she explained in a complaining way, quick-marching after Edgar who strode right by her.

"Well, you tell him to get his things out of my office right now," ordered Edgar without looking at her or any other worker as he made for his office with long strides, nostrils flaring. His door was locked. He stepped back, waiting for the receptionist to set things right.

"See, they're not there," she tried to explain; "they got a deal all spread out in there. They been working on it all week—they don't even let them clean in there. Everybody's out to lunch." Her voice was reaching a whine.

Edgar, to signal the value of his time, glanced at his watch. Unfortunately he hadn't wound it. On its face was some moment the world had already marched past. Wordlessly he stormed out of this resistant camp. Obviously the bank had changed. Instead of projecting the feeling of a cathedral of finance it now was a sanitorium for paranoids. Was there no longer room for gilded columns, paneling and gentlemen like Edgar Barnes?

"Down?" he asked the others on the elevator. They nodded like a condemning jury.

*   *

Energetic business roaches scuttled about the buildings and sidewalks of the financial district as if the nation's capital were food left out in a tenement. No one was letting Edgar in anymore—not Betty, not the bank, not Camilla—had he lost some password? Life had always let Edgar in to higher and higher preserves. That had been his great accomplishment. He dressed the way the businessman did—in fact, better—and he talked better and he had better manners. Was all this to be suddenly taken back? Rescinded? Canceled?

Edgar's briefcase might as well be a hobo's bindle. Wouldn't these three pinstriped musketeers bearing down on him absorbed in some tactical conversation be surprised if the successful-looking presence before them suddenly shot a pink palm their way and asked if they could spare some change?

At least walking seemed to preoccupy Edgar's hangover. Standing still, even for a light to change, allowed the monster to catch up and reinsert, so Edgar kept walking, a route defined randomly by green lights, until he found himself in Chinatown. Every window showed gibbets loaded with mass hangings of ducks the color of women in Palm Beach.

Chinatown wasn't quaint anymore. It wasn't a touristic artifact selling fortune cookies and paper lanterns. It had been rammed full of fresh immigration. The crowds eyeing goods were enormous and Chinese. No, thought Edgar, this wasn't Chinatown, this was Asia. He floated through the alien crowd on his palanquin of tall-ness and tailoring. It diverted him. He would stop for a drink here. This was the place for his brooding, not the Brook Club where men with similar clothes and similar problems could only remind him of his own troubles. Chinatown was the site to blow a couple of hot flashes of vodka off in the arid desert inside himself.

Chinatown. How had he got here? Gulliver asked himself. Was it instinct? Fate? The glittery bottle bank of a bar behind the windows of a restaurant attracted him. He entered and was about to refuse the big tasseled menu and indicate he only wanted a drink at the bar when he read, in gold on black, the name of the place.

"Shanghai Pagoda."

Edgar laughed aloud. He patted the captain on the arm and gave him back his menu. He sat at the bar and ordered a double Chinese vodka on the rocks. "Let the damn Chinese have the earth," he decided, delighted to think if it were to be taken away from him, it would be taken away from his kind, too.

Were they truly his kind? Edgar was fiction, not fact. He'd made himself up. His name had been Sonny in Oregon. Sonny Turchik. Moreover, Turchik was his mother's maiden name, which had never been legally appended, despite Sonny's arrival.

* *

Sonny Turchik in clothes he'd never seen new stood with two other fourth graders on Main Street looking at a rather fantastical sight: a huge, shiny, fire-engine-like vehicle that seemed to be in fact a private automobile, a great, open touring car of the twenties containing an old man in a white cowboy suit aglow with the same silvery sheen as his shoulder-length hair, drooping mustachios and triangular goatee. A black driver in black opened the door and this apparent archangel of cowboys emerged, placing a white sombrero on his head. On his elaborate boots were glittering silver spurs. Wordlessly, he began signing eight-by-ten glossy photographs handed him by the driver and distributing them among the boys.

Sonny looked at the picture. A horse rose on its hind legs. A young cowboy—was it this cowboy? Yes, of course, but way, way before. He held the same white sombrero in one hand and a pistol in the other. The cowboy in the photograph seemed to be wearing lipstick. It was a very old-time, very mysterious photograph. Even though the horse was standing on its hind legs, you couldn't tell what sex it was. Where some sort of organ existed on all the quadrupeds Sonny Turchik had ever seen was smooth, rounded asexuality he couldn't know had been airbrushed on.

"Probly a movie star from the old days," surmised one boy as they looked at their autographed photographs and skipped stones in the Multanomah River.

"Maybe just crazy," said another one.

"He sure is rich," said Sonny.

The local newspaper ran a story on the visitor, but no new picture, because the old cowboy would only allow them to use the same one he gave the boys on Main Street. It turned out he was indeed a matinee idol of silent movie days. He'd been born in the town. He came back for three more years without seeming to notice his hometown had forgotten him, every time performing the same autographing ritual on Main Street from his outlandish car. Then, he never came again. Sonny's mother threw out the four identical autographed photographs of the hero on his horse, but Edgar at the bar in Chinatown could see one clearly: the upraised horse, the smiling, handsome young star with his sombrero and pistol and the elaborate, post-Edwardian calligraphy of the fountain-penned autograph:

> *To Sonny with best wishes and a ki-yi-yippee from*
> *Edgar Barnes and Chieftain.*

Eleven

lease stop this for god's sakes," Betty heard herself saying aloud to her dream as she awakened. The dream and its memory both dried and vanished. She sat up, wide-eyed, still suspenseful from whatever agony assaulted her in sleep, and looked around her room, reassured by the banality of familiarity. Then she remembered Edgar's assault. She wanted to get out of there. She didn't even feel like having breakfast in bed.

Betty reached for the phone to tell Pilar she wanted breakfast in the breakfast room at the same moment a winking light signaled a call was arriving.

"Barnes residence," she heard the butler say. "Yes, is Mrs. Barnes there, Richard?" asked a familiar voice.

"Mimi?" interjected Betty.

"Betty darling, good morning, we're all going absolutely crazy."

"What?"

"About Shanghai Pagoda. It's so exciting we can't see straight. Are you coming?"

"What?"

"Tonight—you have to, remember?"

Even though they were first cousins living on the same block,

Betty had been dodging Mimi for the last couple of years. Mimi knew Betty too well for Betty to feel comfortable in her decline in Mimi's company. Mimi had always acted as if she had Betty's number, which particularly annoyed Betty because Mimi had such suburban taste. Betty had always considered her taste to be more elevated than that of her cousin Mimi. Once, when they were both teenagers visiting Grandfather Bishop's mansion in Palm Beach, Betty had overheard Mimi explaining the ancient Venetian chair Betty adored above all else in that ostentatious house to another girl:

"Isn't it a horror? And Betty always has to sit in it because she thinks she's the queen or something."

Mimi grew up filling her houses and apartments with sentimental stuff: porcelain animals mugging shamelessly, pictures that ran to lost balloons flying over Paris, and piteous portraits of noble animals from endangered species. Inevitably, there were endless framed photographs of people grinning on boats and beaches, on ski slopes and at parties and among ruins.

Pastel colors covered every interior surface of Mimi's domiciles. Pillows winked facetious needlepointed maxims from the laps of fat sofas. Betty considered all this with distaste. She realized she'd forgotten to refuse her cousin's party.

"Oh," she said, "that's tonight, isn't it?"

"Everyone wants to know all about Shanghai Pagoda," said Mimi.

"Yes," said Betty, trying to think up an excuse not to come to dinner.

"Remember when Pangborn won the Wood?" asked Mimi.

To her sudden astonishment, Betty did: they were two little girls standing amid woolly columns of grown men's legs, shouting, "Pangborn! Pangborn!" like the adults as their grandfather's colt was conjured down the stretch by a magician in black and tan whose arms pumped parallel, like a hypnotist casting a spell.

"Are you there?" asked Mimi.

"Yes. Yes, I do remember!" Betty answered, much more excited than Mimi expected.

The memory had surprised Betty so violently because for some time she hadn't been having memories. Depression fixes on the present. It becomes a limitless enclosure, inescapable and unbearably plain, that doesn't come from a past moving through to a future, but only spreads dully in an unremitting now. Betty's drinks and tranquilizers, her official drugs from happy-time doctors and unofficial ones from her hairdresser, were the only things that she'd found to vary her mental state. And drugs couldn't really move it anywhere. They could only bend, skew and color it.

Shanghai Pagoda had cut a clean line down this flat, hopeless perception, a rip she could hear as the crowd roared and he speeded up for a last furlong even faster than the first eight. Through the rip Betty could see the Kentucky Derby. Shanghai Pagoda had marked the first moment of future she'd seen in years, and now Mimi had said something that gave her a glimpse of the past as well. Reality was suddenly, thrillingly, realigning itself.

"Weren't we dressed alike?" Betty asked Mimi on the phone.

"Exactly," said Mimi. "Remember? Apparently there was only one black and tan dress for sale at Best's so we both wound up with it."

"That's right," exulted Betty. "Oh, Mimi—I can't wait to see you."

"Seven-thirty, and we're not dressing," Mimi told Betty in her smoke-and-Scotch-deepened voice which Betty always felt went with her cousin's penchant for heavy gold jewelry. Despite all Betty's reservations and annoyances about her cousin, Mimi suddenly seemed dear and charming.

Betty thought she knew her own mind as minutely and thoroughly as a prisoner in solitary knows his cell. Where could this bright memory of two little girls exulting with Grandpa at Aqueduct Race Track thirty-five years ago have been hidden? Betty looked around her bedroom—were there other memories?

One certainly was available: awful Edgar crawling at her like an alligator across the counterpane, sticking her like a rapist, honking and reeking pure monstrosity. He hadn't developed at all in twenty years. The only thing that had grown about Edgar was his wardrobe.

Betty gave Edgar's door a scowl on her way to breakfast. His good looks had certainly gotten less irresistible. Sexually, his drunken violation was the only thing he'd come up with in ages. Why did she ever marry him? Now he really was what not being had attracted Betty to him, what she'd been avoiding when she met him, a spoiled, well-bred ninny.

Where was that exciting lie she'd married? Where was the thrill she remembered on that distant day when she'd asked, "Where are you from?" as she lit up a cigarette in bed with him for the first time. Instead of drawling out one of those place-names that are all that's left of the country's original occupants the way every American man Betty met seemed to do, he'd sat up abruptly, collecting himself like a horse approaching a jump, and rattled off the first version of an ever-growing tale:

"I don't suppose you ever heard of Mayfield Island?" he began in a way that warned Betty more was coming. She shook her head. His face turned from her and he squinted, like an Apache scout spotting something far away that's going to bring wealth or danger.

"It's not called that anymore. My mother's family is Mayfield. You see after the war—the Civil War—her grandfather Mayfield was the only one left. He was thirteen. Everyone else was dead. There were twelve slave families, eighty-eight blacks, and just the boy to feed them on a looted, burned-out plantation on which he buried every living member of his family. They all lived in the old house—sixty-seven rooms, the rightful heir and the black families, burning Chippendale furniture to cook and paying for flour and beans with Georgian silver. Eventually, Grandfather Mayfield headed west to Oregon. I guess I'm the last remnant of that family."

It was an unusual answer to such a prosaic question. Over the next weeks he sent flowers and notes and telephoned. He did all the things everybody is supposed to do but no one quite manages. He did everything with assiduous correctness. Who has a more desperate attachment to details of authenticity than a liar?

Betty hadn't suspected right away. People did exaggerate and justify themselves to her anyway, as if they felt they had to puff up to the same grotesque oversize as her fortune. She thought Edgar was "trotting out the family spoons," as she called it ever since a remote relative from a penniless tributary of the Bishop family did just that at a flower show to prove to Betty they were related.

"I knew you'd be here and I saw your picture and I said to myself, 'that's our nose all right,' and I thought you might enjoy seeing the spoons that Floyd Bishop Wallop, your grandfather's first cousin, gave to Alma Hemming, who of course became his wife and my grandmother," said the possessed-looking woman producing six silver teaspoons from a big purse. Wondering why the woman brought all six spoons, Betty said, "Please call me in New York," and gave her a wrong phone number.

The bona fides produced by Edgar were more interesting to Betty than old spoons because of their effect on the man presenting them.

Edgar couldn't produce his whoppers without noticeable, physical side effects. His posture improved. His face blackened and grew intense. His voice got a nice, determined edge like a saw going through mahogany. Usually, lying aroused him, as though love-making confirmed and made magnificent whatever he'd said.

Did peacocks make their display when they felt lust, or did the magnificence of their effect cause them to get rapturous, like Narcissus? Edgar made Betty consider such questions.

"How many of your family are coming?" asked Betty during the planning of their wedding. Edgar had reddened and looked at his newly arrived bespoke shoes.

"What is it?" she'd asked, perceiving his embarrassment.

"My mother is dead," he'd said with the dull suddenness of a distant cannon. Betty blinked an apology for bringing up a sad subject.

"Torpedoed on an ocean liner," explained Edgar.

"I'm so sorry," said Betty, "is there someone else you'd like to have—didn't you say you had a brother?"

"My brother?"

"Didn't you tell me about you and your brother once?"

"Rich? Rich was killed in Korea."

"How awful. But I thought . . ."

"Please, Betty. I can't stand all this death. Just leave my poor family in their graves."

"Killed in Korea," continued Betty with a prompter's encouraging enthusiasm.

There was something in the room like that charge of static electricity preceding summer storms. Betty had kept questioning past Edgar's signals to break off the conversation. Although nothing had been said about it, now, finally, he knew she knew he was lying. He also knew she wanted him to keep lying.

"He got through the most awful part; the Chinese had just come in, crazy for war, for death. They did human wave attacks with this horrible off-key bugle noise and he lived through that—there were so many dead bodies all over—it was just so horrible, and then, oh, God, a goddamn tank drove over his tent at night—one of our own tanks which were sent up too late. Crushed him."

Betty had put an arm awkwardly about Edgar's shoulders. He was hot and breathing fast; the big lie made him blush and smirk. His skin was hot and his beard was grainy and Betty's maternal comforting, being slightly perverse since it was assuaging what they both recognized was Edgar's lie, made them look with forbidden knowledge at each other, like Adam and Eve. They made love on the rug that time.

*　　*

At her request after breakfast, both Betty's lawyer and hairdresser made room to see her in their establishments. Both were surprised, because the habit had been for them to go to her, not for her to come to them.

The hairdresser hoped there wouldn't be a scene. Cocaine had funny effects on Mrs. Barnes, but she seemed to expect and want it from him, even though it was, in his opinion, no more her drug than the ponytail was her look.

Despite pink leopard-skin seats ("The thing I love about leopard skin is how it's always been instantly passé," enthused Betty's stylist), new wave tapes and four expensive Warhol "portraits," the beauty parlor seemed to produce the blackest downers in Betty Barnes—even with a noseful of the best. The hairdresser still couldn't figure out why she screamed that time. After that, she asked him to come to her apartment. When she was screaming that time, she kept saying her feet were on fire. "Crazy lady, richer than an Arab. Oh, well, let her come and scream, she pays for it," considered the worldly hairdresser.

Betty wanted to see if she'd shy again at the salon. She wanted to test herself. The time she screamed, a fantasy had overtaken her. She felt she was trapped in a coma at a mortician's, unable to scream her way back to safety as wax was injected and paint applied. There she was under her sheet, paralyzed and mute, waiting terrified for the slap of heat on the soles of her feet as the conveyor belt drew her to the door of the crematorium.

"Mrs. Barnes!" exclaimed her hairdresser, a young man with big eyes and a curly little mustache. "Hasn't it been 4-ever?"

Betty sucked two hot little drills of cocaine up her nostrils. Her teeth went numb. A mild, enthusiastic euphoria ensued. There was no crematorium this time, only her hairdresser talking and clipping.

"One for the road?" he asked after. It seemed such naughty fun.

High and happy, Betty walked a few blocks through a bright, pointy world. People seemed so attractive! Ozzie, her sweet old chauffeur, nosed the car along in traffic, staying as nearly beside her as he could manage. Finally, she smiled at him and he helped her in for the rest of the trip to her lawyer's office.

Yes! Here was Marston Moore's office, a fort of mortared-looking lawbooks, in front of which he was standing, greeting her, a blank man so boring he was outside time. It seemed fantastic, what she was suddenly remembering as she noticed the pat of his shiny, corrugated, speckle-backed hand on her arm. Time, returned to her fore and aft, was becoming like an effusive and drunken and intimate companion, suggesting things to do and places to go, picking up the check and urging a spree.

Huge, awkward quantities of memory presented themselves to Betty's unaccustomed perception. Thoughts just lurched clumsily into focus. As Marston Moore, droning platitudes, took the few steps to his desk after having seated his flagship client, dozens of years ago became the present. Daydreaming Betty suddenly felt the springy lump of lust a boy was rubbing into her at a coming-out party. Harry somebody. Then, in the back of a parked limousine, that Harry had peeled one of her breasts out of its egg-white bra shell. Suddenly he climbed on top of her and started bowing up and down against her like an inchworm, the cloth-muffled bar of his organ working against her upraised groin until a shuddering groan announced he'd concluded. The car windows were steamed opaque. Harry was collapsed like the victim of a beating, his lap a mess of cold glue.

"So this portion of Princess Wilma Bishop von Schleswig-Holstein's income is returning to principal," intoned Betty's lawyer in the present. Betty returned to the period suggested by Harry in the car; it must have been about when she was eighteen.

From Harry's assault on, fornication occupied both Betty's waking and sleeping thoughts. What could it be like? At this period of her adolescence, Betty felt lust rise up just from sitting certain ways.

No boy she knew seemed to have the skills and diplomacy necessary to get on with actual fornication, leaving her temperamental and prone to tears. No wonder contemporary youth drugged itself through this awkward, painful period! What torment!

Maturity wasn't just imposing itself on her libido. It also, because she was an heiress, demanded certain legal rituals. She was sent to sign her will then, in this very office with this very lawyer. Was that all those years ago? How ludicrous time, her sudden, clumsy companion, seemed. Marston seemed so unchanging. His hands, though, had been smooth then, and clear, like ironed pillowcases in fact.

Imagine being sent to sign your will, to consider your death, when all you could think about was the end of your hymen! How strange that meeting had been. Back then, this same Marston Moore had talked on and on while Betty wondered if he could do it. She wondered that about every man she was alone with at this time. He was probably young enough, even though he acted old. He smoked a pipe and wore a three-piece suit. He was being assigned to an heiress he might serve all his life. He was trying to make a good impression.

He explained and explained. The debutante Betty stared at him blankly, thinking only of fornication. She was amused to consider how shocking he would have found her thoughts if he knew. But he kept on, outlining every contingency and safeguard he'd designed to keep her money huge and safe.

Somehow, she began to entertain the notion he understood what she was thinking about. She pretended he was understanding her screaming invitation to spread her and get it in, even though she was only saying mmm-hmmm every time it seemed there was a pause in his legal explanations.

He stood up for some reason and took a step toward some other cache of legal information and, astonishingly, fell down. He'd tripped over his chair. Falling is always a big surprise, and often a funny one. There was all that upright official boredom, twisted on the floor like a tweed cruller.

She stifled a giggle, blushed and ran to help the fallen counselor. Because it was a region she now habitually studied, she noticed at once Marston Moore had a hard-on. Her hand went straight to it and he groaned.

Had Betty touched any other part of him, undoubtedly Marston Moore would have extricated himself from this incident and finished this meeting by offering Betty his pen to sign her will. But her present grip changed everything. Betty joined him on the carpet, never releasing her initial grasp of this lever with which she was determined to open up her world. He had a button fly.

It did hurt and he was squirting way before she had anything like satisfaction but she was instantly proud to have done it, to have joined the sisterhood of fornicating women.

Marston didn't get up. He groaned and kept his eyes shut. He drew his knees up. He certainly looked silly, hobbled in tweed, his white flanks out livid against the carpet. His eyes were squeezed shut and his teeth were bared in a wince. Betty pulled up her sling of panties, wiggling them over her buns and smoothing her dress down in front. Her lawyer had now tipped over on his side, his back toward her, in a fetal position.

Betty left him like that. In the elevator, she folded her hands over the badge of her pain.

How crazy the world was! She had lost all recollection of this incident until now. And there he was! The very man, droning away as if nothing had ever happened between them, just as he had ever since.

"Fix you a drink?" he asked.

"No, thanks."

"What can we do for you?"

"I wanted to find out about divorce," explained Betty, clearly in the present.

Twelve

Shanghai Pagoda nickered and with his head gently hoed the oblong bundle in the corner of his double-sized stall. Harold's straw-embossed, red, wrinkled head emerged like a newborn from the orifice of his sleeping bag.

"Hi there, shithead," he said to the horse just before a bolt of adrenaline went through him. Today was the Kentucky Derby! Harold, by some mad miracle, was in the Kentucky Derby! He got up and stretched. The colt butted him from behind.

"Hey, cut that out," Harold complained happily, like a honeymooner.

Even at the derby, this predawn moment belongs to the animal half of racing as completely as the race itself seems to belong to the human half. A pet rooster was crowing, horse piss was steaming, dogs were yawning and checking their territories.

The media, the public, the owners and the jockeys were still in bed. Trainers came by to make sure things were all right. There were fifteen trainers for sixteen horses (Napa Valley and Uncle Alex, trained by the same man, were coupled in the betting). The trainers ranged in age from thirty-one to eighty. The eighty-year-old was the only one not being goosed by flashes of adrenaline every so often. (He, too, was excited though. His silky old skin wore pink caps on his cheekbones.) These men worried about what they'd find in the stalls. Were eyes bright? Ears perking? Was the sheen still on the coat, or was it gone to the matte finish of malady? Finally their hands went down the familiar shapes of the delicate stalks that held up the thousand pounds of beast.

Once you'd suffered the ax stroke of the four A.M. alarm and wrenched yourself from the peace most of mankind was enjoying, dressed and got to the stables, it wasn't so bad. It was peaceful. It was barnyard. This particular day was even better. There were grins on grooms like the ones on Christmas kids. Hell, the goddamn Kentucky Derby was a piece of American history!

Harold shaved and combed his red hair up into a marquee over his corrugated forehead. Checking his effect from different angles, he could see how he looked sort of like Steve McQueen in a way, and James Cagney in a way and John Travolta in a Clint Eastwood sort of way. New clothes give off a tangy odor particularly apparent to those who rarely experience them. Harold sniffed his spanking new trosseau: Jockey underpants and undershirt, of course, because of the name (even though they cost more than Fruit of the Loom's), a two-tone Western shirt, double-knit stockman's trousers—he even pared his toenails for entry into the sixty-three, ninety-five cowboy boots.

"Some shit," Harold complimented himself sibilantly in the mirror. He walked a little awkwardly in this brand-new rig, unaware he'd left the price tags on.

An enterprising reporter appeared as dawn obviated the bare bulbs illuminating the stalls.

"You sleep with Shanghai Pagoda?" asked the reporter.

"Yes, sir," Harold answered, going about his business nervously. When strange men write in notepads about you, Harold had learned the hard way, you often wind up behind bars.

"Why, Harold?" asked the reporter, grinning. A man's grin, Harold had also learned the hard way, didn't always mean he was going to be nice to you.

"He likes it."

"Keeps him calm?"

"Yes, sir."

"Have you always slept with horses, Harold?"

"No, sir. Just him."

"How did it start?"

"Just did."

"He's a difficult colt I hear."

Harold smiled at Shanghai Pagoda. So did the reporter. As if this were a cue, the colt tried to bite the journalist. It pleased Harold even though he yelled, "Hey, steady there!" The colt had put Harold back in charge.

"I think it's better you clear out now, what with this race and all," said Harold to the educated stranger. The reporter left. Harold patted Shanghai on the neck and even put his cheek to that long smooth muscle, utterly happy and amazed at all this animal had brought him.

"Lord Shiva Appears as a Horse to the Wino Ex-Con Hotwalker" would be the title of this scene in the dawn stall had it been painted in Rajputana, in the sixteenth century.

"How is he?" asked Tommy, more to himself than Harold, picking up Shanghai's feet for a look.

"Real good. Did good," said Harold of his charge's breakfast. They both looked at Shanghai Pagoda. The horse, like all domesticated beasts, accepted this scrutiny with self-conscious resignation. Then he nipped at Tommy, got an admonitory slap from Harold, pricked his ears and pawed the floor to remind mankind he was there because he'd been captured. He was ready. Tommy grinned as he considered it. The hero was ready again to act out a ritual escape, leading a spooked and wearying herd of young studs down that pass between the fence and the howling cliff of humanity.

Tommy turned his attention to Harold. "Are you going to rub your horse dressed like that?" he asked like a mother whose child has dressed for Sunday school too soon. Harold blushed. He should have waited! Harold looked guiltily at his splendid clothes. It was just dawn; the race wasn't until the end of the afternoon.

"I was just trying for size," said Harold, glad Tommy had spotted his gaffe before his peers got on him.

It seemed a shame to let his brand-new underwear suffer the association of his regular clothes, but Harold correctly suspected this day would be so busy, he better leave them on to save himself time.

*   *

Going back two generations in American thoroughbred horse racing put Betty in the aristocracy of horse people who traditionally picnic together in a park near Louisville before the Kentucky Derby. Servants and silver, the casual familiarity of people who feel appreciated by one another for their wealth and breeding, the soft, hospitable Southern manner, and the self-congratulatory implications of reunion (we made it!) always made the picnic a success. These elements were precisely what Edgar usually liked about the event as one of the elect, but this time the knowledge he was included only as an appendage of Betty's was keen because he was a less secure appendage than he'd been on their last trip to Louisville. On that prior occasion Edgar had been the whole show because Betty was too out of it for any more than a very weak appearance at the race itself. At that picnic five years before, Edgar had boomed and guffawed and felt cheerfully masterly as the sole representative of "The See" as the Bishop Stables were called by the cognoscenti.

Now Betty was doing the bubbling. She kept remembering old times with people, times from before Edgar knew her, times he couldn't remember along with the rest of them. Edgar ruminated on cold Southern fried chicken and champagne. She even had the damn trainer Tommy Smithers' arm for her rounds instead of Edgar's. Oh, well, Edgar joked sourly to himself, that's what a trainer is paid for, leading expensive animals.

Churchill Downs was such a dump, Edgar reflected—a rundown, slapped-together lumber facility in the wrong part of a third-rate town. It was just a typical American quickie that prevailed for phony reasons lost in time. It might as well be Oregon.

"Cousin Leslie!" enthused Betty to a fraudulent-looking antique sprinting from group to group like a bowlegged grasshopper. This old bluegrass sharpie rolled over at once to stroke and kiss and handshake them. He wasn't anyone's cousin. He was an inordinately successful horse dealer. ("Cousin" was a useful bit of ersatz Southern charm, like the military title of the Father of Kentucky Fried Chicken, or the "Kentucky Derby" itself. The people who own racehorses are constantly changing. People who got rich are entering the sport as people who go broke are leaving it. In this flux, a man who is everyone's cousin is a hospitable comfort.)

In no time the old gaffer and Betty were reminiscing about times before Edgar and people Edgar never knew.

"She was twenty-five years younger than you even then," scolded Betty. The old lecher gleamed.

"An old cat needs a tender mouse," he observed. Even Tommy Smithers laughed out loud. Edgar dutifully huffed a laugh through a smile-shaped mouth. More and more people gathered around them, or more specifically around Tommy and Betty. Edgar went off to get himself a drink with ice in it because you can't bite a glass of champagne and he felt like chewing on his anger.

How different this Edgar was from the happy bridegroom who had been polite as a courtier, enthusiastic as a salesman and respectful as a fan his first time at the Kentucky Derby. Back then, Edgar's respect for people with money was absolute and sincere. Mouths that had known the taste of caviar and champagne since their first round of teeth could speak no words he didn't find fascinating. Of course they liked him for adoring them.

"Edgar is adorable."

"Really fun."

"Who cares where he's from," said his defenders.

"A complete phony," was said only by the disgruntled jealous men who seemed descended in a line from Woods, a man he met in Korea, a tribe whose sole purpose in life was to doubt the irresistible Edgar.

Now, after twenty years of being married to a fortune, right on the verge of having that dignifying element become his legal very own, he was thrust backward by Betty's recovery. Edgar felt the mantle of the extra man on him again, as tight and comical as trying on his old Marine Corps uniform. It wasn't fair.

He was in the stagline at the bar massaging his morbidity again, watching Betty feted in that miserable park that had this one grand moment a year. Edgar wondered if, like this park, they would all soon walk off and leave him to candy wrappers, cans, condoms and neglect.

*   *

Rubbed and combed to a gloss, his oiled hooves flashing, Shanghai Pagoda knew it was a race day and that he was a celebrity. He shot kicks at strangers who got too close as precise and explosive as the stroke of an expert breaking a rack of pool balls. He particularly struck out at the hideous half-man, half-machine deformities lumbering about, trailing wires, from the television networks. He kept nudging Harold, like an accomplice, on the trip from the backstretch to the saddling paddock.

Harold, stiff with stage fright, was more clinging to Shanghai Pagoda than leading him.

"Hey, Harold!" gibed the familiar voice of a crony of Harold's in the great glacier of humanity looming over them.

"Hey, you redheaded peckerwart!"

It made Harold glad and even more scared to hear his name and not be able to attach it to a face because there were so many in the direction of the voice. Shanghai Pagoda was pumping along in an easy walk, unaffected by the banks of eyes watching. Harold saw Mr. Smithers and Mr. and Mrs. Barnes standing like the groom's party at the altar as he approached with the bride (or maybe as the bride, glad for the knowing confidence of her big strong dad striding alongside).

Shanghai Pagoda continued to pluck at Harold as Tommy Smithers laid out the doll's tea party of racing tack on the colt's back. First came a chamois doily followed by a foam rubber pastry, then the red saddle cloth with the colt's number and name. Finally, the tiny, worn wafer of Montezuma's racing saddle was cinched down and Harold was sent out for his major public performance, a couple of turns around the ring alone leading Shanghai Pagoda, with a great part of the American nation watching.

Tommy Smithers told Montezuma not to go the front until the two rockets from California, Napa Valley and Ballentine, were spent. One of these two, Napa Valley, was half an entry placed in the race so his stablemate, Uncle Alex, could prevail in the more important half.

Montezuma listened impassively. Tommy hoisted him aboard Shanghai Pagoda, who pricked his ears and went up on his toes at once, making Tommy Smithers' heart beat so his binoculars bounced on his breast.

"Montezuma," as he was called because he sat a horse with the stone dignity of an Aztec glyph, was the same black and tan as the Bishop Stables silks. That obsidian colt with the fierce and dignified high priest on his back was such a wondrous sight a huge woman from North Carolina, who was said to be able to see auras (and by that sight give miraculously prescient advice to bettors willing to pay for it), herself laid out eleven hundred dollars, six hundred of it stolen from her own mother, on Shanghai Pagoda to win.

Below the Barnes box, on the infield of the racetrack, were tens of thousands of people milling and partying. Edgar regarded this pond of people ruefully. Was there such a thing as nobodyhood? Would Edgar fall like Icarus into that very sea because he'd risen too close to the solar magnificence of Betty's inheritance? People kept jamming by to poke platitudes at Betty and Tommy and Edgar, who smiled and nodded with an inappropriate wince. A high-school band played "My Old Kentucky Home" as the racers moved onto the track. Even murderers in the crowd got goose pimples hearing that old melody. To Edgar, watching his dark enemy, it sounded like a dirge.

Only ancient, rudimentary plots like a race or an execution can collect and focus the attention of such a silly, rowdy mob as the one at the Kentucky Derby. In T-shirts pulled up to reveal navels and mesh-sided billed hats bearing brand names, they wiggled their hips, hooted and drank. The crowd in the private boxes were

pleased to see companies they controlled featured in the walking
advertisements below them, like barons looking from balconies at
their clods and fardels at a feast.

The volume of the crowd's noise rose as the horses were loaded
into the starting gate. Then it subsided in a dramatic diminution
close to silence, preparing to leap like the horses themselves when
the gates sprang open. That happened, and the sixteen horses
leaped forward in a mob howl. The jockeys rose to slow their
charges and steer them into advantageous positions in the stam-
pede. The excitement made it hard to hold horses back. The riders
were awkward from excitement. At this juncture all of them could
still dare to hope to win the Kentucky Derby, because reality
hadn't yet changed from wings to an anchor between their legs.

The two speed horses, Napa Valley and Ballentine, got to the
front, running like thieves through a crowd. Montezuma had
Shanghai Pagoda in the back of the herd.

Tommy Smithers looked at the board to see the time of the first
quarter. His heart sank. The race was going too slow. The main
body of the race, six lengths behind the front two, were being
gulled into believing the front-runners were burning themselves
out, which they weren't.

"Get up—they're stealing it!" shouted Tommy, feeling a dream-
er's agony of powerlessness. Edgar's eyes widened and he smiled.
He knew what the trainer meant. Sure enough, there was Shanghai Pagoda in the middle of the crowd of marks watching the two
in front draw away with the vapid ignorance of hicks studying
a game of three-card monte. The perpetrators were between eight
and ten lengths in front of the fourteen fools as they entered the
turn. It was like watching thieves stepping onto the international
bridge to an extradition-free country. Tommy was shouting instructions. Betty's fists were up, pounding on an invisible pane of
glass. Edgar's grin widened like the lead of Napa Valley and his
fellow bandit, Ballentine.

Montezuma had horses fore and aft and on both sides. It was as
bad as his dream of being naked before everyone in the Cathedral
of Nuestra Señora de los Milagros back in his hometown, Teguci-

galpa. He saw what was wrong and he couldn't get out. He had been trying all the way up the backstretch. The jockey from California aboard Uncle Alex, stablemate of front-running Napa Valley, was holding his horse as the keystone of a galloping prison. Montezuma couldn't get Shanghai Pagoda clear to run. The conspiracy was clear. Montezuma was trapped. He shouted. He swore in Spanish and English. But no one would get out of the way.

Ballentine couldn't keep up with Napa Valley, even at the slow pace that was stealing the race. When he came back to the duped herd, placements changed and Montezuma sprang at what opening appeared. Shanghai Pagoda got through, and, from the far outside, changed leads and lunged along at a pace that got half a length nearer Napa Valley with every stride, which was gallant, but not enough.

Edgar cheered this big try like the rest of them. Napa Valley would win, Shanghai Pagoda would get a highly praised second. But second was second and Edgar could feel the world as he had known it sliding back into place.

Even if Shanghai Pagoda went on to win the Preakness and the Belmont, the other two jewels of the Triple Crown, he would only be bearably famous. This Kentucky Derby was the big one, the race that got through to the public.

Montezuma felt his horse hit a harder stride. He thought at first something was wrong. It happens so fast when something breaks. The stride loses fluidity, one, two steps, then suddenly they go down like a dog hit by a truck and the rest of the horses are on top of you. But this hardening, this hammer on steel, was also quickening, and the lead horse was coming back at them.

Napa Valley was getting a hand ride straight down the stretch to fame, so far in front the jockey was thinking how pleased his mother would be to see him on the cover of *Sports Illustrated*, when Shanghai Pagoda came alongside with the awful surprise of a torpedo. Napa Valley's jockey hit him like crazy, and got three strides of jump as they hit the wire, but he knew, like everyone watching, that near black bay, with the jock stretched out so smooth and low over his withers they could pass together for a winged horse in a falcon's dive, had won the race.

*   *

There was a roaring and jumping at Churchill Downs you could hear all the way to the nicer part of Louisville. No one could see or hear Edgar's grimace and howl of anguish because they were all howling themselves in primordial witness to something impossible they'd seen with their own eyes.

Shanghai Pagoda was the last horse back after the colts ran through the finish, slowed, turned and came back. He was greeted with the applause and cheering of the crowd's heartfelt approval. It was a more civilized sound than the belly roar that had welled up in those last six strides before the wire. The colt seemed to understand he had driven men mad.

An inquiry sign flashed on the board and the unified voice of the mob came up again, cursing and threatening. The stewards watched the film of Shanghai Pagoda bulling his way out of his trap. The California jockey, keeping the keystone block in front of Shanghai Pagoda, had protested he was bumped in this escape. He was, but the stewards knew they'd be torn to bits by the crowd if they changed the order of finish. Also, it was obvious Shanghai Pagoda had been boxed. Inquiry went off. Official flashed on, and the tens of thousands cheered again and danced jigs and hulas, whooping and holding index fingers up in the orthodox response of televised victory.

Betty held a rein while a garland of roses was thrown over Shanghai's withers. Montezuma sat like a camel driver on this pyramid, unable physically to obey the media's commands and requests to smile. The heat lightning of flashbulbs popped. Shanghai Pagoda pawed and twitched in the tumult. Meaningless remarks tumbled from every mouth.

Only Edgar had nothing to say.

He, Betty, Tommy Smithers and Montezuma were herded into line for a photo against a wall of humanity. Media reporters picked at them with the fine steel probes of their microphones for the prechewed gobbets of cliché left in the teeth after the great feast of victory.

"I din' think he have so much left after we got box so bad," offered Montezuma to the gringo nation.

"He's a great champion with a great trainer and a great rider," said Betty with a generous smile. She was wearing a red, white and blue suit instead of her usual racing tan. With her smile, her beauty and her limitless wealth, she looked on TV like the American flag rippling over amber waves of grain.

"Very nice," mumbled Edgar when the holy chalice of national media attention got to him.

Tommy narrated the race rerun for TV viewers, "That looks like an absolute conspiracy," he said of the praetorian guard surrounding Shanghai Pagoda down the backstretch.

"Are you saying, Tommy Smithers, there was a deliberate blocking intention here?" questioned the artificially intense reporter under a black toupee.

"We were lucky to get loose," replied Tommy.

"They had me box until that four horse come back and shake loose the six and I pull over and show him and he jump right through. This is some horse, mister," gushed Montezuma, who had a reputation for never saying anything.

Gleeful strangers patted the Barneses as though by doing so they could get victory on their hands. A police guard preceded the Barneses' passage through the public. An old woman broke through and ran up to Betty like Jack Ruby getting to Lee Harvey Oswald.

"God bless you, Betty," she offered.

"God bless you," replied Betty with that radiant Hail Columbia smile.

"Hey, Betty," cried another voice.

"Yea for Betty."

"Good going, Betty," said different voices.

Betty? reflected Edgar, The bastards are calling her by her first name! Betty smiled and waved just right. Little audiences formed and clapped. The old God bless woman got her hands on Edgar just before they reached the door that would get them free of the public. Edgar scowled and shook her off.

"Fuck you, asshole," said the old woman. Edgar looked back at all of it: Harold was leading Shanghai Pagoda through the adulation of the crowd: the trembling flash of hundreds of cameras made the gleaming, dark horse shimmer.

Thirteen

The victory party at Churchill Downs included the appalling Mr. Bernie Zilber who owned the entry of Napa Valley and Uncle Alex and had masterminded this pair of operatives who had come so close to sabotaging Shanghai Pagoda. Zilber touched himself and whomever he was talking to continually. He also talked continually. The old racing crowd moved into a defensive, herd pattern around Betty, leaving this toucher behind their backs.

Oppressed by Shanghai Pagoda's victory and the iterating choruses of praise and congratulations reverberating through the Old Guard ringing Betty, Edgar moved through the tailored maze ostensibly to recharge his julep, but privately to get away from that ominous, growing joy building around her. Bernie Zilber, shameless, slapped Edgar on the back, then caressed him, passing off what had just been described to Edgar by a member of the Jockey Club as "the most plainly criminal act I've ever seen at a derby" by saying, "Well, you beat us, Edgar," even though they had not been introduced. Although storm clouds of disapproval shot across Edgar's forehead at this gross familiarity, he was in a tiny way

pleased the little bastard knew exactly who he was. Except for
Bernie Zilber's trainer, who was positively furtive because of what
he'd try to pull off, a small retinue of flunkies and relatives, and,
until she understood the situation, the governor of Kentucky, no
one was talking to Mr. Bernie Zilber at this official victory party,
even though his entry finished second and third.

Edgar would normally have moved wordlessly away from such
a frantic outrage. (How dare Zilber try to cozy up to the very
people he had done everything in his power to cheat? Had he no
shame at all?) But because in his heart Edgar had wished Bernie
Zilber's plot had worked and in his brain he had been considering
things like who might help him if he were expelled from Betty's
garden of wealth, he replied, "You ran a very naughty race, Mr.
Zilber," with a sardonic smile that didn't entirely rebuff Zilber.
Bernie Zilber only laughed, looking to his trainer for a loyal guffaw
(which the embarrassed trainer, shunned by his peers in the room,
barely managed).

"You got some horse there," said Zilber, picking a piece of lint
off Edgar's sleeve as he appeared to scrutinize and admire Edgar's
jacket.

"He come out of that box like Houdini," continued the short,
confident Zilber as Edgar observed Zilber had imposed additions
to his hair.

"Mr. Zilber would love to get in on a syndication," offered
Zilber's trainer.

"I doubt that," replied Edgar, still smiling in a way that didn't
cut things off as cleanly as his words.

"Then I'd sure like to participate if you ever decide to fix a race,"
quipped Bernie Zilber, tapping Edgar three times as he spoke.
Then, laughing so utterly he had to mop at his tears with a garishly
monogrammed handkerchief, he walked away, followed by his
own court, apparently oblivious to all the anuses pointed at him by
the rebuffing herd around Betty.

When Edgar rejoined Betty, the same Jockey Club member who
had described Zilber's machinations in the Kentucky Derby as
criminal quipped, "Did you ask him who made his suits?"

"Or who makes his gold chains," guffawed a man named Lawrence Morris with a visible wince. Lawrence Morris was particularly sensitive to the vulgarity of nouveau riche Jews because, being Jewish himself, he wanted to make it clear Jewish gentility was as appalled as Gentile quality by roaches like Zilber.

Edgar laughed along with them and clenched a mouthful of julep. Zilber was on the other side of the room fingering lapels and plotting with similar riffraff. Edgar, of course, was among superior people. Edgar stood with members of the Jockey Club and the Social Register. Zilber stood with street-gang sneaks who had wormed up through cracks in the great structure of American civilization to be there. Edgar fingered the worn badge on his signet ring. These tiny cavities had come down to his finger through Anglo-Saxon history, from the dawn of Western man through all its great, historic moments. He and Morris and old Jockey Club here were three knights of the round table standing together at the Kentucky Derby. Bernie Zilber over there was some kind of a revolting barbarian, a basilisk they should ride down like Saint George and spear right in the glittery scales of his goddamn Beverly Hills necklace.

Only something in Edgar went over to Bernie Zilber's side. Here was the Royal Navy, there was the pirate, defiant in his cove.

How many generations would you have to go back to find the Bernie Zilbers who made the money that gave the tweedy snobs alongside Edgar their airs? But how could Edgar, always pleased and proud of his acceptance by these people who so clearly believed themselves to be the right sort, want anything to do with the pirates over there? Zilber and his people dressed so badly. They spoke so badly. They didn't know how to act. All they had learned was where they weren't wanted. And this revelation seemed to attract them! First they had got what they didn't have and next they set about going where they weren't wanted.

Edgar touched the worn pits and curlicues of the family ring on his little finger. Looking at Zilber's crowd, Edgar sensed their belief in his gentility and breeding. He stood straighter and breathed as if he were a filling sail on the Mayflower. Edgar did feel

well and anciently bred compared to such stylistic ignoramuses as
Bernie Zilber. The ring felt like part of him, a knuckle repeated
genetically since Druids' days in old England. He gave a patronizing, wintry smile to the posse of nouveaux riches formed around
Zilber and turned back into the genteeler crowd around Betty.

                              *   *

"He's wonderful," reported Tommy Smithers, back from the
barn, entering to congratulations on all sides. Betty hugged him.
Edgar raised his glass in Smithers' direction and chewed ice behind
an insincere little grin.

Then I'd sure like to participate if you ever decide to fix a race, the
pirate had said. Edgar looked at the jovial rich owners. Whoever
assembled the piles they had must have done a few dubious things,
he thought, like what Zilber had tried to do today. Old Jockey Club
could scoff because the dirty work was taken care of by an ancestor.
Lawrence Morris had established distance from whatever crimes
attended the making of his fortune too (just as he'd established some
distance from whatever his name had originally been). Edgar could
see through it all. Beginnings are usually crude. There are always
a few corpses to be found alongside the path to millions. A man
who wants a fortune isn't afraid of such costs.

                              *   *

The word "edge," repeated for muddled reasons, in someplace
yellow, remained in Edgar's memory as he found himself levered
over into consciousness. It was black night.

"Edgar, I want a divorce."

It was Betty's voice in the dark. It was a real voice. Edgar reached
to where a light should be and on flashed some strange bedroom.
What was this strange bedroom doing in his bedroom?

On a twin bed alongside his, Betty had recoiled at the flash of
light like a slug when you salt it. She pulled a sleep mask over her
eyes which stared at him sightlessly.

"What?" asked Edgar.

"Turn off the light."

"What?"

"I've had a little pill and I just decided you should be thinking about it too and we can talk about it tomorrow."

A sudden rage slammed into Edgar. So this was it, what he feared, at last! He pulled open his bed and got up, about to grab her and throw her down. Maybe because her masked eyes or her pill-dulled senses gave her no warning, she made no reaction to this menacing motion of his. Her inert apathy disconcerted him. He didn't do anything. She breathed dryly into a snore, a breathing mummy in satin bandages.

Edgar took a step and reeled from unprocessed alcohol still active in his bloodstream. He jammed arms into a dressing gown and left the bedroom, flinging on lights in his voyage through the strange house to the only destination he remembered: the bar downstairs.

He set off a cherry bomb of bourbon in his mouth and looked around the place. The Plowrights, Jack and Nancy, their hosts here in Kentucky, looked at him from many winner's-circle photographs at the bar. They passed from youth in sepia through adulthood in black-and-white photographs to middle age in color. Unlike the Plowrights, the horses stayed the same age in every picture.

"Jesus," Edgar said aloud, noticing what a sneezy expletive it was. The dormant house clicked around him. "What the hell am I supposed to do?" he asked the empty fireplace.

Edgar spread more bourbon flames in his stomach. His ears rang. He was getting angry. A red fringe appeared at the top of his vision.

"Twenty years, and this is what I get!" he explained to the fireplace.

She surely would have died this year or next of self-administered boredom if that damn horse hadn't dropped that stall door and pranced out to trample Edgar's future. Fuzzed with drugs and booze, watching TV all night, sleeping all day, suffering from increasingly arcane and complex disorders detected by endowment-hopeful hospitals and clinics, she had been withering like a tree in autumn until this ridiculous, unbelievable diversion, this false spring, threw everything akilter.

Everyone knew she didn't have long. Diagnosticians pulled seri-

ous faces and spoke sinister Latin names. The shinier respect Edgar
was getting, shown before her ominous revival, meant the people
they knew approved of Edgar's succession to Betty's fortune. He
had earned it. He'd put in his time. It was all but his anyway. He
was the only one who really enjoyed the Bishop millions—all Betty
needed was a motel room with a TV and a drug dealer. It was
Edgar who kept them entertained and entertaining, who moved
furniture about, bought things—going to London was his idea. If
only they hadn't! His black suit might be draped over a chair in
Camilla's apartment right now as they made love after the funeral.

"Oh, God, all right," she had said heavily, "At least maybe I can
sleep there," and that's where that fateful horse lay in wait for them.

Now the straight bourbon was only a pleasant liquid. Edgar sat
heavily on a sofa. His cock lolling out on the cold chintz gave him
a start. He cupped his balls, drank bourbon and contemplated.

Everyone had been sort of expecting her to die. It wouldn't
surprise anyone, especially if her darling pills were involved. There
were so many of them on her night tray it looked like a painter's
palette. Find out which one would kill her in overdose and fill every
capsule on her tray with it. Leave an empty bottle under the bed.
Everyone would call it suicide.

What was murder, anyway? It was just an old bogey word that
swelled up newspapers and amused mystery readers. Edgar snorted
and cocked the empty barrel of his glass at his mouth. Oriental
armies had tried to kill him for a year and a half. For all he knew
a round from him had stopped a life or two in Korea. He got up
to return to the bar for more of the sweet fuel, knocking something
over in the process.

Murder only applies to the introduction by people of death to
other people. When this courtesy is extended animals it's just killing, or slaughter—it's a kind of harvest. It's how the steaks begin
their journey to our forks. Harvest Betty and enjoy the nourish-
ment of many millions. Edgar knew how to enjoy money. The idea
of turnups on the sleeves of his jackets? That was his idea! Now
other men copied it. Men couldn't help admiring how Edgar was

turned out, how energetically amusing he was—he showed them all a good time. Now it was his turn to have the good time, and a damn horse had trampled it.

Edgar stopped, struck by a thought: murder doesn't apply to the death of a horse. Edgar said "bang" loudly in the empty room. In his mind, Shanghai Pagoda fell into a pile of dog food. Betty's joy ran out like bathwater. Edgar grinned widely at the strange room. Once again he could picture himself in black on his way to Betty's funeral.

Giggling drunk, Edgar headed back up the pathway of light he'd hacked through the jungle of night in the strange house. She lay in the same position he'd left her in, mouth open, lights on, breathing dryly. Without the breathing, she could be in the morgue.

Edgar had trouble entering the bedclothes. He pulled at them, braiding himself in a skein of sheets, blanket and counterpane. He fell into a boozy, writhing sleep, dreaming he was being consumed and digested by a big jungle snake.

* *

Jack and Nancy seemed glad and excited when Betty walked down and said good morning. Like everyone else, they treated her differently since the great event. Glances, now, stayed on Betty a second or two longer than she was accustomed to (and Betty had been accustomed to a bit of staring ever since she first poked her Mary Janes toward the pavement, sliding out of great limousines in front of schools and theaters and museums and department stores). People at the track after the race stepped out of her way when she was near and toward her when she was far.

"Good morning, darling," said Nancy brightly, wiping her mouth and pulling back from a glass breakfast table, prettily set with glittery silver and jams, soft butter and linen and delicate china.

Kisses were exchanged. This freshness and sharpness of everything increased the newness Betty felt about her life. Seeing the wrapped and matted hulk of Edgar in his twin bed when she got up gave her the fancy that his body was something past, like the snake's old skin, like last night's dinner party, something over and done and behind her.

There was particular excitement at Jack and Nancy Plowright's Sundown Farm because a TV crew was coming there to begin a documentary about Betty Bishop Barnes and her champion horse. Betty would be videotaped here in the bluegrass country in tweeds and corduroys, then later in pretty rooms in New York wearing beautiful dresses and at the races in handsome suits. The network felt a documentary about Betty Bishop Barnes was a great idea because it reinforced the fantasies of their most popular prime-time soap about the clothes, furniture and lives of very rich Americans. Betty had already demonstrated considerable and unexpected charisma in her appearance at the derby. The public responded to her. She had a "first lady" quality. She had great clothes, a real smile and a pleasant, unforced enthusiasm. Best of all, she showed a genuine wonderment over her good fortune.

A champion horse is only a sight. To make a beast news, a human has to be attached. Betty looked awfully good to the TV executives designing the documentary.

"What about Edgar?"

"I've met him, he's great. But he isn't too interested in the horse thing."

"What about what I hear about her and the pills and booze?"

"I heard she was croaking, cancer or something."

"Listen, this is a documentary. We shoot what we want. She's been in great shape every time at the races and let's face it, if she has cancer, our story is even bigger," reasoned the network executives before dispatching one of their very best news teams to Kentucky to begin work on the Barnes Family.

*　　*

Edgar felt himself falling off his perch of sleep onto the stones of consciousness. Nothing could hold him off the cruel rock. He let himself plummet and hit. His eyes cracked open under the blood-swollen awnings of his eyelids. Betty's bed was vacant. What little sleep he'd got hadn't bypassed the most painful section of suffering from last night's toxic pleasures.

Poison exuded from every pore. He reckoned a match held too close to his skin would make him go up like a yule log as the swamp gas rising out of him caught. He closed his eyes and fantasized about a hypodermic needle pumping some salvation into him, some potent vitamin that could rid him of his dull, self-wrought agony. A noose, being hit by a train, freezing to death, drowning and a pistol at the temple all occurred to him as pleasant diversions from the pervasive misery of his hangover.

Erect (and woozy from the effort), Edgar found a printed note signed "Nancy" and sealed with a smile face advising the reader breakfast could be taken downstairs, or, by pushing a button on the phone, in bed. Edgar pushed the button, ordered and pulled his hacked hulk to the bathroom for what first aid he could find there.

He needed a drink. How had it happened? Now Edgar was boozing and Betty wasn't. He shook his head and mouthed vows to the man in the mirror whom he had fed and dressed the very best, to fight this demon.

Got to stop drinking. Too much liquid in the face. Jowls like saddle bags on a camel in the desert. Nose marbleizing like the lining of those calfskin volumes in paneled libraries nobody but interior decorators have touched since the eighteenth century.

A screwdriver. That's what his body shouted up at his head. About three screwdrivers now and white wine at lunch and nap off the rest of this killer malaise this afternoon. Edgar heard his breakfast arrive. This sound made him realize he was talking to himself.

His fingers, pink, moist and trembling, got his tie knotted. He pulled on a pinkish tweed he hoped might dissipate the red in his face. He decided to go straight to the bar no matter who was there and make himself an eye-opener—a glass of orange juice shrouding a big, strong, invisible hammer of steel vodka with which he could smash back at the pounding affliction tyrannizing him. He went down the stairs picturing knights clashing, steel on steel, blood trickling out under the plates.

Edgar's antidote lay amid a still life which reminded him of a

Christmas crèche. Bottles like jeweled and caparisoned Magi and angels glinted and glowed around the miraculous drink Edgar devoutly needed. Only between Edgar and his place of devotion was a TV crew filming Betty. White light, like the flares they sent up in Korea to show the crazy horde with their screams and bugles of death, bleached Betty and some horsey-looking girl who was interviewing her. The bottles Edgar needed sparkled in the light as inaccessible as jewels in Tiffany's windows. Jack and Nancy, admonishing silence, mouthed unspoken greetings the way people do in churches.

Betty was the overbright, eye-gouging center of the light. Edgar's shriveled, aching eyes hurt more when they got to her. The interviewer turned smiling toward Edgar and motioned him "come aboard" style. Edgar shook his head and stepped back, but apparently she couldn't see him in the lights. Nancy and Jack urged him forward.

Edgar stepped into the hot, vicious shards of welding-torch light and was pulled next to Betty into a Chippendale armchair glistening like mahogany snakes.

"What was your first reaction to winning the derby?" asked the newswoman, smiling tersely. Then her focus changed abruptly from him as a person to him as an object. "Oh, for Christ's sake, he isn't miked," she said to the wall of light. She looked back at him. "And he needs makeup." Edgar was led out of the scene. "What do you mean you want a divorce?" he had considered saying for openers. That would liven up the interview. But he wouldn't say it. He'd play it straight. He'd pretend she hadn't ever asked him that. After all, she might not know whether she had or not. As a bib was laid over his chest and the soft, dry, not entirely unpleasant powder brush daubed at the balconies under his closed eyes, Edgar considered how the English royal family must live out their lives like this, communicating rarely through whatever cracks or codes they could tap out on the enclosing walls of constant public exposure. The makeup artist stared at him like a spectator studying a drowning down in a well.

"Would you bring me a screwdriver?" Edgar said to the creature.

"A drink—get it over there," he explained louder. Someone hissed at him to stop talking. "I want a screwdriver," said Edgar, enjoying the consternation of the time-tensed TV crew. "Ok, but quiet, please," whispered a voice he couldn't see the source of outside the makeup man's bright lights. Edgar was enjoying himself, despite his headache, his cold armpits, his chemical fatigue. In the solar flare beyond the camera, he could hear the interview waddling along, quacking platitudes.

"You don't own something like Shanghai Pagoda. He's just something that happens," Betty was saying. When you shoot a horse, reflected Edgar, it's like a flimsy coat hanger folding in a suit of clothes. The whole thing drops from orderly, smooth, symmetrical lines to a dark muddled heap on the floor.

When his screwdriver arrived, Edgar didn't jam it straight to his mouth. Just having it as a possession sent a pleasant wave of relief through him which he savored before tasting.

"You're all set," whispered the makeup man. Edgar, drinking in his bib like a good baby, smiled cynically at the sideshow his hosts seemed so pleased to have in their home. Everybody is ready, willing and able to be a media star.

"One more," ordered Edgar, holding his glass into the vague population of flunkies, servants, wired technicians and onlookers.

"He's the one who drinks," the documentary crew reported to the producers back in New York.

Fourteen

dgar figured he must have been to thousands of parties. Those thousands of occasions had pointed him at thousands of women—in fact double the thousands as he politely switched from chatting with the one on his right to find a little fun with the one on his left. Among them there must have been some who had the right specifications to serve as replacements if Betty ever really left him. Betty wasn't the only pile of money in the sort of old monogrammed bags Edgar preferred. He raised his screwdriver like a field commander lifting his binoculars, studying possibilities.

Maybe Edgar was ready for another kind of money now, anyway. He knew so much more than he did when he started. Maybe it was time for him to play Pygmalion to some nouveau riche Galatea. Helping her sort out the right people, the right clothes, and houses and furnishings; giving her the right combination to attack a table setting; teaching her how to perform introductions and how to execute farewells; how to formulate invitations and thank-you notes and menus; who to seek out, who to scorn. Maybe that's just what he should be doing—repaying the wisdom he'd gotten by passing it on.

Edgar scowled. You'd think a place like the Brook Club would have real orange juice in a screwdriver.

Would Edgar be received as widely and eagerly with a new wife as he had been with Betty? Having a last name the same as the first name of a fine old bank guaranteed hundreds of invitations a year. Would those hosts who had always acted so delighted to have Edgar step over their transoms continue their enthusiasm if he were with, say, a pretty little brunette glinting with new jewels whose olive complexion bespoke the hot winds, bobbing dhows and unchristian religions of the Levant?

"Hello, Edgar, my God, what a great horse you've got. Congratulations," spoke a smooth young man, moving gracefully by Edgar toward the bar.

Edgar nodded his thanks and pulled a little bowl of cheese crackers closer. Now, with that bastard's remark, that goddamned horse was present again. Frozen orange juice *without* vodka must be even more awful, considered Edgar, approving again his choice of an abrasive-looking suit of two steely grays. He was having John J. Walker, chairman of the Bishop Bank, to lunch here at the Brook Club. He was going to ask Walker about a job. This warrior weave of woolly mail seemed handsomely apt.

John J. Walker, chairman of a bank manipulating more money than most of the countries in NATO, was a string Edgar had never before pulled. Betty always treated the banker with a deferential enthusiasm that amused Edgar because it expressed so plainly in its attempt to convey no such thing, her sense John J. Walker was her employee. He wasn't, of course, and no one thought he or she believed this better than Betty. Still, it was called the Bishop Bank and he got a salary to work there. It was her concentrated efforts to show John J. Walker she considered it his bank in which she was just a depositor (albeit a freakish one) that made it plain she hadn't outgrown that impression childhood gives that things with your name on them belong to you.

John J. Walker, like Edgar, had sprung from, or, more accurately got the hell out of, a lonely nowhere. The yearning caused by being both plain and from the Plains was, in Walker's case, intense enough to fuel the manly drive for success all the way from social mediocrity at a small midwestern junior high school (the prettiest girl in his class wrote in his yearbook, "To Tubby, a real brian") to the most powerful boardrooms of Wall Street.

Outwitting the frauds, sharpies, financial geniuses, foreigners, smarty pants, idiots (and idiots are occasionally, John J. Walker was thinking en route to his lunch with Edgar, the most formidable challenges of all), politicians, liars, weather, wars, market quirks and unforeseeable coincidences had never lost its appeal for Walker. Almost as soon as he opened his eyes the excitement his work caused him started. His home, including the wife in it, the driver taking him away from it and the underlings through which he passed on the way to his office all served as little more than a ground across which he painted his money-vivid day. He breathed by sucking intelligence out of telephones and blowing commands back into them. It was out of his way, off his rhythm and a pain in the ass to go have lunch with a nonentity like Edgar Barnes, but anything concerning Betty Bishop was special and sacred to John J. Walker.

He'd first laid eyes on her at Hopewell, her great-grandfather's estate which perfectly matched Walker's farm-boy dreams of grandeur—probably because it had been built by one (Betty's great-grandfather, Bernard Bishop, had also begun with his grip on udders).

Walker had pushed the heiress in a swing that long-ago day, not taking off his jacket despite the heat because he wanted to keep the burst seams attaching sleeves to his shirt hidden. She was a little girl and he was a trainee at the Bishop Bank, astonished to be plucked from his work and driven out to the chairman's house by his boss.

The house, the garden and the little girl crystallized Walker's ambitious dreams. Now he personally had such things, and he barely noticed them. His model had been matched but never equaled. Bernard Bishop's life, which had been John J. Walker's dream, was gone but not forgotten. Now Walker worried about

Betty Bishop Barnes like a priest or a historian watching the disintegration of a relic or an artifact.

Walker's feelings about Edgar, however, were not of this sacred tone. Watching Betty slide into the confusion that so often besets American heirs as they copy the national striving with neither the need nor the support less-enfranchised citizens have (an agony treated with the same sort of general sympathy as the menstrual complaints of transvestites) pained John J. Walker. The likely outcome of Betty's decline, Edgar getting that holy fortune, galled the banker. To think that vain popinjay, that unemployed clotheshorse, might actually wind up richer than himself was an outrage. John J. Walker had added many of his own ingenious touches to keeping the Bishop fortune out of the hands of the only worse beneficiary than Edgar Barnes he could imagine, the U. S. government.

Of course Edgar wouldn't get title to the capital itself. Trusts had been devised to preserve blood ownership of the mighty wad, but even just the income blowing off the holy mountain was fortunes. The stupid son of a bitch had never worked a full day in his life to Walker's knowledge. Edgar had spent horizontal what little time he actually did put in at the office they kept for him. He couldn't even read a balance sheet. Edgar Barnes was just a damn gigolo. John J. Walker was audibly growling when his car stopped in front of the Brook Club.

*   *

Edgar frowned, winced and took another sip. There was just no comparison that could be made between fresh and frozen orange juice. They were elementally different. This frozen stuff was acrid, flat, metallic and mean. Its cloudy, pale yellow color was almost bronchially repulsive. The financiers who owned this frozen juice industry should be, like their product, gelded, Edgar decided. This notion and the little lift beginning as he lowered the level of his second screwdriver cheered him up.

"Edgar, I love your horse," said Lawrence Morris, approaching as if to embrace Edgar.

"Damn good," affirmed Edgar, pursing his lips to affect conviction, unhappy to be poked again by this touchy topic.

"Seriously, that's once in a lifetime," advised Morris, growing
rapter as Shanghai Pagoda swung around the turn of Morris' memory. "One in a million lifetimes. My family has had a stable racing
here for one hundred years, year after next, and we never yet have
had a horse like Shanghai Pagoda," noted Morris, thereby congratulating both of them.

"It's still a little early, Lawrence, three races."

"But, my God, what races." Now Morris was sitting with Edgar,
staring awestruck slightly above Edgar's eyes. What was up there,
a halo? A pair of dark bay ears pricking?

"It's Betty's horse."

Morris' eyes returned to the real world of Edgar's face. "What
about a share?" he asked.

"I really don't know what her plans are."

"Please let me know when she starts thinking about a syndica-
tion," said Morris, spreading his fingers and rising off them, giving
Edgar a pat and leaving to greet his own luncheon guest, a tall man
Edgar could see also had a hangover.

John J. Walker arrived, rising up the stairs and into the barroom
with an escort of verbal banter from excited clubmen. The chairman of the Bishop Bank was their own kind of celebrity. The gibes
and greetings with which they strewed the banker's path among
them affected genial clubhouse equality, but by their volume and
eagerness revealed their recognition of his exalted status.

"Saw Johnny Walker at lunch, great guy," was bound to be
casually slipped out this evening as drinks were mixed in Green-
wich and Manhattan. This attention pleased John J. Walker as he
found Edgar.

"How are you, Edgar, how's Betty?"

"She's all right, Johnny, how are you?"

"Gee, she looked so swell on television. Great."

"She's a brave girl," responded Edgar with an expression suggesting the victory glow Betty got from a bolt of national network

exposure was an impermanent flash. "What'll you have?" Edgar asked, waving for a barman.

"Tab," said John J. Walker evenly. Edgar reflected this was going to be tough going. The banker started popping the little yellow cheese crackers into his mouth as if he were eating gold coins. Entering clubmen scanning the barroom stopped for a flutter when they detected the mighty chairman. Now that Edgar had his fish landed, he didn't know what to do with him. "Could I have a job in case Betty leaves me?" seemed a pathetic, panhandler's plea, ludicrously inappropriate considering the circumstances.

The dark barmen saw two mighty white sharks feeding on cheese crackers, working their gills as they sucked at their glasses. Edgar was bigger and more handsome, fitter and better dressed than his tablemate. Wouldn't the barmen or a visiting scientist from another galaxy studying earth's biology presume Edgar the more powerful of the two? He mustn't ask for a job. At least not until he'd had a bit more to drink. It would certainly be easier if Walker would have the fraternal decency to drink with him.

"What can I do for you?" asked Walker abruptly, barely restraining himself from employing the starker phrase "What do you want?"

"It's sort of complicated, Johnny," Edgar heard himself speaking as if he were calculating something complex and international, a tone he believed was appropriate for addressing a bank chairman. Listening to the familiar tone of bullshit, Walker wondered if Edgar Barnes were so presumptuous a fool as to have asked the chairman of the Bishop Bank to lunch for a stock tip or a touch.

"First of all, I couldn't get in my office the other day."

"Why not?"

"But that isn't why I asked you here," Edgar continued, brushing his inconvenience aside. The banker waited. Edgar was horrified to find himself so quickly in something like a duel with this glinty-eyed computer. The subject had to change, the entry angle had to get more oblique, or Edgar would burn to a cinder entering the ruthless banker's denser atmosphere.

"I asked you here for a glass of the greatest white wine I've ever tasted, come on." Edgar rose up and got Walker out of his battle crouch at the cocktail table. He was pleased to note cracker crumbs sticking to the banker like mortality as they headed for the paneled dining room upstairs.

On the stairs, Walker thought, *The lounge lizard is hurt when the little playpen kept for him at bank expense to no useful purpose gets put to real use. For this he takes up the multimillion-dollar minutes of one of banking's supreme officer's time. The peckerhead lies stupidly in one of the hugest, most ingeniously contrived and protected nests of private wealth in the country, ignorant as a nigger lottery winner bitching about bird shit falling on his Cadillac.*

Edgar, behind the banker on the same stairs, considered his guest's lack of taste in clothing. Walker's unseemly calves rose and fell like clumsy pistons in front of Edgar, bulging the spider-web plaid of the financier's trousers with a kind of cumbersome violence. Walker's prestige and power, noted Edgar, deflected attention from the mediocrity of his taste and physical form.

In the dining room the entrants nodded to nods and unfolded napkins onto their laps. Edgar signaled and winked at a waiter who was expecting this command.

"Wait until you taste this, Johnny. It's the greatest Chardonnay ever made in California. This is the one that beat the greatest French wines in a blind tasting." Edgar had correctly assumed such patriotic, combative attributes would appeal to John J. Walker.

"I guess we hadn't seen you in so long we didn't know you still wanted to use an office with us," said Walker with barely muffled sarcasm.

"I'd like to talk to you about that," said Edgar, disgruntled by the bald way Walker put this subject back between them, "but first I want you to taste the stuff that beat the greatest wines of France right there in Paris. Did you read about it?" The wine arrived mercifully quickly, giving Edgar time to get a little spit and spin on his petition before returning it to play.

"Imagine how those Frenchies must have felt when they found out they'd picked a California Chardonnay right there in Paris," amplified Edgar patriotically, delighted by the way Walker scrutinized the bottle as if it were a pleasing municipal bond. The big buttery Chardonnay did its work admirably. Yes, Walker liked the idea of springing a great American wine on some conceited European greaseball sometime. He even wrote down the name in his tiny, precise, serial-number-style handwriting. Edgar was relieved.

"First class, first class," enthused Walker. Food and wine were becoming earnest concerns of farm boys like Walker raised on overcooked meat, mashed potatoes and milk. They wanted to live up to the privileges of their bank accounts. Edgar smiled like a cardshark at a mark, and took a draft of wine himself, scouring screwdriver off the walls of his mouth with the luxurious detergent.

"I'd like to be more involved with the bank, Johnny," said Edgar after the wine had pinked Walker's cheeks.

"What do you mean?"

"A job, a regular, salaried job. I want to do it for Betty."

"How's that?"

"For the regularity. You see, she's kind of using me for a crutch sometimes, because she feels I'm available. I hope you understand I don't mean this is something I regret or resent, I just think if I had a business day for her to plan against, she'd rise to it. She'd like to see some form and discipline to set herself against, I just kind of feel this on instinct. Gosh, I hope this makes some kind of sense."

"You mean you want a job?" asked Walker, a little startled.

"Exactly. I think Betty and I would both be better for it. I just wish I were some good with figures. Is there something there for a man who's good with people?"

This took Walker by surprise. Edgar Barnes looking for a job? Edgar had always reminded Walker of Albert Acquistapace, leader of Walker's boyhood 4-H Club. Acquistapace was a womanizer who used 4-H meetings to neck with a sewing instructor named Ellen Suggs. Forty-five years ago, Walker and his 4-H clubmates sat in the dark, watching a magic lantern slide of a champion sow curl and burn on the screen while Acquistapace's activity back in the dark behind the projector produced sounds of clothes rustling as well as those of moaning and sucking. Finally, a titter from the boys broke up the petting and the blank left by the burned sow was filled with a diagram of alfalfa. Ever since this boyhood glimpse of human sexuality, Acquistapace had served as Walker's model for his concept of womanizers. Edgar Barnes had immediately impressed Walker as this Acquistapace type. But, perhaps Betty was behind Edgar's request, reflected Walker. She should have a working husband. Every woman should. No doubt Betty had told him to get off his duff. Good for her. But what good was a fifty-year-old clotheshorse in a bank? Walker drummed his fingers and took another sip of the fine wine. He hadn't thought in thirty years of that evening Albert Acquistapace burned up the magic lantern slide.

There was a man at the bank with a vice-president's title named Llewellyn Battle Boggs III, whose job was mainly to be someone with a name like that who could show important clients a good time in New York City. A commander of impressive service at "21," a member of the Racquet, Links and Brook clubs, Boggs's purpose was to make outsiders feel they were on the inside track in New York. The mortality rate in this job was high. Livers burned out like the batteries in Christmas toys. Llewellyn Battle Boggs III himself, Walker remembered hearing, was taking the cure somewhere.

"There might be something. I'd like to check things out before I say anything concrete."

Edgar dented his cream soup, his lower lip in a pout and his brows knotted by a dark thought: employment. What was it like? Edgar had arranged this job for himself without really considering the inconveniences that were occurring to him as he faced his pallid disc of crème velouté.

Alarm clocks, those self-administered wounds with which workers began their days—could Edgar bear such interruptions to his matinee of entertaining morning dreams? Would he have to read things that bored him, the worn information glazed and fuzzed by copying machines on unpleasant-feeling paper? Would he have to keep himself in the difficult yoga position of man-at-desk when he would rather lie down? How about accepting the outrage of commands from others? How much was enough money to enslave yourself when the whole reason you sought money was to free yourself? These dour questions kept Edgar bowed over his soup plate, slurping softly, considering, if he weren't careful, he might be getting what he wanted once too often.

"Edgar, I'm curious. What the gee whiz are you looking for a job for?" asked Walker as the waiter recharged his wineglass for the fourth time.

"Betty's hitting the booze and pills too hard," said Edgar. "As I said, I had the idea if I was leading a more regular kind of life, it might shape her up, too."

"Bad as that?" Walker looked puzzled at his wine. Edgar nodded. Walker had thought Betty looked great at the Kentucky Derby on TV, but the last time he'd seen her in the flesh was at a lunch where she'd lost her shoes and slid down her chair trying to hook them with searching feet until she slipped. Hung by her chin from the mahogany, her ineffective limbs swimming drunkenly in the dark grottoes under the table, she imprinted Walker forever with this definitive image of dissipated decline.

"Trouble is," said Walker, "the job I was thinking of would involve a lot of late nights and all that; do you know Llew Boggs, Edgar?"

"Battle Boggs?"

"That's right. Llew is in the hospital and I was thinking along the lines of you picking up in his area."

Edgar's own fourth glass of wine atop the solid base of screwdrivers he'd built while waiting for the chairman had now opened the way to smooth, serene thought cushioned by pleasant feelings poised at an Olympian perspective. Much was coming clear. Many good things had been accomplished by this lunch. At least Edgar now knew how vividly he did not want a job. Better the complaints and tyranny of joining some poodle in the companionship racket than entering the morning commute to a living death. Maybe Edgar was the type who actually had to feel the rough jute prickles of the noose around his neck to decide against hanging himself.

"I'm afraid that's no go, Johnny. Nights are the rough time for Betty. I've got to be with her."

A smooth reply, Edgar complimented himself, to a grotesque offer. Battle Boggs, greeter and glad-hander, industrial gigolo, pimp and paid companion to visiting executives—is that how John J. Walker perceived Edgar Barnes? How revealing! This banking hen who pecked all day at digits couldn't see life beyond the shit, seeds and pointy tracks of his printout chicken yard. Even now, Edgar observed, Walker was refusing himself another sip of wine after reviewing its possible consequences. He was looking at the glass of wine in his hand like a loan to a shaky enterprise. Edgar had chosen this Chardonnay for its color. He thought Walker would like to drink gold.

Edgar felt he and Walker were two similar success stories, ambitious boys, whose parents hadn't even achieved listings in the phone book, washing down shad roe with Chardonnay at an exclusive club—couldn't Walker admire Edgar as his soul brother? Edgar concluded the crafty teachings of banking had deformed as powerfully as they had enriched John J. Walker.

Walker, meanwhile, was thinking better of Edgar than he ever had. Managing Betty must be like—there it was again, a flashback—trying to make Betty Jean McAllister's doll play something besides dead. This was hard because it was an old, old doll, its elastic was gone. Lounging was its only capability. Betty could be like that. Walker had propped her up at times himself. What was it about Edgar that made Walker think, as he never did, of these images from his rural boyhood? Walker imagined Edgar had grown up in urban wealth—maybe even gone to one of those schools in England—and yet when Walker was around Edgar, he often recalled his farm-boy days.

"This is too good to drink alone," complained Edgar, filling Walker's glass despite a shudder of protestation.

"I've got to get back, Edgar, but thanks a lot. I'll let you know how you can help us."

Edgar glugged. The gulp of wine plummeted into him like a creamy meteorite. He rose to accompany Walker out. The barrier of employment had risen between them. Breaking off pleasant lunches, considered Edgar, was yet another disadvantage of working for a living. Walker had closed the lunch like a desk drawer. He was resolute, like a warrior leaving a maiden to return to combat.

The comradely pleasures which the lunch had brought forth were apparently less important in Walker's world than they were in Edgar's, he reflected, walking Walker out of the dining room. Edgar felt the lunch would only have improved if it grew through the afternoon, watered by golden showers of Chardonnay. Walker felt how far tankers had moved through the Suez Canal in the hour and a quarter he had extracted from his life for this lunch.

Seeing Walker out of the club, Edgar was pleased by how well he felt, by how he had now clearly decided not to look for a job. He admired how he had reinforced Walker's worries that Betty was in a serious decline. Furthermore, Edgar sensed Walker's low opinion of him had risen. There was instinctive comradeship between them now. Walker climbed into the dark den of his limousine after a jolly farewell.

Listing a little, Edgar strode beneath the big glass boxes of executives lining lower Park Avenue like a shelf of breakfast foods, wondering if Camilla's lunch was also over. Whatever he was going to do about Betty's dangerous changes, he would have to do soon, before the interruption in her decline became widely known. He headed for a pay phone. Reaching for the receiver, Edgar was presented with a Polaroid shot taped to the front of the phone of a man's erection blooming from his blue jeans. He grimaced, disgusted, and left the receiver dangling. The pervert was probably thrilling himself watching reactions to his phone display. From a lobby, Edgar saw the perpetrator replace the receiver and duck back into hiding to continue his game. He looked like a business executive.

Men are so cruel, so base, so disgusting and offensive, thought Edgar. What a ruthless thing that picture was, ruining anyone's day who saw it. What if a little girl chose that phone? Edgar decided to thrash the man. He was an anonymous, fiftyish white male in a business suit, loitering among office workers taking the sun on a plaza.

But when he drew near the deviate, instead of hitting him, Edgar just continued walking by without looking at the creature.

Edgar made his intended call from another phone, dreading the sound of Camilla's recording machine, unprepared when her raw, actual voice inquisitively said, "Hello?"

"Camilla?"

"Edgar!"

Edgar was heartened by her tone of enthusiasm. Instead of plotting a date, he asked, "May I see you right now?"

"Oh. Well, sure, where are you?"

"I'm out on a walk."

"Well, whereabouts?"

"Couldn't we just meet there?"

"Here?" She'd never let him see her apartment.

"Yes."

"It's such a mess . . ."

"I'm on the way. I'll help you clean it up."

There was a pause, then, "All right," she assented.

Her acquiescence reminded Edgar of the suddenly sweet passivity of a conquered ballerina at the finale of a pas de deux or the hen curtsying in front of the rooster after her indignant squawking has ended, or a cat come to the finish of her sex fight.

*   *

New York City brownstones, like conquered Rome camped in by barbarians, have become mere warrens of shelter. High-ceilinged rooms, in one of which, Daughter played the piano while Father read his Emerson, and in another of which (that one upstairs), Bridget did the sewing, while in the one below her uncle William, back from the Orient (and still unmarried) quietly locked his door and smoked opium, are each one now a stranger's home. Hellish light quivering out of fluorescent tubes illuminates a passage hacked through lobbies and stairwells and between added walls inside the old home through which the modern tenants can

get to their piece of the place without walking through one another's lives.

Edgar climbed stairs round shouldered from laminations of car-
peting (each one of which gave a muffled complaint) to Camilla's
floor, number four according to the silver decal on the hideously
overpainted wainscoting of the vandalized town house. It reminded
him of his first apartment in New York.

Metal clanked and chains rattled before the door opened. There
she was, real! She looked perfectly beautiful to Edgar, cocking her
head to one side with Eve's own smile of recognition of what was
to come next.

"Would you like a drink?" she asked. A sweater, trousers, slippers—Edgar had never seen her unappointed for public appearance
like this. She seemed sweetly vulnerable and mortal to him.

"No thanks," said Edgar hoarsely, pulling her into an embrace.
A metal rod triangulating support against forced entry to the high
old door hit the floor with a bronze clang. Camilla didn't use it as
an excuse to stop Edgar's embrace. Instead, she stepped backward
in tune with Edgar's momentum. He saw a brass bed filling a room
or closet off the main one as fully as a garaged car.

At last the irredeemable garments were off. With his left sock still
on and his clothes twisted in worsted pretzels leading like elephan-
tine footprints to the bed, Edgar entered Camilla.

When it was over, Edgar was surprised to find himself clinging
to her, trading smiles and kisses. She was so happy, so willing, so
beautiful—how had he doubted her? Just when he was about to
dismiss her from his daydreams as a flirt, she welcomed him to love.
What had he done to change her interest in him so markedly?

"I was afraid you were going to dodge me forever in New
York," confessed Edgar.

"The time just wasn't right, darling," explained Camilla.

Edgar resisted the urge he felt to love her utterly. He pushed
back the great stupid oaf of love crowding up inside him. He looked
up atop a cheap wardrobe at expensive suitcases staring back at him
with brass eyes. Camilla was all clothes and trips. Who paid her
bills? She was much poorer than he'd guessed from their meetings

in Newport and London. No wonder she'd never let him come over. How dear! She needed him!

"When did you decide to see me again?" he asked, smiling.

"I just all of a sudden realized how I felt about you," she said dramatically.

Edgar's heart pounded. She'd realized she loved him. Nothing had changed and now she loved him. Maybe he really could utterly love her. Maybe he was free for love at last, in a life at last his own.

"When?"

Camilla looked at Edgar and smiled.

"When I saw you on television in the winner's circle," she said, playfully shaking her blond hair so it whisked Edgar's face.

Edgar was wounded to find her motive sprang from that shallow spectacle. But his wound comforted him. She loved him for the wrong reason so he didn't have to love her back: the Kentucky Derby, that horrible horse, the phony grandeur of publicity.

Justified doubt at once rushed up to congratulate him on knowing all along Camilla would fall in love with something like a television appearance. Fine. The surge of feeling he'd felt had scared him. Doubt was far more manageable than love.

Besides, love can leave you witless and at this moment Edgar needed all the brains he could get. If Betty dumped him, this could be his apartment, a little penniless place stuffed with the possessions of someone moving past such circumstance. Only unlike Camilla's residency here, Edgar's habitation of such a place would not be an ascendant pause. It would be on the way down.

Camilla jumped up, kissed Edgar and exited. He heard her run a bath in some other grotto of her little cave. Camilla returned in a robe as her bath deepened and asked the ancient mistresses' refrain, "How long can you stay?"

"As long as you can stand me."

"Dinner?"

"Wherever you want."

There was a world-weary timbre in Camilla's voice now. Edgar looked at the expensive suitcases and the expensive clothes. Of course she thought he was rich. Expensive suitcases in an inexpensive apartment explained she was living in suspense, waiting to choose the man who would make these suitcases look at home. Edgar recognized Camilla's urge from his personal experience. The day he'd married Betty he was down to four thousand of the ten thousand he'd brought back from the Korean War.

When she was in her tub, Edgar dozed off.

Fifteen

 onny Turchik crouched down so people on Main Street wouldn't see him driving with his mother in their dated sedan. When she looked quizzically his way, he pretended he was tying his shoe or looking for a dropped penny. Normally, Sonny managed to avoid riding in the car with her, but she was taking him to the doctor because she feared he might have polio. Polio was a horror then, crippling and killing children in a plague. Iron lungs and wheelchairs were regularly photographed with their young inhabitants in solemn photo essays in *Life* magazine.

"Just growing pains," said Dr. Wood to Irma's vast relief after going over her son. Sonny was truculent, but glad he didn't have polio and even gladder no one from his school was there to see his mother, of whom he'd grown ashamed.

Advertisements in the magazines in Dr. Wood's waiting room showed happy, attractive women smiling in gloves and hats outdoors, and grinning delightedly wearing aprons indoors. These, Sonny was sure, were the right kind of mother. His was fat, limped, and spoke English with an accent. At home, she glued sequins on paper birds from kits she'd got for answering a matchbook ad that said:

"Milliners wanted. Make valuable
decorative birds at home. Earn
extra money."

As for fathers, there never had been one, leading Sonny to presume in Sunday school that he and Jesus shared a shameful secret.

"Church is good," enthused his mother.

"Then how come you never go?" countered Sonny. She just shook her head for an answer, just as she did when he asked about his father.

When she drank, a smile Sonny hated came over her face. This smile meant he would have to prepare his own food, and that she would snore.

At school, Sonny liked a boy named Richard, who liked him too. Sonny could tell from Richard's brand-new clothes every first day of school that Richard, like his nickname, was rich. It was at Richard's birthday in the fifth grade that Sonny found out how rich. Richard must have had other birthdays in other years, but this ten-year-old one was the first to which Sonny got invited.

"What's your phone number?" Richard asked.

"It's out of order or something." replied Sonny.

"Then how can your parents bring you to my birthday party?"

"When is it?"

Multanomah was small enough for Sonny to get to Richard's on foot. It was a long walk, including, at its end, a driveway along which trees grew at regular intervals which Sonny realized meant they'd been planted that way for the entertainment of Richard's family. This imperious reordering of nature itself impressed Sonny no end. But the house was even more impressive. It was huge, with clean windows, fresh paint and beautiful wallpaper. The kids were all in party clothes, stuffing themselves with pastel drinks and running around on a lawn mowed down snug as a crew cut. It was immediately apparent Sonny should have brought a present. A pile of the gaudy things was added to with ostentatious generosity by each arriving guest.

When Lee Elder, a classmate, ran out on the lawn after putting his offering on the pile, Sonny noticed Richard wasn't looking. Sonny picked up this present and handed it to Richard who thanked him. What was wrong with that? Sonny didn't claim he'd brought the present. He just handed it to Rich to help out.

Sonny grinned. The party was exciting. Before him cavorted children he knew, renovated and painted up brand-new, dressed like presents themselves. The sort of glamour that pervaded the first day of school was present. They'd all come their prettiest, ready to squeal from mysterious excitement.

This was a wonderful, incomparable day for Sonny, a glimpse of something fine and grand. Parties were obviously fabulous improvements of life. The plates on which the bright, delicious sweets were heaped all matched. They had fascinating pictures on them of elephants, umbrellas, castles, clouds, bridges, trees and distant mountains.

After they began to ruin the baker's sculpted cowboy and Indian scene, Richard unwrapped a treasure hoard equal to the whole toy section of the Multanomah Woolworth's. Lying piled like spoils in the Arabian Nights were books, toy weapons, the most expensive baseball mitt, a stamp collecting outfit, and so much more Sonny lost count.

The children played games organized and refereed by Richard's mother. She looked like that woman running through advertisements. Sonny could imagine her stepping out of Packards with a veil stippling her beautiful, happy face to enter stores and restaurants filled with ideal Americans. Sonny couldn't believe anyone could be as lucky as Rich. He wanted to stay and live like this. As the party ended, Sonny lingered.

Cars came. Guests embellished with party favors were sent back to thank Richard's mother when they forgot. Manic and cranky with party fatigue they tumbled into the homebound vehicles with histrionic motions of being shot or jumping off a cliff. Only Sonny was left. He couldn't tear himself away.

"Can Sonny spend the night?" asked Richard. Sonny looked hopefully at Richard's mother.

"We'll have to ask your parents."

"They said it's ok," said Sonny.

Dinner was formal. The arrival of the father was awesome to Sonny, who had never seen one arrive at his home like this. He smiled and reached a hand toward Sonny, who was first startled, and then relieved to figure out this was something he'd never had from a grown man, a handshake. The man looked more important than a school principal as he laid down his leather shield, removed layers of armor, bestowed kisses and then awarded himself the golden prize of a cocktail from a bottle that looked like a trophy.

Although he was exhausted by the excitement and Richard had fallen asleep, Sonny couldn't sleep. He stared wide-eyed into the darkness, picturing Richard's presents, Richard's mother, Richard's father, Richard's house. It was so wonderful, so perfect—why wasn't it his?

The horror of what happened next still arrived in Edgar's worst dreams like the Mongol horde sweeping into the gardens of the Song Dynasty's bliss. A plaid pattern of light chased itself around the three walls of the room where Sonny and Richard lay. It was from the headlights of an arriving car. There was a banging and then grown up voices. House lights flashed on. Sonny sat up, holding his breath to hear clearly what his worse suspicions had already previewed: his mother's loathsome squawk.

The door to the bedroom opened softly, a widening parallelogram of light like a blade over Richard's father.

"Sonny," he whispered. Sonny bounded out of bed and ran, heart beating, to be punished for the lies he'd told about approving parents.

"Your mother's here," said Richard's father in a disturbed way. He wore a bathrobe. He had also been waked up. Sonny half ran to his fate.

"I worried you is kidnapped," she said in her Middle European accent. Sonny knew this was all a lie, that she was dressed for a party, this party. She even had a prize of hers on, her fur stole, which always looked to Sonny like a chain of long linked rats, some of which had bead eyes and some of which had only the tiny sockets from which the beads had fallen.

Richard's mother and father stood with their arms crossed in their bedclothes.

"Them is cute pajamas, very cute," hailed Irma Turchik. Richard's mother left the room.

"Why you no tell me where you was? I find out from Ray Pinole when he come with some deer meat," she prattled. Richard's mother reentered with Sonny's clothes, folded in a pile. Sonny reached to pull off his beautiful pajama top, speckled like a prince's ermine with tiny pictures of cactus, sombreros and cattle brands.

"Oh, you keep those pajamas if you want—and you put these on," said the beautiful mother. She had slippers for him, into which she assisted him as he stood with his arm around her, looking at his own, unsatisfactory mother. Richard appeared to check out the cause of this nocturnal excitement. Sonny saw Richard's eyes go big and his mouth open in astonishment when he looked at Irma Turchik. Sonny's mother had on so much face powder she looked masked. Her penchant for dress-up, for too much makeup, the hairy wurst around her neck, her homemade sequin bird hat and painted nails were all there, out on parade. She looked exactly the way Sonny most feared she might be seen by the boys in his school. Sitting next to her, Richard's mother looked pretty and natural, like a movie heroine meeting a movie monster.

Irma Turchik would dress up at home sometimes like this, waltzing alone to radio music and drinking Tokay with her little finger cocked while Sonny glowered at her from his hiding place behind the hot-water heater.

Why did he have to have this European apparition for a mother in America? Ever since Sunday school he'd seen how other children gaped at her. He'd done everything in his power to keep her away from elementary school, to keep her his shameful secret.

At home, Sonny cried himself to sleep, trying to keep his sobs inaudible until he heard his mother's snores. The only balm for his unbearable desolation was the beautiful pair of pajamas in which he lay.

*   *

Sonny played hooky next day, afraid to face Richard. He threw rocks at a gaunt old tire reflected into a moaning mouth by the oily water flowing slowly through it in the drainage ditch behind his unsatisfactory home. He bitterly imagined Richard telling the others at school what had happened—all about her, every detail.

"Whassa matter you?" she kept asking him at breakfast. Stripped of her makeup and finery she also looked shocking to him, so oversize and pink. Her eyes were tiny without mascara and the ridiculous eyelashes she glued on them.

Sonny jerked away from her soft hands after him at breakfast.

"Sonny boy?" she called after him when he ran out of the house. Tears ran down his cheeks as he hid, watching her come to the door to stare after him.

Some mother. Instead of a pert, cheerful, bobbed and aproned housewife throwing up her hands and grinning to call the family in to fresh-baked cookies and milk, he had a monster who thought she was Salome or the Queen of Sheba. Rigged up in scaly satin, wigged and rouged and glued and scented, she had some kind of lovemaking sessions with Ray Pinole, the married laborer who liked to hunt deer. Pinole only had about three teeth, but Sonny heard his mother croon flowery phrases to him in broken English and old country language. There was slapping and laughter and remonstration and the sound of movement he wished he didn't understand.

Undoubtedly she thought she'd made a grand appearance at Richard's.

"At my house always give a little drink, something to eat," she'd observed indignantly of her reception by Rich's parents as her old heap shuddered across the railroad tracks to their side of Multanomah. Didn't she notice how they stared at her, how she'd interrupted them?

"Why you no tell me you was over there?" she cooed, her hand cupping Sonny's cheek. He jerked away.

"You is a good-looking boy, Sonny. They gonna love you," she exulted, not noticing the murderous expression on her son's face.

*   *

At school the next day Sonny stared at the picture in his history book of Christopher Columbus landing in the New World, not daring to look over Rich's way. Later, at recess, the boys were playing tops. The blunt wood tops had a steel point. Spun off a wrapping of twine with the right whipping motion, they would knock tops already spinning out of the victory circle in high, surprising bounds like deer. Sonny glowered at the game from behind a tree. Sonny could see Rich's orange top was winning. Rich had everything and always would. Sonny hated him now.

With no explanation Sonny entered the circle of boys and hit Richard as hard as he could. The top game broke into an even more interesting schoolyard spectacle, the fight.

"What's wrong with you?" howled Richard, holding the arm he'd managed to get up the last second of this surprise attack.

"Fight, you chicken," taunted Sonny, "you rich chicken!" At that, Rich fought back. After a few blows, they circled each other, weaving their fists as if they had secret training to scare each other off. Rich struck Sonny's cheekbone, grazing his nose with a gong of pain.

"He's bleeding!" observed a spectator. Sonny touched the hot wet squirt.

"Quit?" asked Richard. Sonny hit him in the face. When they fell to rolling, Sonny got a top, point up, in his back. That hurt more than the blow.

"It's stuck in him!" called a horrified boy. The fight was over. This wound was real enough to call in the adults and their sterile bandages.

At home, Irma was horrified by her son's wounds.

"What happen?" she kept demanding, adding dressings from her own folklore to the work of the school nurse.

"Who done it?"

"Richard."

"Nice boy with the party?"

Sonny nodded.

"Oh, Sonny, how come?" she pleaded, trying to cradle him against her buckets of breast. He squirmed miserably against this hateful mothering.

"Because of you," he finally blurted, causing Irma to release him.

"What you say?"

"They called you a battleaxe hag of a shit-witch!" shouted Sonny, stalking out of the room. As soon as he said it, Sonny felt it was true, even though they had said no such thing. More and more, Sonny began to sense things he made up were, if not true, at least as good as true, and usually even better.

*   *

In the tenth grade, romance provoked Sonny further into an investigation of the superior prospects suggested by his invention. Despite the hurdles and handicaps of his family and his poverty, Sonny had managed to win one of the prettiest girls in the school, a cheerleader whose father worked for the telephone company, the beautiful redhead, Mary Geiger.

"He is white trash," explained Mary's father in one of their battles over her infatuation with Turchik. The Geigers were terrified of Sonny almost from the moment they laid eyes on him. He was precociously smooth, sexual and good-looking. In towns the size of Multanomah, the background of everyone required no research.

Sonny Turchik's meticulous flattop haircut, expensive Day-Glo socks, V-neck sweater and dark blue suede loafers didn't impress Geiger as they had his daughter. The man-hours of minimum wage labor represented in these acquisitions aroused no admiration in the anxious father.

When Sonny actually got a car, a Chrysler Airflow for sixty-five dollars which Mr. Geiger dismissed as a "jalopy," the Geigers realized they were losing control of the situation. The grotesque sedan was a movable tryst.

Every kissing session advanced the amorous technology of both Sonny and Mary. They could kiss for hours without getting bored, drifting in sensual exultation. Sonny finally got ahold of Mary's bra strap catch long enough to release the smooth strange shapes into the moonlight. After this liberty had been given, they both pulled off their shirts as soon as they parked. Topless, they toiled like sweating coal miners in the shaft of the sedan's tatty backseat.

The father's interdiction only added desperate poignancy to the romance. The couple understood the play *Romeo and Juliet* better than anyone else in the tenth grade.

"If only it was different," lamented Mary.

"What do you mean?"

"If you know, it was different at your house," she unnecessarily explicated.

"That's not my mother," said Sonny on an inspiration.

"It's not?"

Sonny shook his head, marveling as vividly as Mary at the possibilities opened up by this claim.

"I got left with her because my parents got torpedoed on an ocean liner."

Once again, as he spoke, Sonny felt he had found a profounder truth than the one provided by circumstance. Mary made a gesture to mother the sudden orphan in her arms.

"They were from England," added Sonny spectacularly.

"His folks happen to be dead from England," shouted Mary through her tears to her furious father.

"Like hell," he shouted back.

"How do you know?" challenged rebellious Mary.

"Because I was stationed in England!" triumphed the recently returned veteran of the Second World War.

Sonny's dead English parents were, next to Mary, the happiest encounter he made in his whole life up until then. Even though they couldn't reach across the void of death and fiction to take

Sonny away from the terrible circumstance in which the Nazi torpedo had left him, the vision of them, handsome, beautifully dressed, leaning across a picket fence entwined with roses, the father waving with a briar pipe of sweet-smelling tobacco and the mother, that advertisement mother, smiling wistfully through her tears and canting her head in apology and admiration toward her unreachable son, was a great comfort to Sonny Turchik.

"Their name wasn't even Turchik," said Sonny to Mary during a lull in their lovemaking.

"What was it?" she asked.

Sonny stared bright-eyed into the sparkling vision of his fabrication. Perhaps it was this very glitter that reminded him of the cowboy.

"Barnes," he said, "Mr. and Mrs. Edgar Barnes."

He seemed spectacular at this moment, as irresistible and unstoppable as the Maid of Orleans when she found her vocation. Mary at last let Sonny go all the way.

*   *

Edgar sighed. Camilla shook his arm.

"Hey," she said, "it's getting late."

Edgar woke up deeply refreshed by his nap. He called a car and took a shower. He was happy to be there, with his fine-looking girlfriend. Electronic flatulence announced the limousine he ordered was waiting for them.

he Odeon in SoHo suited Edgar fine for his dinner with Camilla. SoHo was a youthful and raffish district of New York off the track of Betty and Edgar's crowd, who now occurred to him as a dull and elderly lot. Edgar was thinking of the fun of a bright new life with Camilla. She was wonderfully good-looking. The sight of a woman like this could ruin a man's day. Pine away, boys, thought Edgar when men looked up. Camilla had long been aware of her position as a gentleman's trophy. Since adolescence she treated strange men's glances as her annoying due.

When they entered the unfamiliar place, Edgar took in the tubular chrome chairs, venetian blinds and hat racks.

"It reminds me of a barbershop," he joked. Camilla didn't react to the witticism. She waved to people she knew.

"Edgar Barnes," she introduced him. "Edgar just won the Kentucky Derby."

Camilla's friends seemed to Edgar to travel in table-hopping packs, kissing one another but peering around the room as they did. Edgar wondered if this would be his crowd if he and Camilla came together. Would they entertain these carefully styled people who seemed so glad to be among one another in the fashionable café?

Edgar and Camilla had a certain radiance from their tryst which brought her friends to them. Edgar was handsome and famous from the Kentucky Derby. Somebody had heard his incredibly rich wife was terminally ill; how perfect for Camilla!

A sparse, decorative dinner was brought by a girl in a crew cut (part of the barbershop theme? wondered Edgar). Camilla's friends and acquaintances waxed and waned at the big table at which Edgar insisted on paying for everything, which pleased Camilla both because it proved he was rich and generous, and because it gave her a certain sort of power.

Confidences were whispered down her neck by an effeminate young exquisite which caused Camilla to widen her eyes and say, "No. I don't believe it," in that husky, worldly timbre Edgar had begun to notice. She was obviously popular and important among these people. Would he fit in? He always had fit into situations. One of Camilla's friends wanted to know all about Edgar. Camilla was interested too, because she hadn't yet talked to Edgar about his schools and family.

"Saint Ambrose in British Columbia. It doesn't even exist anymore," had been Edgar's prep school since he thought it up fifteen years earlier in Virginia. This Canadian notion provided a basis for his increasingly English accent. British Columbia had been handily obscure and untraceable as a site for Edgar's education, but he was careful not to talk about it to Canadians. He explained to Camilla's friends that he was slated for Cambridge when the Korean War broke out. He told them about the boys with whom he signed up for Korea:

"The Groton Mystics—I don't suppose you ever heard of them, did you?" he asked the group.

"It sounds sort of familiar," said a young man who'd been to Groton.

"Yes, well you know that thing for the Lafayette Escadrille they have up there?"

"The monument up at Groton?"

"That's it. A lot of the Lafayette Escadrille were from Groton, that American fighter group in the First World War—romantic as all hell, of course. Anyway, it inspired these chaps I knew from

Kenya to join the marines to fight the yellow peril—oh, please excuse me," said Edgar to a modish Asian among them whose sex he still hadn't determined. The person giggled. "Anyway, we'd shot rhinos together and all that and Hemingway and Africa and that monument up at Groton just convinced us all it was something we had to do. We sort of felt we owed it, you know, because we'd been given so much sort of thing. Sounds like pure romantic nonsense now, doesn't it?" laughed Edgar, but he felt Camilla was impressed. Edgar had long since discovered that his fabrications made him attractive. The stories animated and intensified him; he had to be careful and daring to tell them so no one would challenge or question or cross-check his story of himself. There was a sense of excitement he felt and communicated when he stepped into the minefield of fabrication. Camilla stroked his hand as he talked and even the Asian was obviously fascinated.

* *

Sonny did know the Groton Mystics in Korea. He met them in a whorehouse. Edmond De P. Courcy, William Woods and Frick Strongworth all thought Sonny Turchik was a deserter and a pimp when he sat down among them for the first time at the Girl Pussy Club in Seoul. Sonny was raffish, wearing a Japanese robe instead of fatigues and pulling out a roll that included yen and dollars as well as Military Payment Certificates. They looked over his cheap good looks and decided he was some Korean War version of a towny. But at least he broke the gloom congealing around these three as they waited to see who would go first with the chubby whores. When Sonny bought a round of beer in the socially unstratified accent of a Westerner, they accepted that beer as their due, like the familiar blandishments of proprietors trying to attract the carriage trade.

"Are you a reporter?" Courcy finally asked Sonny. How else could someone out of uniform be explained?

Sonny smiled at the question, frostily delivered, but lighting all their eyes. "I do the same thing you do," he answered.

"First Division?" asked William Woods. Woods wanted to ask

why Sonny was out of uniform and what rank he was, but neither question seemed appropriate in the Girl Pussy Club.

"How long have you been here?" asked Courcy.

They were all staring. Sonny at once deduced from their eagerness that they hadn't been in combat yet. They wanted to know what it was like up where the metal was flying. Instinct told Sonny not to tell them he was a supply sergeant in Seoul, that he'd played out some ingenious schemes to get out of the shifting death zones and that he had actually got rich in a small but flashy way in the black market—things of which he was ordinarily proud—because he sensed at once the values of these three Eastern snoots were not built on the usual human ones of staying alive and getting rich. These three marines exuded frustrated heroism. They wanted to die right.

"Have you got laid yet?" he asked, throwing the threesome into jaw-clenching, foot-shuffling, napkin-tearing retreat.

"Get Ginger," he advised. "Hey, Lee, where's Ginger?" Sonny called to a Korean in a Hawaiian shirt whose answer was to inflame his Zippo with a clank. "Ginger's got the biggest jugs in Korea."

Ginger arrived in a shirt filled like a sack of melons. She grinned and stuck them out. Courcy fell out of his chair. Woods, Strongworth and Sonny all laughed. Courcy hit William Woods when Woods tried to help him up. He grabbed Ginger's arm and marched off with her. Woods and Strongworth looked at each other big-eyed and rocked with unreleased laughter.

"Have you been with her?" Frick Strongworth asked Sonny. For an answer Sonny nodded and rolled his eyes in wonderment over what he had experienced. Strongworth actually blushed. When Courcy returned with Ginger, Strongworth rose. Ultimately, William Woods had her too.

Boys make blood brotherhoods by commingling the fruit of pinpricks and taking oaths together. By commingling semen in this Korean vessel, Sonny felt he was becoming the fourth of these three.

"You never fucked any Missy Montgomery," howled Frick Strongworth at William Woods after five or six more beers had loosened the conversation. "The captain told me she threw your ass out of the cabin and you went up on deck and jerked off every time you got expelled." Strongworth's accent fascinated Sonny. It was a superior sort of braying that knew nothing of poverty.

Sonny joined in the derisive laughter directed at William Woods who found this familiarity on Sonny's part cheeky.

"Woods was on my father's boat last summer," explained Frick Strongworth, "trying to get in my sister's roommate's pants the whole way to Sweden."

"What kind of boat?" asked Sonny.

"Just a touch under a hundred feet," Courcy mocked Frick Strongworth's voice.

"Fuck you, Courcy," replied Strongworth.

"No, it's a beautiful boat," Courcy relented.

"You're damn right it is," Frick continued. "It's a steel-hulled Rasmussen yawl," he said to Sonny, presenting his case. "We're going to sail her around the world when we get back."

"Ginger already took you around the world," joked Sonny. Courcy and Strongworth snuffled sardonically.

"What's it to you, mister?" challenged William Woods, who hadn't taken to Sonny as easily as his pals. Sonny laughed off this belligerent challenge. Woods rose and stormed off with Ginger.

Marine officers weren't drafted, Sonny was thinking. *Why did people with hundred-foot boats want to get shot at by Chinese?* When they reached for beer bottles, Sonny noticed both men wore identical loops around their wrists, sort of a leather wire.

"What's that?"

"Elephant hair. Good luck," said Courcy.

"Big medicine in Kenya," elaborated Strongworth.

When Woods came back, Sonny observed he too wore an elephant hair. They didn't seem to be queers, at least not tonight. Why did they all wear these identical bracelets? Sonny asked Woods what the bracelet was. Not liking Sonny, he didn't answer. The story came out slowly from the others as they drank themselves drunk and visited Ginger.

"The elephant has no enemy but man," Courcy told Sonny

portentously at some point. "Groton" was said a lot too. By this time Sonny had figured out that the three of them had gone to Africa together during summer vacations from a school called Groton at which boys had accents like snooty butlers in old movies.

Despite the obscenities and horseplay, there was a spiritual resignation about these three that explained the nickname he later heard for them, the "Groton Mystics." There was something of the quest in their attitude, as though war was simply a place to make a courageous gesture. Imagine considering Korea a heroic opportunity instead of a sordid, deadly calamity! Sonny was attracted to this superior attitude of these aristocratic, military sportsmen.

"What is your name, anyway?" William Woods had finally asked him another night in the same club.

"Sonny."

"But I mean what is your last name and your rank and who the hell are you?" demanded the combative Woods. Sonny didn't answer and the gentler Strongworth once again called off his terrier friend.

Eventually, considered Sonny, if I'm going to keep up with them, I'm going to have to be someone.

"What are you, some kind of military intelligence creep?" persisted Woods. A sip of beer under a level gaze provided an ambiguous enough reply to Woods's speculation. Sonny was delighted his enemy's suspicions were so sophisticated. A "military intelligence creep" sounded good enough to Sonny. The truth was nowhere near as interesting.

At eighteen Sonny Turchik made the sort of mistake for which the judge gave him a choice of probation or the Marine Corps. He was arrested for breaking and entering. He had broken into and entered Rich's house, knowing Richard and his family were away for the summer. When Richard's family packed up and went to an island in Puget Sound to play, barbecue, water-ski and slam through the waves in speedboats, Sonny climbed a tree, popped a screen deftly off an upstairs window and glided inside their home. He'd been doing it for three years. Richard's spurned residence was Sonny's summer house. He never took anything and he left it exactly as he found it. He just liked pretending he lived there.

Naturally, the police presumed he was burglarizing the place when they caught him sitting at the dining-room table in Richard's father's clothes. Richard's family agreed to drop charges if Sonny joined the Marine Corps. Richard wanted nothing to do with him anymore. From then on, anytime a member of Rich's family couldn't find something, they presumed it was part of Sonny's haul. Mary Geiger's father gave five hundred dollars to the church for answering his prayers.

Despite danger and difficulties and Woods's unswerving enmity, Sonny managed to continue his acquaintance with the Groton Mystics, all the way into combat.

Strongworth was the first to go. He fell on top of Sonny when he died. Sonny heard the very shot that killed him after Strongworth fell. Sonny had worked so hard at maintaining friendship with these fellows he had actually, insanely, gone out on a moonlight patrol with Strongworth for the hell of it, for sport. Another burst of rifle fire came. Sonny imagined its preceding cluster of bullets looking for him, passed right through where he'd been standing.

Death was all he was going to get for forging a friendship with them. How stupid! Sonny should have remembered from Rich how dangerous the rich were for him. When he heard the Chinese patrol nearing, Sonny pulled the stiffening corpse of Strongworth over him like the portrait lid of a mummy case. He could hear the Chinese soldiers grunt and breathe and whisper. The jolt of the bayonet into Strongworth's body was so frightening Sonny felt piss bubble out of him. But they went on, leaving Sonny secretly alive.

*　　*

Eventually the Groton Mystics were all killed.

"Woods too," said a laughing sergeant, who lacked teeth, to Sonny as they passed out stolen sleeping bags in the dark to a Korean who was buying them at five dollars a throw.

"Whattyou mean?" asked Sonny, feigning ignorance.

"Yer fancy buddies is dead," said the sergeant, wind whistling through his chops.

Woods too. They were all dead. Sonny held a bag from midtoss until an interrogative Korean communication from the blackness below the deuce and a half returned Sonny to the present. He threw down the sleeping bag. It was the future that had arrested his black market motion. Sonny had a big idea, the biggest one of his whole life.

*   *

The East turned out to look very different from Oregon. There were many more people in this population. The trees (second growth after early agriculture) were skinnier. Korea's surprise included a foreign language and another race. Here in New York were different, but recognizable Americans, but many more than there were in Oregon. There were so many bridges over the rivers it was obvious many people had lived here for many years.

Sonny wasn't surprised the house of Frick Strongworth on Long Island was brick and as grand as the mansions on folding money and pipe tobacco cans. He stood locked into the attention brace of a marine officer when the door opened, slashing off his cap in a saber stroke. The woman jumped. From under his arm, Sonny produced a box. Of course the mother cried when she saw her son's effects.

It was evening, so a father (like Richard's) was inevitable. He rushed to his undone wife's side. When the loss-reminded couple recomposed themselves, they asked the marine officer if he would like "a drink or something." They stared at him. Sonny was a fantastic piece of evidence that their son, Frick Strongworth, had lived out there where he had died. His death was all they knew of him since he gaily and gallantly went to war. That he had lived as well as died in Korea never occurred to them as an actuality until they saw this handsome lieutenant with whom he'd served in Korea.

"I'm sorry, I didn't get your name, young man," said the father.

"Edgar Barnes, sir," said Sonny.

"Lieutenant Barnes."

"Please, sir, call me Edgar."

The man cried too.

They wanted him not to leave, not to take away this contact they felt with their dead son. This attractive young man had served with Frick in Korea! That fatal life Frick had breathed and eaten there was at least represented in parallel by the charming, living young lieutenant standing before them, apparently so embarrassed by his doleful task.

Frick Strongworth had been dead for six months when Lieutenant Edgar Barnes walked in with that box of his things, so the shock of his death was not so much a part of his parents' reaction to this arrival as was a desire to remember and memorialize the brief, handsome, stolen life of their son.

"Can you stay a little?" asked Mrs. Strongworth, "Please?"

"We're having a party for our daughter," explained the father. "It really would be wonderful if you could stay here this weekend, you know, Frick's sister."

* *

Every time Sonny said, "I'm Edgar Barnes," at Ellen Strongworth's debutante party, it rang truer. The young lieutenant, so handsome in his dress blues, so much more glamorous than the mere boys fidgeting in dinner jackets, was immediately and inordinately popular. Sonny Turchik's bronze star was, ironically, the only part of that handsome uniform that was authentic. And yet to its wearer, Edgar Barnes, the medal seemed the inauthentic part, belonging, as it did, to the man he no longer was.

"My God," said the debutante when Lieutenant Edgar Barnes told her a slightly altered version of the story of Frick Strongworth's last patrol.

She let him play with her breasts, but pushed away his efforts at her crotch.

"What's this?" she asked during a truce.

"It's an elephant hair. Good medicine in Kenya," he said in his

new accent, got, like the elephant hair bracelet, from the Groton
Mystics.

*   *

Ironically it was William Woods, the Groton Mystic who never
showed Sonny much more than scorn, who was the most valuable
to him in New York. It was William Woods's mother who offered
the now demobilized (a marine who can award himself a commis-
sion can also offer honorable discharge to himself at his conve-
nience) Lieutenant Edgar Barnes her son's room and his clothes
and William Woods, Sr., who got him a job as a stockbroker.

For six months Edgar Barnes, who had replaced Sonny Turchik,
lived in the life vacated by William Woods, scion of a family which
had worn neckties since the American Revolution. The trouble was
Mr. Woods, like his son, didn't take to Edgar Barnes the way his
wife did.

The old man would drink enough to reduce his normal reserve,
and glare at the handsome young man to whom his wife had
become so devoted. Woods, like his son, was a homely fellow. He
resented his charity to what he had come to perceive as a professional charmer, a lounge lizard and a ladies' man. Maybe he was
jealous of his wife's patent infatuation. They sat for hours together
with Edgar listening enraptured to her boring family stories about
her grandfather's fate in the Civil War. She told him how he'd
grown up alone in the ruined mansion with the confused slave
families, burning Chippendale furniture to stay warm. God how he
would listen to her! William Woods hated it. "And, after the war,
do you know, he became a courtier in the court of Emperor Maximilian down in old Mexico? Well, of course, that was ill-fated, too
—and so was his participation in the Alaska gold rush, and so he
just gave up and married Grandmere, you know, Otterbeck Beer."

Edgar answered the father's sullen scowls with deference and
courtesy. When Mrs. Woods ran up to her room to find a photograph of herself at Vassar ("See if you would have gone out with
me!"), Edgar found a glare so intense coming at him from the plain

visage of Mr. Woods he expected the broker must be having a migraine headache.

"Who are your people?" asked the old man.

"Sir?"

"Who is your father?"

"I lost my parents, sir. They were on a liner that was torpedoed in the Second World War."

Mr. Woods took a sip of his highball without breaking off his stare. Corpses seemed to patch over any access to information about this intruder in the Woods's household. William wasn't alive to ask who Lieutenant Barnes was, and neither was Frick Strongworth. Now the boy's parents, also, turned out to be accessible only to marine archaeologists.

"What do you think?" asked Mrs. Woods breathlessly, returning from upstairs. In the photograph a dozen period virgins were modestly kicking up their knees in a chorus line in front of Matthew Vassar Hall.

"That's you!" marveled Edgar Barnes. Mrs. Woods nodded delighted that he'd spotted the right girl and blinked shyly at the young man. Mr. Woods stood up abruptly and left the room.

Later that week, Edgar rented a room in an old house broken up into apartments. Every morning on his way to work he took another parcel of William Woods's clothes there. At work, he called other stock brokerage firms and arranged interviews. Finally he asked Mr. Woods if he could have a word with him.

William Woods, Sr., slipped on his jacket before admitting his late son's self-appointed substitute. There was nothing definite or specific he could pin on the young man, but it was as if just not quite off the scale of human hearing came a sour note when Edgar Barnes was present. Unconfirmed suspicion tormented the senior Woods. He wished to be either disproven or justified. Edgar Barnes was considerate, and so ostentatiously polite William Woods had the idea he was practicing from a book on manners (which he was: Emily Post).

"Good morning, sir."

"Please, sit down."

"Thank you."

"What can I do for you?"

"Sir, I'm afraid, I think that I should be moving on."

"Oh?" (William Woods almost sang this expletive.)

"Please don't imagine I haven't enjoyed every moment of your generous hospitality. It's just that I think I've got to begin to make my own way."

"I see. Yes, that's probably the right thing," said William Woods, deciding as he did to take an inventory of his household goods after this departure.

"Well, Edgar, let me know if there's anything I can do for you," said William Woods rising, steering the young man toward the door, delighted by this development. He had to admit Edgar Barnes had tact. Just as he was beginning to wonder how to get rid of the creature, Edgar volunteers to exit on his own. It warmed the old man to him for the first time since the impulsive invitations which had landed Edgar on his doorstep.

Exiting Edgar hesitated and turned back to his mentor.

"There is something, sir."

"What's that?" reacted William Woods, not without a note of suspicion.

"Being on my own like that, I mean you've been a family to me, well, I was thinking it would be nice to have somewhere in the evening like the Brook Club . . ."

When William Woods got Edgar Barnes into the Brook Club, he was surprised Edgar insisted on paying his own initiation fee. Woods figured that was going to be the price of getting rid of him. Having Edgar pay his own way only made William Woods feel a little more badly about his suspicions and low opinion of a young man who had, Woods had to admit, fought for his country and behaved impeccably under Woods's roof. William Woods was to spend the fifteen years remaining to him vaguely hoping Edgar Barnes would justify his unrelenting suspicions of him, but such satisfaction never came.

In the first personal residence of his life, a large room with a fireplace in a brownstone house partitioned into apartments, Edgar

Barnes copied the taste of the William Woodses, the Brook Club, the Strongworths, and the Ivy League haberdashers patronized by his fellow stockbrokers. Although he'd never hunted foxes, engravings of the sport hung on his walls. Leather furniture was the only kind he wanted, so the place was furnished as slowly as the occurrence of such items in antique, junk and secondhand stores permitted.

The ten thousand he had from his black market activities in Korea had gone down to five from his investments in the stock market. When luck shot his worth back up to eight, Edgar sold himself out of the market and put away his endangered capital. His clients' accounts (Mrs. Woods had fifty thousand with him, the Strongworths two hundred thousand and a couple of debutantes he'd known about a hundred and fifty more) moved often to pump him commissions, but it was obvious early to Edgar that he was not as clever at stockbroking as others at his office.

From his acquaintance at the Brook Club and friends he'd made at debutante parties, Edgar began a much greater success socially than he'd managed with the stock market.

"God, you have such incredible manners, it's just great," said the girls.

"What was the war like?" said the males.

When he first saw Betty Bishop, Edgar had all but settled on a very pretty red-haired girl (Mary Geiger had set a romantic pattern for him) whose father was a respected doctor. He'd already heard who Betty was. Besides the Bishop Bank there were hospital pavilions, a foundation and even a university by the same name. She was thin and strikingly handsome and older seeming than her contemporaries. She was trying to get the top off a jar of stuffed olives in the butler's pantry of a country house when Edgar, perspiring from tennis (a sport he was trying in public for the first time after intensive, and expensive private lessons), saw her.

"Can you?" she asked.

"Say that again," he answered.

"What?"

"Can you—you said 'can you' and I want to remember our first words. Let me show you I can."

Betty looked again at the handsome man. That was amusing. So was the shape of the cylindrical little jar and the provocative way he eased it through her fingers. What a pleasant surprise to find an amusing man even before her first martini.

The redhead had never had such a thudding experience of being dumped before. Edgar Barnes, a man who had sent flowers and opened doors and finally proposed on his knees with a two-carat diamond ring in his pocket, suddenly didn't appear to be capable of recording her existence. Right after doubles that morning at Mimi and Falwell Barnes's summer place he didn't just go cold, he completely lost track of her. He walked right by her carrying a drink with Betty Bishop. At first the redhead, Annie Spinks, thought he was kidding. When Edgar sat with Betty on a bench in the garden a hedge away from the tennis court, Annie walked up behind him and said "boo." He turned, smiling, and laughed at her. His eyes were as blank as if she were a gardener. He didn't seem to recognize her! Then he turned back to Betty Bishop.

Dumbfounded, and then enraged, the dropped doubles partner served a ball with all her might at Edgar Barnes and knocked Betty Bishop out cold.

"Really, I'm fine," said Betty, coming to in Edgar's arms as he carried her past the sofas of the sitting room to a bedroom. She touched the back of her head. What a pleasure it was to ride in his arms, the handsome man she'd found with her olives.

"Well, you certainly *can*," she said afterward.

"It's like those cavemen who conk you and carry you off somewhere," she added.

"What's your name again?"

"Edgar Barnes."

Edgar knew all the magic there was in the world had suddenly become his.

"Are you related to my cousin's husband?"

"Who?"

"Falwell Barnes, Mimi's husband."

"I didn't realize she was your cousin," answered Edgar ambiguously.

"I never got in bed with a man this fast in my life."
Edgar kissed Betty.
"Edgar just sort of knocked me out," Betty told people after that.
The dropped redhead eventually married a lawyer.

*   *

In bed that night, after he met and made love to Betty Bishop, Edgar lay under *The Kill*, the final engraving of his fox hunting suite, with the name *Bishop* beating in his heart. It was enormously consequential. The Bishop Bank was probably as well known, even to people like the queen of England, as the name Donald Duck. Taxi drivers, receptionists, ballerinas, debutantes—even charwomen and street vendors—had the name permanently enfolded in their brains. Betty was beautiful and famous and not just rich but richest—and Edgar Barnes had made love to her an hour after meeting her!

He levered up in the dark, his grin glowing, and shook his head. No lottery winner, Nobel Prize recipient or newly crowned Miss America felt much different from Edgar as he stared into a darkness writhing with promise. Edgar turned on his bedside lamp and got out of bed.

He decided his clothes shouldn't be in a pile on the chair he'd paid over a hundred dollars to have upholstered in tartan (like the one he'd admired at the woolly Anglophilic clothing store where he'd bought the very tie drooling off the casual heap of trousers and underwear)—not now that he'd arrived at the Bishop level of American life. Picking up his clothes, Edgar particularly admired the combination he happened to have selected for Annie's fateful invitation to Sunday in the country.

Annie Spinks. Edgar paused, pulling the crease in his trousers taut. He hadn't thought of the redhead once since he'd seen Betty Bishop. And Annie was his fiancée! Or at least she had been. Edgar laughed aloud at the thought of this engagement. The ring had cost him two thousand dollars. Edgar frowned. Would he ever see that money again? Unlikely. That left him only six thousand with which to court Betty Bishop, Elizabeth Williams Bishop—Betty

Bishop Barnes? Mrs. Edgar Barnes? Edgar was so gleeful he did a little jig with his jacket before filing it among the hand-me-downs from the late Groton Mystics in which he had blended so quickly and smoothly into the genteel society of bird shooters, tennis and backgammon players, yachtsmen and skiers among whom he'd found, at last, Betty Bishop.

Annie Spinks, daughter of a doctor, member of a country club, privately educated and listed in the Social Register, had been Edgar's *belle ideal* of the female possibility until he had stepped into that pantry on the very day that had darkened into this very night. Annie had told him what a Social Register was:

"Don't you know? It's a stud book!"

"How do they get in?" he had asked, thumbing thin pages of names of people he imagined living happily ever after.

"You're supposed to be born, or marry, but they *add* people," she had said with an ironic drawl and roll of her eyes about these *added* people.

Everything about Annie had seemed to Edgar like a privilege: her clothes, her parents, her possessions and her home were all the right ones. Edgar knew he had advantages. He'd been the teacher's pet in every grade even though his clothes were ragged. Women had always adored him. Irma Turchik, who so grotesquely imagined herself a lover, treated her son like one. "You is damn good looker, Sonny," she had said to him a thousand times, shaking her head in happy wonder.

People accepted and made way for him. They always had. And Annie had the main thing he hadn't, background. Where she had cousins in prep schools and law firms and down neat, crackly driveways, Edgar had only that freakish harridan, powdering and painting and drinking the truth away as best she could. Where Annie had clean, genteel, handsome and wealthy parents, he had a living, hidden birthmark from which he had seen people turn away. Annie had everything he lacked and Edgar had counted himself fabulously lucky to have her.

Signing Annie's parents' names for hamburgers at the Yacht Club, with attractive contemporaries of hers adjusting their grips on tennis rackets and golf clubs as they bantered on the terrace, had been a vision of paradise Edgar was happily accepting as his lot until this afternoon. Now Annie's once grand circumstance seemed a pathetically minor sinecure. The Bishop Bank, Bishop University, the Bernard Bishop Foundation, Parnassus Casualty, Williams Square, W. A. Williams and Company, the Williams Fund, Foundation, Hospital and Symphony Hall—these institutions were all parts of that woman pumping beneath him whose howls he'd covered with his hand so as not to inform the other guests of their activity in the guest bedroom after the tennis accident. In his present, nocturnal review, Annie Spinks instantly underwent the shrinkage return to childhood circumstances can provide: everything so much smaller than you remembered.

Edgar paced around his apartment. He walked through the comic strip sequence of his treasured fox hunting pictures, *The Meet, Breaking Cover, Tallyho! Gone Away, Gone to Ground* and *The Kill*—this very sequence had entirely happened to him today with Betty Bishop! Annie had taken weeks to allow Edgar into her, and it was weeks more before she ceased looking like a shipwreck victim clinging to the side of a lifeboat as Edgar adjusted angles, rhythms and outcries to make her let go, but Betty hadn't wasted a moment. Did she make love to anyone? It was something Edgar had to consider. Maybe she was merely rich and promiscuous. Well, so what? Who wouldn't be with all that? The advantage Edgar Barnes had over suitors who might be shocked and threatened by Betty's sexual proficiency was the legacy of Sonny Turchik, who was in fact a part owner of the Girl Pussy Club in wartime Seoul.

"I'll call you tomorrow," he'd whispered breathily in Betty's ear before closing the black shiny steel of her car door. "Please do," she'd said aloud.

Mimi, Betty's cousin, had looked bemused when Edgar returned to the house to get his things.

"I think your ride went back to New York," she'd remarked with irony about the departed Annie Spinks as Edgar stood with his tennis racket, staring triumphant at his hostess.

"Falwell will give you a ride to the station," she said next, looking with private amusement at the back of her hand as she flexed and fanned her fingers with nails painted like pistachio nuts.

Edgar felt a certain challenge implicit in Mimi Barnes's tone. "You don't think I can get your cousin? Just watch!" said Edgar's shining eyes (but not, of course, his smiling mouth).

*   *

Being engaged for two years to Bertram Hull Woodruff attracted Betty to Edgar Barnes with the intensity of escape. Woodruff had won Betty's finger, but not her hand, through the boring erosion of patience and determination. He was wooing her with inevitability. His fortune was grand enough to preclude needing hers. His breeding featured late nineteenth-century title hunting after a fortune resulting from the invention of a packaged dessert by an upstate New York pharmacist.

He, too, could point to ancestral names incised in the pediments of buildings erected to administrate improvements in human society and recall a grandfather with a private railroad car. But Betty worried Woody Woodruff would bore her to death. Besides "Betty Woodruff" sounded unbearably plebeian to her. Edgar Barnes's scintillating entry couldn't have come at a more diverting moment.

*   *

Her telephone was unlisted! Edgar sat at his stockbroker desk looking at the receiver with anger before replacing it. Of course it was unlisted! Betty Bishop was too rich to appear in a phone book. Why hadn't he gotten her number? They were already lovers. He hadn't even told her where he worked because unlike every other woman he'd met in New York, she hadn't asked him what he did. So far, his name and where he was from were the only lies he'd told her.

Edgar had to discover Betty Bishop's number. When he tried the office of Falwell Barnes, the man married to Betty Bishop's cousin Mimi, Falwell Barnes turned out to be in Chicago on business. The maid at the Falwell Barnes residence took Edgar's number, but no one returned his call. Edgar was aghast and furious and frustrated until he thought of calling Annie Spinks.

"What do you want?"

"I just would like to talk about things."

"You go to hell!"

"Please?"

"No."

"Let's just go out and have a drink and talk."

"You just want your stupid ring back!"

"No. I want you to keep it."

"I'm going out to dinner."

"Let me just drop by a minute after work."

"No."

The last no tottered like a domino about to fall. After work, Edgar went to Annie's apartment, correctly expecting to be allowed admission.

When Edgar appeared in her apartment, Annie looked like she was going to kick his ankles.

"Help yourself if you want a drink," she said sarcastically, turning at once to leave the room, which is just what Edgar wanted. He crossed the stain-spotted white rug, noticing for the first time how small her sitting room was, to the reproduction chinoiserie desk, relieved to see the monogrammed leather address book under a display of invitations in front of silver-framed photographs of the parents he had earlier envied. Now they looked average, even mediocre, to Edgar.

Bishop, Betty, BU8-0007 he read in Annie Spinks's book.

"What are you looking at?" said Annie harshly from across the room. Edgar turned, closing the address book behind him.

"Parties you aren't going to be able to go to?" she continued sarcastically, taking a step toward him. Edgar smiled and sighed.

"I'm sorry," he said, raising his palms in benediction.

"You bastard!" shouted Annie, bursting into tears. Of course she expected to feel his supportive arms when she clenched shut her wet eyes and trembled with a sob. But when the moment for him to embrace her passed unfulfilled, Annie opened her eyes to discover she was alone in the room.

*   *

"I can't," said Betty when Edgar telephoned and asked her to dinner. He waited for her to say why not, but she didn't. Edgar found that impressive. He decided he would act this way someday, above explanations.

"What about next Wednesday?" There was a pause during which Edgar wondered if he were being assayed.

"Nope," said Betty. "Nope" was an interesting word, too—so typically American. It was the kind of word Edgar didn't use anymore, worrying it was proletarian, but when Betty Bishop said "nope," it sounded almost patriotic in its implication the Bishop fortune didn't stand between her and the country from which it had been extracted.

"Well, when is good for you?" asked excited Edgar, afraid she wasn't continuing the enthusiasm she'd expressed in flagrante delicto. He cleared his throat to drive his voice down from too obvious a pleading tone.

"What are you doing the sixteenth?" she asked, relieving Edgar from his growing doubts about his welcome.

"You tell me," he offered in a husky, lowered voice that pulled her into an embrace. She chuckled.

"There's some kind of a dinner dance. I guess if you came by about eight."

"I look forward to seeing you," said Edgar in a boudoir purr. Betty chuckled again.

"Black tie," she said, and she hung up.

Edgar's nostrils flared as he sucked in a battle breath, grinning tightly. That abrupt way of Betty's, just hanging up, not asking him even what his number was let alone what he did or where he lived, the regular old "nope" and the absence of explanations, apologies or even platitudes challenged and thrilled him. The climb was over. This was the view from the top. Everything less than Betty was small and far below.

Edgar's genius, in his own opinion, lay in his power of recognition. The notion that the urchin glowering at the harridan gluing sequins on felt birds from his hiding place behind the hot-water heater in a hovel in which a couple of kicks could link inside and outside would grow up to play tennis on the court of a country estate with rising young executives he knew from his membership in the Brook Club was fantastic enough, but linking that waif to Betty Bishop, probably the premier heiress of the entire nation, bordered on hallucination. He'd accomplished it by the instinct of recognition that led him to Rich at school and the Groton Mystics in Korea and Annie in New York. He'd known who to go after and how with an instantaneous conviction and accuracy that were explicable only as a genetic instinct.

Having no father was something of an advantage in Edgar's Himalayan social climb. That particular blank could be filled in any way he wanted from the growing store of information about life in the upper classes to which he'd added every day. Maybe Irma Turchik, like her ancestors in medieval Europe rolled over in potato fields by passing knights, had combined with a prince to conceive Sonny. The father could have been a touring aristocrat from Europe, the scion of an American industrial fortune, a movie star or even an antecedent bastard who didn't know his own father was the czar of Russia who had dallied with a chambermaid in his cabin on his cousin the kaiser's steam yacht during the Russo-Japanese War.

Then again, Dad could be a failing salesman with newspaper keeping the wet kiss of pavement from coming through holes in the cheap soles of his pointed shoes, or a toothless wino whose bones rattled around in his filthy old suit like golf clubs, or a grocery delivery boy, a department store Santa Claus or a horny policeman.

It was Edgar's good looks that allowed him to entertain the nobler possibilities of his ancestry. How else could his fine form have emerged from Irma Turchik? Only as a baby had he resembled her, and only that because she resembled all babies. Even awful

Irma could be seen by Edgar as something of an advantage now. It was escaping her that set him out on his course among the finer things of life. If she had been the American mom he had pined for as a child, he might be delivering mail in Multanomah or canning salmon in Seattle instead of making these ever more refined choices that had moved him up to the summit where he stood tying a black tie around his neck to take Betty Bishop, Elizabeth Williams Bishop, to a dinner dance at the Metropolitan Museum of Art.

Edgar had been choosy at the formal wear rental place. He had avoided the cheaply tricky modified suits suggested by the clerk and chosen the simplest formulation. He knew from coming-out parties the genteel didn't wear "showy" tuxedoes.

"Do you want the shawl collar?" asked the salesman. Edgar cursed himself for not paying closer attention to lapels at those dinner parties at which his marine dress blues had set him handsomely apart.

On a hunch the double-breasted, wide-lapeled jacket was old-fashioned, Edgar rented the notchless lapeled "shawl collar" model and prayed, as he draped it on (after retying his tie for the fifth time), that he'd made the right choice.

Superb! he thought, walking stiffly in his unaccustomed costume. Cold as it was, Edgar didn't wear an overcoat because the Irish tweed former property of Frick Strongworth didn't seem correct to Edgar for evening outer wear.

Conserving capital, Edgar took a bus to Betty's neighborhood. To his surprise two other men in tuxedoes, one of them black, were sitting in the tin whale across from him.

"Where's your gig?" asked the black one. Edgar saw they had musical instrument cases.

"Private party," answered Edgar.

Annie's apartment house with its uniformed doorman, lobby plants and piped music in the elevator had impressed Edgar as luxurious and expensive when he'd first entered it six months ago. But Betty's building made it seem like a tinny geegaw by comparison. A doorman with a high starched collar and gloves as white as Mickey Mouse's smiled and bowed Edgar in.

"Edgar Barnes," said Edgar, proud to put his name in the paneled lobby with its big black-and-white marble checkerboard floor, its leather furniture and eighteenth-century portraits. Recognition again served Edgar instantly. He recognized how much better this place was than Annie's as completely and quickly as he'd known Edgar Barnes was a better name than Sonny Turchik.

The doorman looked at him quizzically, holding up Edgar's progress to the elevator, where another attendant awaited details of Edgar's ascendancy.

"Barnes?" asked the doorman. For a terrible second Edgar expected the doorman to continue his sentence:

"Don't you mean Turchik?" like a sarcastic detective in a movie. But the doorman only looked at him with a sort of helpful, urgent confusion. Edgar shivered from his walk from the bus stop.

"I'm here to see Betty Bishop," Edgar explained.

"Miss Bishop," said the doorman repairing to the lobby telephone. Edgar wondered if the doorman were correcting him. He wished he'd said "Miss Bishop."

"Mr. Barnes is here to see Miss Bishop," intoned the flunky into a telephone, with an undertaker's discretion.

"You can go right up, sir," he enthused with a smile as he returned.

The elevator man watched the well-known plot of passing floors unfold again. He pulled the shiny brass gate back and Edgar found himself in a vestibule with a big door. It opened at once, revealing a man who recognized as quickly as Edgar did that he was wearing a better tuxedo.

"How do you do, I'm Edgar Barnes," said Edgar offering his hand. The man stepped back with a bow.

"May I get you something to drink, sir?" he asked.

"Scotch and soda," answered Edgar. It was a butler! Christ! Turning away his blush to look at rooms of ecclesiastical proportions furnished and hung with a grandeur more refined than hotel lobbies, Edgar sharpened his wits like a burglar entering a house. He mustn't make a second mistake like this initial one. The notion a twenty-five-year-old girl lived alone in such parental, regal splendor astonished Edgar to the point where he had to clear his throat not to reveal his jaw was gaping. His drink came atop a little snowflake of a napkin on a silver tray.

The butler's tuxedo made Edgar's feel pointy and shiny by comparison. Edgar sat down until he decided that pose was too humble and waiting-room like. He paced around looking at pictures in honey-colored frames as curled and coiffed as women's hairdos, furniture painted and carved into fantasy, great bunches of unusual flowers, and draperies as elaborate and luxurious as ball gowns. She was behind him when he turned around.

"Hi," she said. She was holding a glass of champagne.

Edgar's lust bolted through him. It wasn't unappreciated.

In the morning Betty laughed, carrying Edgar's clothes into her bedroom from where they'd fallen to earth in the sitting room and vestibule after the party.

"This is the worst dinner jacket I've ever seen," she remarked. "I'm so glad it was only rented."

*   *

Betty liked telling Edgar to call it a dinner jacket instead of a tuxedo and to get one from a tailor instead of a rental agency. She liked showing him what clothes to buy and where to buy them. They made love at least once every day for weeks, even after they were married.

*   *

Inside the inside pocket of the tweed overcoat Edgar had inherited from Frick Strongworth (the one he hadn't worn on his first date with Betty) was the label. Above Strongworth's penned name was that of "Pollifax and Pollifax, Bespoke Tailors" and their London address. Clear back in Korea listening to the speech patterns and ideals of the Groton Mystics, Edgar had recognized how these superior, wealthy Americans aped and revered the English (the major commanding the Gurkha rifles of the UN forces brought fully as much respect to William Woods's eye as Sonny did con-

tempt). This label was what came to Edgar's mind when Betty
suggested they go to London for their wedding trip.

He was thrilled by the suggestion. Not only did it mean Pollifax
and Pollifax would soon be outfitting him, it confirmed Betty was
going to marry him.

"Why don't we go over to London for our honeymoon?" she
said brightly, making fun of the sentimental old word, stretching
and rising to wash up after they'd made love.

"Sounds like fun," he suavely replied as if he'd been there a
thousand times, wondering if they really drove on the left side of
the road and dropped monocles in their soup.

He all but shouted for glee once he heard precipitation in the
marble-and-mirror rain forest of Betty's grand bathroom. He laid
his head back in the crook of his elbow and smiled bright-eyed up
into the vortex of the pleated canopy over her bed.

London! What next, Paris? Everything he'd dreamed of was
coming true! Edgar grabbed up and twisted a hank of downy
pillow encased in lacy linen: tartans and Spitfires and salmon kills
occurred to him. "Mr. and Mrs. Edgar Barnes chose England for
their wedding trip," he mouthed. And that's exactly what the
caption under their photograph read in *Country Life* magazine.

*   *

When word of his forthcoming marriage to Betty Bishop got
out, Edgar's fellow stockbrokers couldn't hide their awe and envy.
Members of a profession based on dreaming of millions suddenly
found that Edgar, one of them, had escaped into that very dream:
millions and millions. Edgar was pleased to notice glances and even
stares from the telephoning brokers in the trading room. They
quickly turned away when Edgar caught their eyes on him, jerking
their heads up to watch the parade of millions on the tape, a parade
Edgar Barnes had now somehow joined.

There were lots of parties. Edgar was welcomed with kisses,
hearty handshakes, food and wine. People with houses and enormous apartments celebrated the new couple with what Edgar

began to detect was more or less the same herd gathering over and over again. He loved every minute of it.

Like Rich's seminal birthday party, these celebrations of his engagement to Betty held for Edgar a thrilling sense of newness, excitement and treasure. Even the same maids seemed to turn up at different parties. Without asking Betty why maids and butlers were repeating their appearances in different households (which, he suspected, might be a revealing inquiry), Edgar deduced by himself the parties were being catered. The same investigative observation informed Edgar what florists, magazines, hors d'oeuvres and even candles were in favor with this handsomely dressed herd, who Edgar never doubted was socially the very highest ranking one in New York City.

Betty refused to have the wedding at her parents' house or at their apartment. When her cousin Mimi offered the country house where the couple had met for the occasion, Betty still refused. She had her own ideas about her wedding.

"City Hall," Betty replied to every offer.

Like her habit of occasionally chewing a stick of gum, an activity Edgar considered a class stigma, Betty's choice of City Hall for her wedding ceremony seemed to Edgar to be deliberate and facetious, a kind of slumming that amused her.

Fine with Edgar, just so it actually went ahead and happened. Edgar wouldn't have minded if she chose the dog pound as a site. Could it be? He still wondered. Only clenched in the fit of orgasm, with nothing smaller or more specific than the entire universe visible, was he free of worry.

Betty liked this part of the courtship too, so they made lots of love. For Edgar, the Bishop millions were aphrodisiac. For Betty, sex was a treat.

"It's fun, but is it enough for marriage?" questioned Mimi over a filet of sole she hoped would cancel the half box of chocolates she couldn't resist that morning. Betty eagerly nodded. Edgar was more like a toy than any man she'd ever known. He wasn't connected, like others, to some knowledge or occupation that took up his attention and gave him authoritative airs. He was all hers. It was fun to teach him finer points and fun to watch him marvel at finer things. He was attractive, enthusiastic and wonderful as a lover.

The Bishop fortune had begun to tyrannize Betty at this time in her life. As a child, her wealth was presented like a religion: a lofty, distant responsibility, as big a deal as death. As she grew older, her distance from the thing, the fortune itself, shrank and the stink of it grew the closer she got. It turned out to be different from either the philanthropic instrument or fabulous shopping tool she'd been taught to expect. It turned out to be a kind of embarrassment.

Other people wanted her to make them rich from it.

"It's all deductible if you lose," explained investment seekers. "I hope it doesn't affect our friendship," they said they hoped. But, of course, it always did.

Sometimes Betty acted poor, pleased no one knew she was rich and other times she made damn sure everyone knew she was rich. Wealth was a weird appendage, an afterglow, a bizarre reflection that never let her appear without it.

Often, other people seemed personally proud of Betty's wealth, proud to be seen with her and it, as though they were gilded by its glow. No one seemed able to perceive Betty without it. Did they presume she would be a failure without it? Would she? Wealth, that rare and dangerous advantage, was becoming particularly infuriating to Betty as the time for marriage arrived.

Lawyers, family, trust officers, accountants, cousins, friends and even strangers at parties made it their business to warn Betty that her wealth made her a mark, a target, an irresistible attraction to society's ruthless ambitions. The worst possibility envisioned by all these advisers was marriage to an unknown, a man with no money at all. But if she did marry Bertram Hull Woodruff, her fiancé whose fortune defused such doubts, she'd never know exactly what she'd avoided.

Edgar Barnes had slept with her an hour after they were introduced. That amused Betty. There was something shady about him. That amused her too. As a lover, a doubt and a novelty, he perfectly embodied all they'd been warning her against as long as she could remember: this man was the epitome of what she'd been drilled to abhor. Only he could show her why she shouldn't have married him, and only if she did marry him, could she discover the reality of this reason.

Those who advised her could never really know, themselves, what it was they were advising her to avoid. They could only surmise it, the way people surmised what it was like to be as rich as Betty. There was only one way to find out.

At the ceremony when Betty said "I do," Edgar's vision went black for a moment. It cleared and he felt his pulse beating the whole room like a pile driver. His grin stayed on so long his gums began to dry. They kissed. Betty's maid Pilar threw a little rice on them outside on the street before they got in the limousine. Now, they were married.

"Betty Barnes," mused the bride aloud on the way to a reception at Mimi's. "Thank you, Edgar." Edgar could only grin. He couldn't even think. He believed the impossible had actually just happened. Betty wasn't the only one whose name had truly and finally changed at this momentous ceremony, his was now truly Edgar Barnes, gentleman, handsome millionaire, envied aristocrat. He squeezed Betty so tight she said, "Hey, ow!"

The grinning guests at Mimi's reception looked to Edgar like the heavenly chorus. Sputtering glasses of champagne never got all the way empty. A little band in the other-side-of-the-tracks-style dinner jackets Edgar now clearly recognized after his own mistaken rental, played jumpy, dated music that got Mimi snapping her fingers and, after an hour, even shaking her hair.

When Edgar made his way through a two-step with Mimi, she had the unchanging, wiseacre grin Irma Turchik often achieved after hours of Tokay. She bounced her bulgy body, like a big bunch of grapes, into Edgar on the turns.

"You bad man," she said in her deep, whiskey-fragrant voice, winking. Edgar didn't reply.

"Bad, bad man," she repeated, rolling some parts of herself into Edgar's loins and chest.

"Great party," said Edgar.

"Poor Annie Spinks," said Mimi in a high note, making a face-tious pitying expression on her face. Edgar's smile didn't check, but his eyebrows darkened when they bumped together between his eyes.

"You sure dropped her, Edgar," said Mimi with a knowing grin. "Fine girl."

"You dropped her like, like Kleenex you're through with," laughed Mimi, pantomiming such a drop. "God, Edgar, we all saw the whole thing. One look at Betty Bishop and poor little Annie Spinks was yesterday's fish."

Edgar didn't know what to say to these remarks of his hostess.

"You're bad," she said, nuzzling into his chest. Edgar swung her around, wishing this style of music wasn't so interminable.

"You're bad," she said again when he took her to her husband, Falwell Barnes.

"Where are your Barneses from?" asked Falwell as Mimi con-tinued right past him, leaving Edgar with the husband where he meant only to deposit the wife.

"Tennessee."

Falwell Barnes brightened and appeared to scrutinize the newly-wed.

"Knoxville?"

"No, the river."

"The Mississippi or the Tennessee?"

"Fanville."

"Because my family is from Tennessee—maybe we're kin, Edgar —well, I guess we are anyway." Falwell Barnes raised his glass. Edgar smiled and raised his.

"Congratulations, cousin," said Falwell Barnes ironically.

Marking these relatives of Betty's as possibly dangerous, Edgar recalled the hostility of William Woods, Sr., only unlike Woods, Falwell Barnes wasn't a successful businessman. In fact, from what Betty'd told Edgar, he'd laid back on his oars once he'd married Mimi. Maybe that's what he meant by his sarcasm, they were both now appendages of the great Bishop trusts.

Betty was also noticeably tight. When Edgar danced with her, everyone drew back the way they did when Fred Astaire began to dance in an old movie. Betty didn't really want to dance. Edgar's theatrical turn almost tripped her. The guests politely raised their glasses and looked busy when the new couple failed to enchant them with dance display.

Betty made her Bronx cheer at the music, and Edgar escorted her into Mimi's breakfast room.

"Happy, darling?" he asked her. Betty began to kiss him with her tongue lolling, squeezing impersonally against him. Edgar responded, but his heart wasn't in it.

"Oh!" enthused a guest stepping around a corner. "Excuse me!"

This interruption returned Edgar's own enthusiasm and swept away the cold and congealing doubt that had begun with his dance with Mimi. This witness reminded Edgar of the figure he had come to cut in the world. As Edgar Barnes, married now to Betty Bishop, he felt a bolt of joy he easily transmuted into lust. He shut the doors, braced chairs against them, swept a pair of porcelain squirrels onto the floor where they shattered from cuteness into rubble and pulled down Betty's pants. Betty couldn't have been more delighted. Now she was sure she'd married the right man.

Seventeen

efore she incontrovertibly awakened, Betty wondered whether she could be happy yet another day. Her fret it was bad luck to notice how well things were going flickered across this still semiconscious moment, too. Then she really was awake—and everything was still just fine. A smile had opened with her eyes.

She was at Bothwell, two days before the Preakness was to be run at nearby Pimlico Race Track. Betty lay in a bed covered and canopied in her black and tan colors. What a wonderful bed it was! Twenty years ago this bed caused much comment in a famous magazine spread that showed Betty and Edgar's glorious advantages to the less fortunate (who, Betty had considered about this time, included just about everybody else there was). On the slick color pages of the magazine, Edgar's monogrammed velvet slippers pointed at this very bed from the super old Caucasian rug like a pair of Moslems at prayer. This picture, like all the photos of their property and persons back then, showed the world you *could* have money and style and looks and breeding and youth and fun all at the same time.

One time when Edgar and Betty got out of a car together in front of the apartment on Park Avenue, a plain girl passing stopped, looked and unashamedly burst into applause. Betty didn't miss children, really, and after a halfhearted interview at an agency decided to skip adopting some. Edgar was in many ways her child then. So eager and ignorant and good-looking, he was the boy she had raised to this present middle-aged juvenile delinquency.

Racing back from her decorator's twenty years ago with the very canopy now stretched above her bed in the trunk of her Ferrari, Betty'd been stopped for going a hundred miles an hour in a twenty-five-mile zone. The police officer was curious and dazzled by the patently rich and beautiful young woman in the vicious elegance of an electric-red foreign sports car. Ice cream dripped over a cone in her hand. A poodle looked up from under the dashboard. An exclamation point from what could be either anger or worry had formed between the inscrutable plates of her dark glasses.

"Please, officer, I'm sorry, really. The thing is I have to hurry. My ice cream is melting and my dog has to piddle," she explained, then she cried. The policeman was too astonished to give her a ticket. She simply didn't seem earthly enough to regulate with a summons.

Eight-thirty said Betty's watch. A bedside clock did too. It was morning! This was the earliest into morning Betty had penetrated from the correct side. She'd got there too often from the dark side, watching day crack squares around her drawn curtains, as old movies gave way to the variety shows of nosy interviews by smiling anchor people. Eight-thirty in the morning would make her whimper, then, and order a bullshot to wash down a sleeping pill. But this eight-thirty was a boon, a real one, got to through the front door.

The dining-room sideboard at Bothwell held salvers of breakfast in the English fashion for a houseful of guests. Except for Tommy Smithers who had risen at four and gone to Pimlico Race Track, Betty was the first one up.

That wonderful effect of being pleased by physical objects grew with everything Betty saw. The pinky sheen of polished Georgian

silver and the rich clatter of old bone china made her shiver with
delight as she poked and sniffed under lids. She felt so grateful, not
only to whatever glands were serving happy chemicals and electri-
cal charges to her nervous system for a change, but even outward
from herself to all the wonderful little people who did their best to
serve, furnish, tend, groom, clean, repair, supply and maintain her
life. At this exact moment of Christian consideration, William the
butler entered with strawberries and cream.

"Good morning, William."

"Good morning, Miss Betty."

"Oh, how yummy."

To her detailed inventory of the morning's pleasantries, Betty
now added old William's form of address, "Miss Betty." William
was from her father's time. "Miss Betty" sounded good both because it proclaimed Betty's childhood an enduring treasure from a
historical past and because it sounded so unmarried.

Edgar wasn't due at Bothwell until the next day. He was in New
York on business, whatever that was supposed to mean. Was he
buying clothes? Taking college girls to expensive restaurants in
limousines? That ridiculous little marshmallow he found in Newport? It didn't matter, really, his days were numbered.

Now that she could stand up and see beyond her toes and TV,
Betty thought it was slightly fantastic she'd ever married Edgar, let
alone stayed with him all this time. He was like an embarrassing
relative, except being a husband, he could be expunged from family
connection. It was inevitable Edgar would wind up chasing girls
when Betty thought about it. He wasn't equipped for life beyond
thirty. Soon he would be just another of those comical dirty old
men of New York, buttless in blue jeans, the sides of his hairdo
fading the same silvery white as his washed denim knees, offering
collegians cocaine to keep him company.

Betty frowned at her strawberries, but the frown didn't last. She
snorted sarcastically. Being penniless, a likelier scenario would just
have him arrested for loitering near the residence of some tender
tots, a wrinkly old bum in the rags of Savile Row suits, coiled in
a bush like the snake in the Garden of Eden, hissing with toothless

gums to attract gullible cuties on their way to receptionists' jobs or secretarial schools,

William tarried, adjusting the flames under his salvers before he left. Betty understood this meant he worried the guests would be too late to eat his breakfast while flavors, textures and appearances were at their peak. Except for the sour thoughts about Edgar, everything worked for Betty these days, so she wasn't at all surprised to see the door open and, outfitted for a horseback ride, Jack and Nancy and Mimi come in bubbling compliments and greetings as a relieved William disappeared into the paneling.

"I slept like a log."

"Oh, how yummy."

"Isn't this a beautiful room? Now Betty is this a Herring?" enthused Nancy squinting at a horse painting.

"No, darling, it's a kipper," joshed Jack peering under the silver canopy of a chafing dish. Betty laughed, delighted at how everything was getting used again: houses, silver and servants. Jack and Nancy and Cousin Mimi were perfect for the room. They looked and acted just as the interior decorator would have hoped people would look and act in this setting. Cousin Mimi's husband, Falwell Barnes, in bright pastels entered to further kisses and exclamations.

No county home in England could have been more English than this breakfast scene. The breakfasters sat in Georgian English furniture with English silverware of the same period moving an English breakfast from English china to their mouths. Only old William, being black, and their eggs having been laid by Rhode Island Reds might tip Sherlock Holmes the County of Kent or Northamptonshire didn't stretch beyond these walls.

"Isn't this marvelous," enthused Nancy in an accent Holmes might also find difficult to place.

"When is Edgar coming?" asked Falwell. Betty's smile tightened and her eggs held a minute on their climb to her mouth. The tension between Betty and Edgar that Jack and Nancy had suspected in Kentucky seemed to be confirmed. Jack and Nancy exchanged a glance. A little charge had come out of Betty, nothing you could exactly see or describe, but something long-married couples like Jack and Nancy picked up on their connubial oscillo-scopes simultaneously.

"Tomorrow, I think," said Betty a beat too late and too coldly to belie the doubt and tension Jack and Nancy had felt between Betty and Edgar at the Kentucky Derby.

"Do you think Edgar and Betty are headed for the rocks?" Jack had asked Nancy in the dark in Kentucky.

"Don't you think?" Nancy had answered.

"I do think she's looking rather marvelous and he's obviously drinking too much."

"Isn't it funny how first it all seemed to be running out of her and into him all these years and now it just seems tipped the other way, doesn't it? I mean now it looks like it's running back out of Edgar into Betty, don't you think?" (Anglophilic Jack and Nancy had adopted the British mannerism of following every observation with a request for confirmation.)

"Aren't we fortunate in our equilibrium?" Jack had replied to his wife's comment in his ironical, snooty lisp.

"It's the little insincere things that hold a marriage together," he had once said to Edgar in the same tone at a drinky Brook Club lunch, "don't you think? I mean really, more than the sincere ones. What could be more insincere than the celebration of an anniver-sary, my God. Sincerity is much too volatile an ingredient for keeping the peace which is what marriage is. It's all compromise and hypocrisy, after all, isn't it?"

Apparently Edgar hadn't followed Jack's advice. In Kentucky, Edgar had gotten awkwardly alcoholic. Jack soon guessed it was Edgar he'd heard bumping about Sundown Farm late at night. He'd considered burglars until he sat up and saw that whoever it was was turning on lights, something burglars didn't do. His ever ready fear—black men would swarm up from below decks killing, raping and ruining their nice old things—switched to the more benign image of drunken Edgar, bulldozing his way through the eighteenth-century mahogany underbrush.

Then later, when everyone was up, Edgar had openly ordered morning drinks. Jack sympathized somewhat with Edgar's circumstance. Nancy's was the money that bought the boots Jack was tucking under Betty's table at this Virginia breakfast. Betty was more spoiled, less grateful for Edgar than Nancy was for Jack. Nancy was homelier, which helped. Betty was beautiful as well as much richer, which Jack suspected made her more troublesome to a husband.

"How scrumptious," Jack said feelingly of his breakfast.

"I love your King Charles spaniels," enthused Nancy of the dog portraits stacked on one wall. Riding later with Jack she said, "Those decorators are just loading up people with portraits of King Charles spaniels all of a sudden."

"They're probably painting them in the Philippines to keep up with the demand," guffawed Jack. They both stopped talking and jumped a fence together.

When their horses got back to a jog, Nancy said, "I think having portraits of dogs that weren't in your family is even worse than having other people's ancestral portraits around."

This complimented Jack two ways. His were the ancestral portraits peopling the walls of their apartment, farm and country house. Even the old dog and horse pictures were of family stock. Nancy's money had supplied the walls. Jack's fine old penniless family brought things less ancient families had to acquire at auction houses and antique stores. Nancy's gratitude for Jack's lineage sometimes seemed even more profound to him than his own gratitude for her bubbling financial resources.

The other count on which Nancy's indirect compliment pleased Jack, as they rounded a turn and found themselves riding beside a glittering pond, was its implication of marital solidarity. Nancy felt she and Jack were a superior combination. When Jack saw what was happening to Edgar, he felt grateful. Yes, he and Nancy had come to a stage where they were grateful they'd chosen each other. A wild goose and her goslings appeared on the pond, pedaling in a perfect isoceles triangle, mama in the lead. Finding your natural order and relenting to it was Jack's philosophy. He clucked and his gelding went to a trot. Nancy's followed suit.

* *

Shanghai Pagoda's breakfast resonated handsomely as he ground it up with his big square teeth. He blinked sweetly as Harold rubbed him lovingly. Tommy Smithers' arrival caused the colt to pull his head out of his feed tub for a glance, a flick of shoulder skin and a slash of his tail. Tommy felt his legs: smooth and fast and cool as swords.

Tommy and Harold were both smiling.

"Ain't got no odds at all no more," complained Harold. He didn't really care because, as of the Kentucky Derby, Tommy had cut him in for a percent of the purse. Now Harold was somehow in on the fat cats' side of the great fix called American life.

Tommy and Harold simultaneously gave up all pretense of activity in the stall to stare a moment at this big midnight-colored miracle. The colt threw up his head, stopped chewing and, pricking his ears, listened a beat for saber-toothed tigers, always a danger at dawn. Hearing none, he shit and returned to his feed tub to sweep the corners with his plucking lips.

"He's a doer," Harold noted with pleasure. Tommy shook off the spell he'd felt come over him and headed for his office to look at paperwork for the Preakness. On the way there he heard the pleasant wet click of eggs being scrambled in a bowl, the tiny whine of a radio on a country and western station, buckets banging and the nicker, thud and tail sweep of the great equine presence. Tommy sighed through his grin.

* *

Flying toward Bothwell and the Preakness, Edgar remembered a ride on a troop transport plane taking him toward the quilted killers scrambling down through Manchurian hills to end American lives with primitive artillery pieces pulled by ponies. There was much less upholstery on that plane (and on Sonny Turchik) and the seating was down the sides, but those doubts (would a MIG open this tin can of tender flesh with cannon fire? Would the bayonets be used this time?) suddenly introduced their descendants to Edgar Barnes: would Betty turn him out? Could he begin again? Would there be no money? *No money?*

Next to Edgar sat a high-school girl reading a magazine article about Shanghai Pagoda with her mouth open.

"May I have a double this time?" Edgar asked the stewardess.

"Are you going to the race?" he asked the adolescent.

She nodded, openmouthed. "He's the greatest. You too?"

Edgar nodded.

"They say their guns is old Springfields and shit and don't work," a soldier had said of the Chinese Commies they were traveling to face on that Korean air ride.

"They say their bayonets work," another had replied.

In the airport, luggage moved around slow motion racetracks as Edgar looked about for someone from Bothwell to drive him home.

"We didn't know you was coming in, Mr. Edgar," pleaded William over the phone. That was impossible. Betty knew. She hadn't ordered anyone to pick him up. Would there be linen on his bed? At dinner, would he sit at a blank place as food was served to people on his left and right?

Without that horse Betty would be back where she was. That big, stupid, dark animal was Edgar's mortal enemy now. That bite was proving to be only the beginning of the wounding the animal had in store for Edgar. Shanghai Pagoda was the quilted Chinese horde coming across the Yalu River in suicidal commitment to the postponed death of Sonny Turchik.

"I'm sorry, we don't rent to people we feel are inebriated," said a man with a carefully cut and combed hairdo that left only the lobes of his ears exposed.

"I'm only here because there are no more limousines," retorted Edgar.

The man turned away.

"Darling haircut you've got there," commented the refused car renter before he marched off from the agency.

Edgar bought a breath mint and approached a car-rental franchise wearing green silks instead of the yellow stable that had the "feelings" about his drinks. He kept his conversation minimal and his bearing imperious, winning a pair of keys for his efforts.

The car was small and bright red, like a painful boil, a Bloody Mary or a nasty kind of anger. Edgar didn't want to go back and argue about this choice for fear the inebriation issue might return. He should have ordered a car to come for him from Bothwell and waited in the bar, arriving plenty tight and going straight to bed, but it was too late for that now, he was out in traffic.

The Preakness tomorrow might take care of Shanghai Pagoda for Edgar. After all, the colt had only won three races. Even if you admitted one was the Wood and another the Kentucky Derby and that the style in which he won was impressive, winning three races was somewhat less than a historic feat in racing.

Still, you could tell. Even loathing the creature, watching him through eyes squinting with anger, Edgar received that mysterious signal that left the fans screaming sure of the Chinese magic of Shanghai Pagoda.

A car honked at Edgar, who sped up and resolved to concentrate more on his driving. This was no time to be arrested for drunken driving. Weakness and failure were inappropriate attributes for a man in Edgar's position. Appearing a little tight with a cutie in SoHo was fine, but a drunk-driving arrest, a stumble in public, falling down at the theater—Edgar had seen those pitiful thrashings come from men on the way to ruin before. He wanted no one to see them from him. Once they get the scent of blood, the piranhas strike.

"Edgar Barnes? I hear he's been given the boot. He's broke and drinking. Let's not let him in anymore." More honking. Edgar's knuckles were white on the wheel as he suffered the anxieties unleashed on him by Shanghai Pagoda.

Kill the horse, of course, and if Betty showed no inclination to return to her decline, kill her too. He'd served her for twenty years, he'd earned what was lowering toward him with each passing day until the calamitous turn of events brought on by publicity. The therapy of celebrity was bringing her back from the grave. Kill the horse and the publicity would die with it, reasoned the angry, drunken driver.

The horse must be at Bothwell with her, considered Edgar. No doubt a car had been sent for the horse. A truck, a police escort and a brass band too probably.

Edgar wasn't sure he'd made the right turn and he was becoming certain the headlights which had followed him off the main road belonged to a cop. He lurched abruptly up a street. The lights followed. Edgar pushed his accelerator to the floor and began careening through a strange little housing development he eventually realized was composed of moored or grounded house trailers of the largest size. He banged something metal on the way out of the tin maze and turned up a modest-looking road into trees.

With his lights and engine off, Edgar's heart predominated his senses. It pounded his blood through him as he awaited the appearance of the probing lights of his pursuer. No lights appeared.

He had been so merry so recently, so controlled and hopeful. Why should fear come near a man most could only envy? His wealth and looks and taste and acquaintances were all of the highest grade, the topmost part of the topmost part. The cold gray fear coiling through Sergeant Turchik that wretched combat winter in Korea was nonsensical recurring in a well-known gentleman driving from the Dulles Airport to an estate that had been publicly featured in steel engravings even before it had been photographed for magazines, a house that had itself been a rich celebrity for over two hundred years.

No lights arrived looking for him like the flares that blanched the charging Chinese horde— Stop thinking that way! Edgar ordered himself. He opened the door of the awful red contraption which buzzed warnings at him.

"Fuck you," shouted Edgar at the admonishing car. He threw his head abruptly back. There were stars in the sky, an extraordinary display. Except for the audible warning of the nervous, hateful little red car, it was silent.

Edgar's anxiety washed away as he made water, staring at the stars. A small but viable rapture came down over him in the starlight. He threw his head down to concentrate on the jet of urine.

"I'll make it," he explained aloud to the universe.

*   *

The driveway to Bothwell was long and ceremonially attended
by files of ancient trees, which passed with the rhythm of spokes
in Edgar's headlights. When the rhythm broke, it wasn't just a gap,
it was an explosion, a collision: the horse! Edgar saw Shanghai
Pagoda stand and shudder an instant before they hit. The dark
horror seemed for a moment to have eaten him, like Jonah. Edgar
saw the big eye ringed white in terror or passion against the wind-
shield before he slammed into some force and the car rolled over.
Edgar went unconscious, unsure whether he'd hit the horse or the
horse had devoured him.

His door was open to stars and men were reaching down to him.
Nothing hurt, but his left arm didn't work as he ascended up
through a car now sideways to the earth.

"You ok?" asked familiar faces.

"Look out now, Donny."

"Oh, shit."

And other phrases came to Edgar as he emerged. The horse was
down, writhing in front of him. It was too fantastic, his enemy, the
Chinese dragon, lay in mortal throes at the knight's feet.

"Kill it, Donny, get the hammer," shouted the man holding
Edgar like a combat buddy.

"Oh, shit," said the boy with grief as he swung a blow between
the creature's eyes. The animal's legs shot straight up, like Tan-
talus' fingers toward the grapes, and then the whole monstrosity
collapsed into death.

"You all right?" they asked.

"Dead?" asked Edgar.

"How could he have got out?" said the boy with the hammer,
who was crying. He was swaying over the horse's corpse.

"How could he have ever got out?"

Lights of a car, serrated by trees, beat toward them from the
house. Betty and Jack emerged from a car. Betty screamed and ran
to the horse.

"Oh, no!" she cried.

The boys drove Edgar to a hospital in a truck. No one spoke. The hammer boy kept snuffling. The other hand, an older man, kept admonishing.

"Quit it."

At the hospital it was determined Edgar's left shoulder was only badly sprained.

It was only riding back to Bothwell that Edgar was able to consider what had happened. With no act of his own will, he had killed Shanghai Pagoda. That embodiment of disaster had met disaster.

"How absolutely horrible," he said to the farmhand.

"Must've jumped the fence," said the farmhand.

Edgar was astonished to be told Betty was asleep when he at last entered the house. Jack gave him a drink and asked how he was with a solemn air. Edgar thanked him and went upstairs. He decided he must speak to Betty before he went to sleep. Something awesome had happened. He had to carry out its ceremony.

"Betty?" asked Edgar reverently.

"What is it?" she answered in a surprisingly prosaic, complaining tone.

"I just wanted to tell you how dreadfully sorry I am."

"Thank you, Edgar."

Something was quite wrong. Her tone was at the most merely annoyed. Had Edgar got something wrong?

"I know how much he meant to you."

Betty switched on her light and pulled up her sleep mask.

"Who?" she asked.

"Shanghai Pagoda," ventured Edgar with solemnity.

To his astonishment, Betty began to laugh. Her laugh got all the way to hearty. Edgar considered he must be in shock, that this laughing of Betty's was a hallucination. Perhaps she was screaming and sobbing in reality, but the trauma of the accident and an admittedly substantial intake of alcohol must have altered his senses dangerously. Above all, Edgar knew he must be careful. Perhaps his perception of Betty's reaction was weirdly distorted, or perhaps the loss of her *raison d'être* had driven her mad.

She looked at him with a squint that was checking to see if he was serious. In pain, confusion and shock, Edgar waited to see things clearer.

"That wasn't Shanghai Pagoda, Edgar," said Betty with another outburst of laughter, "You killed the teaser."

Edgar blushed as crimson as his late car. A teaser is a stallion kept on horse farms to excite mares so the management can tell which ones have come into season. When mares back up to the teaser's fence, winking the labia of their vaginas, they are taken to the breeding barn to be serviced by the high-priced racing stallion.

The teaser, always exciting, but never rewarded, is breedings' dupe. Edgar realized he had been in a fool-to-fool collision.

"Are you all right?" she asked, looking at his sling. Edgar nodded and stepped back from this embarrassing audience. Before she turned over and went back to sleep, Betty wondered why Edgar hadn't laughed with her.

*   *

The next morning Edgar awoke to a patchwork of physical pains from his accident. Downstairs, everyone was happy and excited about this afternoon's Preakness.

"Oh, Edgar, this is for you, darling," said Betty. She handed him a big, very pretty scarf in which to hang his arm at the Preakness. Edgar was astonished. It was so sweet, so friendly. Had he got everything wrong? Did Betty still love him? Was all that divorce business just a passed whim?

"Betty, that's wonderful," but when he moved to give her a kiss, she moved away as if she hadn't noticed.

"I want a drink," said Betty.

"Good idea," complied Jack, ever the correct guest, jumping to fix her one. Betty was at a sort of spoiled princess stage now in her recovery. Edgar's pretty scarf was the result of a thought she had about how he was going to look in her retinue.

Edgar was glad to have a drink with the group. Maybe he was still part of things.

"Are you going to ride, dear?" he asked Betty.

"I'm going to take a little ride," answered Betty, marveling at her own decision.

"You haven't been riding much, have you, Betty?" asked Jack.

"No, but I'm going to have a little ride today," she answered in the imperious baby princess tone she'd got for her big day, her Preakness day.

"We'll just take a little walk to the lake, get you limbered up," Jack offered. "You too, Edgar, come on."

"I really can't with this thing," answered Edgar.

"We're just going to walk," challenged Betty.

When they approached the barn, Edgar felt he would possibly die on this ride, from the pain and misery and depression infesting him. Why couldn't he have managed things as effectively as Jack who was so eager and so well turned out to ride? Why had he agreed to ride at all? He hated horses. He'd just killed one. One was killing him by Chinese torture, a piece a day of his flesh.

Six horses were waiting saddled, held by a couple of hands all slicked up for this relatively rare event of a ride taken by the masters of Bothwell. Nancy was already in her saddle and Jack was giving Mimi a leg up when a perfectly awful thing happened: the dead teaser was raised up in the mandibles of a tractor and swiveled toward a waiting dump truck from a tallow company. Everyone stared frozen at the stiff, mechanical spectacle until the corpse rang the bed of the truck, and that cumbersome vehicle drove off.

"Who did that?" shouted Betty at the no longer cheerful lad holding the rein of her mount, "Who did that?" she demanded again.

"Sorry, Mrs. Barnes," said a mortified authority of the stables.

"God, what bad taste," said Betty, and she made her Bronx cheer.

"I don't want to ride anymore," she said, throwing down her crop. Edgar picked it up and accompanied her back to the house as the guests discreetly trotted into the background.

"I just don't see the point," she said to Edgar at the house.

"What do you mean."

"Why do you do such unpleasant things?"

"You mean our marriage?"

Betty looked back out the window at horses grazing.

"I think we have to give ourselves a chance. God, Betty, this is twenty years."

"So what?"

"Don't you think we should try."

"Try what?"

He wanted to shake the life out of her like a champion ratter. The complacency of her kindergarten debating style left him no grip, no purchase, on her high stone walls.

"Try to find whatever it is we're not doing right—whatever it is that's suddenly coming between us." Edgar was standing, orating without conviction. He saw his good hand posing in midair.

"You mean like your little girlfriend?"

A bolt of panic went through Edgar. He'd forgotten there was anything unseemly about his life as he defended their marriage.

Betty didn't say anything. He felt like the animal thrashing in the pit for the savages' amusement before they throw boulders at its head.

"Listen. I talked to Johnny Walker about working for the bank. Don't you think maybe if I had a job, things might be more sensible for us and all?"

"Did he give you a job?"

"He sounded like there were possibilities."

"Are you going to live in New York then?"

"Then?"

"With your little girl and your job?"

Edgar drained the last traces of red off the cruel ice in the bottom of his drink. "Let me get you another," he said, reaching for Betty's glass. He tried to think of things to say all the way down to the bar and back.

This was the sort of conversation a master of quick thinking and cross-examination could probably turn things around on, regaining control and hope. But what were the right things to say? Where were the questions and arguments that would win?

When Edgar got back, Betty was locked in her bathroom. He

knocked, but that only turned on a big, mocking cascade of water within.

*   *

Edgar, a geisha's distance behind Betty, saw awed smiles pointed their way as they stepped through the crowd at Pimlico Race Track like worshipers on the way to their pew. Betty put down her inevitable clutch of things: a program, a racing form, binoculars and a candy bar. She didn't even bother sitting and looking around, although she hadn't been to Pimlico in years. She knew perfectly well where she really was: she was in an unfolding, inevitable myth which would sweep her to victory and Edgar aside. After her territorial deposit she left her box to get near her reason for being, the dark angel who had landed on earth to save her from the deep blue death of her long, lonely bedroom nights.

At the Preakness, horses are saddled on the infield. Edgar didn't accompany Betty on this promenade. He didn't want to go back to the box, either, her box. Goddamn it, he kept saying to himself. He didn't want to sit in her box, brooding like a caged hyena under the dull scrutiny of zoo goers. Instead, he found a bar in the seediest zone of the run-down Pimlico Race Track. A woman with unmatching parts—a tiny face on a big head under hair a tint of red that reminded Edgar of his recent car rental—moved strangely made, Popeye-the-Sailor arms to present him with a drink, part of which came from a hose. Gimps and gumps, jerks and boneheads, creeps and thugs, chicks and scumbags, dudes and jailbait milled. Might Sonny Turchik have been one of them? When Betty ejected him, should Edgar change his name back, give his beautiful clothes away and roll up his shirt like the man standing next to him, so his navel could also prance in public?

Above the gaudily dignified rows of plastic-beaked liquor bottles was a television set mounted like a stuffed head. On it or in it directly mocking Edgar's hiding here in the crowd, a camera was panning Betty walking with Tommy Smithers to Shanghai Pagoda held by grinning Harold. There was a close-up. Betty was saying something to Tommy. To Edgar and his company at this bar, it was the unhearable conversation of gods. Down the bar the wizened horseplayers' faces studied this spectacle like sailors watching weather. Edgar had the liquid out of his drink in three sips. He rattled its skeleton and replaced it on the bar. The woman who seemed fabricated from limbs found at some sort of surgical dump refilled it.

"Where does your hose go?" asked Edgar.

"What's that, honey?"

Edgar waggled his finger at the hose she held.

"To tanks," she explained, hanging it up like a phone and moving away.

Edgar stared at the hose, at ice, at fluorescent lights, metal and plastic. Where he was going if he continued to do nothing was probably somewhere like this. Good-bye paneling and upholstery; good-bye candles and silver; good-bye art and society, thought Edgar. A brutal-looking little metal shovel lay on its side in the ice, like the sled of a lost polar explorer.

*   *

When the gates opened at the Preakness, Montezuma felt Shanghai Pagoda's first stride was like that hard strike that had scared him coming down the stretch at Churchill Downs. Standing in the irons and pulling back, he tried to save some fuel for the critical return passage back here to where it all began. But the colt ran out from under him. He looked back four lengths to the herd behind around the first sharp turn. Now there was a steady rhythm to his flying horse's reunion with earth, but that fast start had to have cost precious energy. On the back stretch Montezuma tried to relax Shanghai Pagoda. "*Descánsete, hijo,*" he cajoled like a lover, gently pulling back. But the Chinese horse didn't seem to understand. He wanted to run. Montezuma almost physically felt how the coming turn would curl like a hook in the lungs under him, and pull Shanghai Pagoda back. They would fade like a car he remembered stinking as its locked brakes began to burn and fitter tourists flew shinily by.

Looking back in the turn Montezuma saw no other horses. For

a moment it unnerved him—had he jumped the gate and run out before the race? *No—imposible.* He clearly remembered the other horses. Where were they? Where was the rest of the Preakness? A great avalanche of noise was falling down over the stretch ahead. Montezuma rode straight into it, crouched now and giving the reins every lunge the horse's shoulders made as if he were sculpting speed. Shanghai Pagoda never let up until he was past the wire. Montezuma stood in the irons. Montezuma's knees, strong as bridge couplings, were shaking. He looked back—there they were, only now running down the stretch like cartoon cops, absurd and too late. Shanghai Pagoda had entered the stretch at Pimlico over ten lengths ahead of the nearest contestant. At the finish, his lead was fifteen lengths. The time was a new world's record for the distance.

*   *

Edgar banged his glass down on the bar, but he couldn't hear the report of this gesture, because there was so much noise coming from the racing fans. They milled about under the stands grinning and already bragging, as they would for the rest of their lives, that they were there. If winning the Kentucky Derby had given Betty the courage to mention divorce, her present victory, considered proportionally, could lead her to order Edgar beheaded.

"Where's your badge?" asked the cop in a surprisingly high voice after Edgar had, working his body against gaps to loosen his passage through the dense, tense and hideously dressed crowd, got to the winner's circle gate.

"I'm Edgar Barnes," he shouted above the noise at the officer, who was, he noticed for the first time, a woman. She was a big one. She looked like a sixth-grade boy bully inflated to parade proportions.

"Pass," she demanded.

Edgar remembered the packet of tags and badges he had casually left behind, not wanting to decorate himself in homage to the horse he hated. The police valkyrie looked him over. Edgar's sling could contain an assassin's pistol, she reasoned. Still, he had pretty good

clothes on. Yep, he had that wealthy stink and he was American.
Why would a rich man alone wedge up to the gate in such an
undignified way unless he had to?

"Al," she called to a fellow officer who was staring with con-
temptuous impassivity at the glittering hamster eyes of the mob
tiled into diamonds by cyclone fencing.

"Yo?" he answered in their superior, praetorian jargon. He sauntered over to where Noreen held a guy in a sling at bay.

"Edgar Barnes?" she asked Al.

"What's that, like Betty Bishop Barnes?"

"I'm her husband." Edgar was begging at the castle gate.

"That's the owner." reasoned the big woman.

"You're her husband?"

"Yes, I am." How humiliating, thought Edgar, begging on
Betty's name again. Edgar Barnes was important enough in most
places now. In twenty years his name had outgrown the paren-
theses that had dangled behind it through the first ten years of their
marriage in gossip columns and photo captions (whose wife is
Betty Bishop Barnes) (husband of Betty Bishop) (Betty Bishop's
hubby) (as in Betty Bishop Barnes) like training wheels on a begin-
ner's bicycle.

"You got like a marriage license or something?" queried the
suspicious male cop.

"I don't carry a marriage license with me!" retorted Edgar with
enough contempt and indignation to convince the big female he
ought to be allowed in. It was a Lionel Barrymore–type outburst
she recognized from old television movies.

"Jes let's have a look at that," she said, gesturing at his sling.

"It's fer yer own protection," consoled the male cop, reaching
in like a teen dater trying for a breast. "He's clean."

Shanghai Pagoda floated like a pool toy on the pates and hats and
hairdos of the select mob inside. Betty was holding his bridle and
smiling as strobe light flickered over her new suit. Tommy, grinning, was guiding the horse tugboat style, pushing him into his
pose. The jockey sat with the menacing grandeur of a gargoyle
against the egg-white Maryland sky. Harold, dangling tack, and

bearing a black and tan blanket, waited like a wardrobe mistress for the ballerina to come offstage. The great bellows of Shanghai Pagoda's lungs slowed down as he stared at mankind with his fire dragon's eyes. Edgar readjusted his paisley sling.

Suddenly two burly men in black suits with dark glasses and neat, mouth-hiding mustaches lunged at Edgar, one of them grabbing his sprained arm, sending a bolt of pain through him that made him give a yell. They pushed him aggressively against a wall. People were jumping away and staring. The men felt his cast and sling and ran hands quickly all over him, even giving his balls a surprising, strangely exhilarating soft squeeze.

"What the hell?"

"Who are you?"

"Boys," called the man standing with Betty, "boys, it's all right. That's Mrs. Bishop's husband." Like big steel vultures, the television cameras turned back and forth, recording this interchange.

It took Edgar a moment to realize this man addressing his captors was familiar because he was president of the United States.

"Sorry, sir," relented one of Edgar's attackers.

"See, you don't have your pass—and the sling and all and you made a funny move," explained the other Secret Service man.

"Edgar always wears a sling at Shanghai's best races," reminisced Betty.

"Right, just like the Wood," confirmed Tommy. Everyone had a good laugh.

"We had him all checked out," said the male and female state troopers who had rushed over, at first terrified they'd made a disastrous mistake, then filled with indignation their local police craftsmanship had been questioned by these federal interlopers. Edgar tossed back his head to see if God were right there munching popcorn and laughing at the slapstick routine just added to Edgar's torment. But the sky was a blank white, an unpleasant, eyeball white.

The worst of it for Edgar was how this whole clumsy, embarrassing outrage had been televised to provide an amusing vignette to go with Shanghai Pagoda's wondrous solitary stretch run on the evening news. After the chuckling President called off his Dobermans, the face Edgar had made was caught in a superb close-up—the big-eyed glance up at the absurd gods of fate—worthy of the great silent movie comedians. One network held this close-up in freeze frame to close the evening news. It was just the note of fast and funny whimsy to finish the evening's vaudeville of international grief and horror on a day when villainy and cataclysm were minor enough to permit a fade-out on gently chuckling anchormen playing with their papers, showing the public how warmly human they really are.

*   *

Everyone had seen and loved cornered Edgar's comical reaction. Only Edgar didn't know he'd become a peculiar sort of celebrity. Having missed the evening news, Edgar hadn't seen his interchange with the president and his guards. If that camera hadn't got Edgar's perfect, hilarious "Why me?" face just right, the incident might have been actually troubling, reminding our assassination-wracked country what a cracked and dangerous place it is, showing how wrong police can be and how helpless citizens are and how dangerous American life is. But Edgar's funny expression had defused all that. Our national paranoia had been called up and then magically dissipated with the touch of a good laugh.

William, the butler at Bothwell, greeted Edgar with Edgar's own, unbeknownst to him, nationally famous grimace, before turning with a wheezy deep chuckle and bowing him home. The butler wasn't the only one copying Edgar's turned-up, big-eyed, endearing woefulness. It was instantaneously becoming part of the nation's vernacular. It was to be used the following Monday morning by secretaries to each other as the boss walked away having delivered an impossible command or an undeserved redress, by motorists stopped by traffic cops, by badgered wives and even by children ordered to make their beds. They all would copy Edgar's televised reaction. The brotherhood of the unfairly accused, wrongfully oppressed and dignity-stripped had found their secret handshake.

The smarter papers and newsmagazines were all in the act of

laying out photos of Edgar's woeful grimace in their Preakness stories even as Edgar, still wondering at the butler's clowning, headed down to dinner at Bothwell. In the time it took him to reach the dining room from his dressing room, a columnist had speculated on his word processor about why that moment at the Preakness was so instantly charming:

> Why should a man who obviously has everything have communicated so perfectly in that facetious look how helpless and silly we are, how alone and comical before the very same greater powers of privilege and rank for which he, Edgar Barnes, stands? He looked like a man whose world has crumbled about him, as though insult had just been added to injury, and yet his horse, Shanghai Pagoda, had just won the second jewel of the Triple Crown in the most spectacular fashion anyone can remember ever seeing. Maybe it was a quirk of the camera or Edgar Barnes's digestive system, but it gave us the great look of our time.

All this of course was still in the works when Edgar sat down at the great mahogany pond in the dining room at Bothwell, teeming with the glittery toy navigation of the polished silver and plate of the great victory dinner. Guests joked about Edgar's television appearance, but the enormity of Shanghai Pagoda's victory was hugely more important to Betty's guests who were, except, of course, for Edgar, horse people.

Betty was chirping like a bird and pecking up glasses of champagne like golden oats. Tommy Smithers was also getting smashed. There were a dozen people already drunker than Edgar, a strange reversal of his recent role in society. Betty was toasted again and again. She graciously lavished attention on Tommy Smithers.

"It was Tommy who spotted him," she piped with sweet, birdsong modesty. "He told me to go have a look."

"There were four horses at Small-Granger's stud," Tommy retorted equally modestly. "I liked all of them, but Betty only brought back the right one."

Edgar was never signaled in these toasts, which had got to the jockey and even Harold the hot-walker, who was led in a like a pony by prearrangement.

Standing next to dinner-jacketed Tommy Smithers, glittering with embarrassment and intoxication, Harold grinned under his red cowlick like the world's oldest little boy as the gentry muttered approving noises both at Harold and at the good form of congratulating the help. William, brimming with family pride, brought Harold a glass of champagne. Harold, brimming with racial prejudice, tensed up a moment before taking it. He didn't, however, wipe the glass with his sleeve before knocking it back as he had momentarily considered. *Shit,* he thought almost out loud, *this is the way things is sposed to be.* He even managed a smile at William. When Harold held out his glass for seconds, outstaying his dramatic usefulness at the joyful party, Tommy signaled him out with an impatient jerk of his head. But Harold stayed on until Tommy rose, plucking a bottle from the sideboard and with an arm around Harold's shoulders, buddy-style, headed him back out through the kitchen and down the stairs.

"They're partying at the barn, Harold," Tommy told the success-dazed hot-walker.

"He done it, Mister Smithers," enthused Harold. That statement and Harold's blue-eyed wonderment made Tommy stop and to his eternal surprise, burst into tears. He sat down on the stoop with Harold, both of them drinking out of the bottle, gazing at horses in the fields, vague in the moonlight.

"All they ever do is eat," observed Harold, "even in the dark."

"Eat and run," laughed Tommy. Harold cackled uncomprehendingly. All was equally antic to him now. Tommy stood up, blew his nose and headed back inside.

Betty got to what Edgar privately noted as the bicycle stage of her drinking pattern. There was some spinning spokes motif in her movements now, some circular speed that usually, like the faster and faster steps of a toddler racing the inevitability of a fall, wound up on the rug.

"How'd you get the name?" someone asked her. Everyone was interested.

"I was going to name him for Edgar's new ring," she answered, rising spinnily for a toast.

Edgar felt the thud of the first brick of a wall being shoved over on him. Betty was waggling her little finger. Edgar's signet ring abruptly throbbed like a tumor. "I mean old Edgar's old ring. His family couldn't be with us today because they're so old. From before the Civil War or the Revolution or anything, the dinosaurs?" Now she looked at Edgar, laughing, close to careening, "But maybe they saw him on television tonight in their old estates." Betty was wobbling, and no one but Edgar knew what she was talking about. When she seemed to be just hanging there, holding out her glass like a Christmas ornament she was trying to place on an invisible tree, reentering Tommy Smithers drew up beside her, put his arm around her and finished what he believed to be her toast.

"To Edgar."

What were they trying to do, wondered Edgar, humiliate him? Did they talk about him in bed, or in the straw with that heinous horse? Everyone laughed. How red and naked all their drunken faces looked, like writhing babies. It wasn't just going to be the ax Betty was preparing for him. Humiliation seemed to be in store too.

*   *

Edgar was moving against the bias. When his crowd drank, he stayed sober, and vice versa. You can't do that forever and stay a part of such a set. In bed he closed his eyes and saw the racetrack crowd around that seedy bar. The outlandish clothes and shapes appalled him. It was his mother cloned and costumed a thousand ways. It was what he had spent his life escaping. Sonny pulled the corpse up over him, it took the bayonet. Then he pulled Edgar Barnes up over him and now Betty was going to laugh it down so when they rammed in the steel blade this time it would go straight to Sonny Turchik's own secret heart. Edgar's knuckles were white on the counterpane pulled up now over his head; he threw it down and sat up in his bed.

"Thank God you called, darling, I've never wanted to talk to you so much in my whole life and I didn't dare call you down there. What happened to your arm?"

How totally unexpected and gratifying Camilla's caring response was. Once again it seemed as if maybe Edgar had got everything wrong, as if his life were fine if he would only stop worrying about it. This passionate devotion put everything in order. He suddenly, even while talking to Camilla about how desperately he wished they were together right now, remembered how totally drunk Betty had got at the party—as bad as ever, and right in front of all those choice witnesses.

Edgar had gently carried her away, out of her chair, and told them to keep the bright blaze of the Preakness victory party for his return. He'd been the perfect host and she'd been the embarrassing drunk. He'd stayed in control and now his girl loved him. Once again it became obvious Edgar Barnes had it made. Why did he suffer those doubts? He was way off base, cowering under his coverlet. He wasn't an endangered loser about to be dropped into the masses from which he'd so ingeniously stolen. He was a swashbuckling gentleman with a throb in his penis at three in the morning talking to a live cutie of the sort other men could only dream of or hold in the other hand as magazine photos while they angrily pounded their fistful of lonely flesh.

"Wait until you see the papers, darling, you're in every one."

Edgar presumed she'd made a mistake. After all, he'd gotten to the winner's circle too late to appear in the photograph. But what did it matter as long as she thought he was famous enough to love, he couldn't care less why. Her voice was that of a woman in love, a flower open and troping toward the telephoned sun of Edgar Barnes.

"I wish you were here," she said again. "I want to pull you up over me to cover me like covers," she poetically expostulated.

ow, even though summer was approaching, there was so much mail Betty's part-time social secretary Miss Dowdell was working full time and had taken on a part-time assistant, Miss Dufour. The mail was sometimes just addressed to Betty, often to Mrs. Betty Barnes, to Betty Bishop Barnes, to Mrs. Barnes and most of all, to Shanghai Pagoda. Betty was determined to answer all of it. Miss Dowdell or Miss Dufour would type, for example:

Dear Mr. Wojyk,

Thank you for your kind letter about our super friend, Shanghai Pagoda. No, I'm sorry, but I can't mail you a million dollars.

> Your friend,
> Betty Bishop Barnes

or

Dear Marie,

Thank you for your kind letter about our super friend Shanghai Pagoda. He is seventeen hands and he weighs one thousand and seventy pounds. He's an Aquarius, but almost all racehorses are because we try to time foaling as near the beginning of the year as we can. You see, the official birthday of all race horses is January the first.

I know he loved your letter and that he counts on your support.

Your friend,
Betty Bishop Barnes

Betty would sign these letters with a new signature she'd developed just for this aspect of her life, three plump joined Bs. Uncoiling these Bs after looking at the fan letters and often personally dictating responses to them gave Betty her first real feeling of being joined to the regular old world, the one she imagined from what she gleaned on the news and looked at through tinted windows all her life. What incomparable fun it was!

The eight-by-ten color photographs of herself in the winner's circle with Shanghai Pagoda she sent on requests from fans brought a reproof from her accountant, Mr. Abrahams. He projected the costs of such generosity and suggested she send only postcards, a suggestion she took. Her triple B autograph looked fine on a postcard, and it seemed less ostentatious to her than the big, gaudy, shiny photo with its mailer. After all, she had learned at both her grandfathers' knees the phrase, "There's no such thing as something for nothing," and something for nothing was exactly what the autographed color eight-by-tens in their special packing paraphernalia were for these public strangers. If you gave them that they would want more. They would start by filling their pockets with your bibelots, then they'd carry away your pictures and furniture. You had to be careful. Just look at Mr. Wojyk, asking for a million!

Some people asked for less than a million. A woman in Syracuse, New York, asked for $9772.36 to pay for a cataract operation. Betty told Miss Dowdell not to show her the ones about sickness, handicaps and accidents. They were depressing and often crooked.

After all, how could a woman with cataracts have seen the Kentucky Derby? But little girls still got eight-by-ten glossies, no matter what grandfathers and Mr. Abrahams advised!

Betty loved the public with a bright novelty to which the public responded. She'd spent a lonely childhood warned about kidnapping, walled and guarded from this mystery of the great mass of people who really had got nothing for nothing, as both Grandfather Williams and Grandfather Bishop proclaimed was just. Now that she was presented to them at last on this glorious pedestal of her champion horse, she adored them, and they loved her for it. She beamed and smiled with genuine, pent-up affection at the public she'd spent her life locked away from. Her affection was contagious. They loved her back.

The media knew she was a winner. She'd watched enough television to know better than ever to do less than perform when the camera was on her. Let stupid Edgar mumble and act furtive. Betty would simply shine for them.

Betty had put her divorce on hold not just because she was too busy and too happy to bother with such an unpleasant complexity, but also because she didn't want to hurt her new children, the public. She had queenly responsibilities now. Maybe after her horse's campaign, in the winter, when it was dark and there were so many balls and dinners, she would get it over with. When Betty thought about it, she pictured Edgar in a trunk dropped in the East River at night. She ran the silver prong of her letter opened down a sleazy envelope addressed in leaky ball-point.

> Dear Betty, my darling,
>
> I love you. It probely seems crazy coming from one you haven't never met, but it's so. You are so beeutiful. When you was on the Preakness I felt true love. I want to have kids with you. I will start by touching your . . .

"Not this one," chirped Betty, holding it by the tail and dropping it on a card table covered with correspondence for Misses Dowdell and Dufour to giggle with her about.

*   *

Edgar was appalled. He reached up to touch the sudden throb in his neck. He looked at the other posters in the window: a girl tennis player pulling down her panties to show her ass, a baby grinning through the muck of a bowl of spaghetti poured over its head, a grossly fat hag bending into a refrigerator, a pair of rhinoceroses fornicating and Marlon Brando leaning on a motorcycle early in his career. That was the company kept by the poster that was causing Edgar to breathe through his mouth. Edgar's face, eyes rolling in his comic mask of despair as the Secret Service men at the Preakness frisked him, had become a poster.

The proprietor of the store was an impassive Pakistani. Edgar asked him who manufactured the poster. The man didn't know. Edgar asked where he'd bought the poster. The clerk was annoyed by what he suspected was going to be a fruitless negotiation.

"Please, are you intending a purchase? I have other customers to attend to," the dark Moslem informed Edgar in a perfect, radio announcer's voice bent comical by his chirping accent and Victorian grammar.

"How did you order it? Is there a catalog?"

Gem Novelties titled the Edgar poster "Frisked." As Edgar left the store with the glossy paper tube rolled into a wand, he saw a camera-hung tourist point him out to his wife, who smiled and nodded. They had been gaping at his face in the window the very moment he stepped out of the poster store. The man suddenly threw back his head and grimaced like the poster.

Now what? This unexpected horror must be illegal. So this was what was meant by the *invasion* of privacy! It was like an invasion, like the Inchon landing—the public pouring out of landing craft firing cameras on the beach of Edgar's being. He had already endured a week of guffaws following the appearance of this photo in the news media; wasn't that enough? *Basta la commedia!*

The filthy little grotto of the cab's interior wasn't safe either. Edgar saw the driver check his mirror in lengthening glances.

"Say, are you a celebrity?" grinned the driver.

"Certainly not," scoffed Edgar, twitching the rolled poster and blushing as he looked out the window.

"Sorry, I don't know. You look kind of familiar."

"I am not familiar," Edgar nearly shouted. Damn this. How dare they do this? Horse of hell!

At least the receptionist buzzed Edgar through the big door without a word, but his desk hadn't been cleared at all. Edgar didn't even sit down. He called John J. Walker standing up.

"Yes, Mr. Barnes, Mr. Walker is in a meeting; is it something I might be able to help you with?" purred the Magog guarding the chairman's door.

"My office has not been cleared out," said Edgar. "My desk is piled with a goddamn pile of litter addressed to . . ." The letter Edgar angrily plucked from the heap was addressed to him! They all were—it was his mail.

"Never mind, there was a mistake. Sorry." Edgar looked at the stuff: letters, manila envelopes, bills, all of it forwarded from Park Avenue. Was she kicking his mail out first? Would suitcases follow? Edgar looked around his office. How long could he hang on here? Could he sleep and shave and eat, carry out his whole life cycle in the midst of workers coming and going? The only things with continuous lives in offices were plants. Perhaps Edgar could serve instead of a palm tree, out there in that barren waiting room.

"Look, I'll need a secretary to sort out all this mail," Edgar finally said, pushing at the scaly pile of postal droppings. The "Edgar Barnes" on all the envelopes came to him as mockery, a whispered chorus of vindictiveness.

This figure addressed by fans wishing an autograph on that absurd picture was the work of the same cruel lunatic God who was riding his life out from under him on that damn horse, who gave him Camilla as long as he pretended he was close to that horrible horse, who dropped the teaser on his hood, who was raising Betty from the dead with the same black magic horse to sweep him from the glory just about to be his. His creation was being taken out of his control. Edgar Barnes was turning like a monster, on the man who'd made him.

The boredom of baby-sitting bombed Betty, the years filling time with tailors' appointments and trips, with entertainments and shopping, decorating and dressing were for a perfect goal: the production of the magnificent sort of fellow Camilla adored. Now that dashing figure was becoming a comic poster vision for the public, an object of scorn for Betty and, for himself, a menacing burden of pain and depression.

Betty's sudden fun with her advantages was got at a price Edgar found appalling, the removal of those advantages from him! Instead of applauding Betty's improvement, Edgar could only dread it. Now she could do without him. Now she owned a much more interesting stallion than Edgar.

It was all timed and arranged with the perversity of a fun house. Just as he hits full speed, the steering wheel comes off in his hands. The messages and mail he sorted through on his desk were, of course, full of tricks and mirrors. He called back the number left by a television network and air jets shot up his pants legs:

"No, thank you. I don't want to be on television."

"Really, Mr. Barnes? We had Mrs. Barnes on, you know, Thursday?"

"I know."

"Wasn't she great?"

"She likes it. I don't."

"But you were the best thing on television this whole month."

"I didn't know I was on."

"Did you know Johnny has your poster in his office? I'm not kidding. He wants to talk to you personally, in fact. Have you got a minute? I'm going to put him on."

"I don't want to be on the show."

"You're serious?"

"I am saying no."

"I get the picture. Well, look, call us if you change your mind, ok? And like, if you want to talk it over personally with Johnny, he has expressed a personal willingness," said the network woman.

Edgar would gladly have appeared on this show at a more confident moment. But now he had a growing feeling of estrangement from the Edgar Barnes they all wanted. The expression that had come over his face and made it famous at the Preakness wasn't the marvelous joke of a highly placed and richly privileged comedian saving the nation's good spirits at what looked for a terrible moment like a tense turn—it was the naked truth of a fool. The granite rock of Edgar Barnes had been pulled back to reveal squirming Sonny.

*   *

When a secretary appeared, Edgar gestured to his paperwork and told her what to tell everybody:

"I have nothing to say to the press and I won't give any interviews."

As she picked through the mail, Edgar unrolled the poster, and, scrutinizing the "Gem Novelty©", called his lawyer.

"I'm afraid the photograph is in the public domain, Edgar," explained his lawyer. "It would be like those marines raising the flag on Iwo Jima asking for royalties."

"These are personal; do you want to see which ones you want me to look at?" asked the secretary. Since he couldn't imagine anyone he knew writing him a letter, Edgar was going to ask her to deal with all of them, when the address on the top one, in a cramped, ball-point, topsy-turvy hand on a cheesy envelope, blazed up:

> S. Turchik c/o Edgar Barnes
> c/o Shanghai Pagoda
> Belmont Race Track
> Elmont, New York

Edgar shoved it into his pocket like incriminating evidence and sorted through the rest of the personal mail.

"Take all that out and answer it and make me a list," he ordered. When the secretary left, he pulled out the letter addressed to Turchik.

Dear Sir,

My dad says you are the son of his late friend Mrs. Irma
Turchik and so you should know she is dead. My dad is not
good with letters so he asked I write and tell you she is dead
and gone and she thought it was you. If it's you, don't fret;
it was a peaceful demise and there wasn't no estate. My dad,
Ray Pinole, is out of pocket three hundred dollars for burial
and he's too proud to ask anybody so I am, if it's you, in
memory of Mrs. Turchik.

S. Pinole

Route 2, Box 128
Lumber City, Oreg.
P.S. Mrs. Turchik was proud of you.

S. Pinole

"What is it, darling?" asked an annoyed and fatigued Camilla,
throwing down Edgar's slack tool like anything else she couldn't
get to work.

"I don't know. Jesus. I'm just worried about something."

"Is Betty much worse?"

He nodded morosely. Despite her efforts, Camilla didn't look
erotic to Edgar. She looked merely anatomical.

"Darling, it doesn't matter. Can't we just be cozy and sleep?"

How could Edgar sleep here? She had the damn poster framed
above the bed! His nerves were raining nails.

"I'm going to get another drink."

"You know it will just get you all depressed tomorrow."

"What do you think I am now?"

"Darling, I'm just too exhausted." She turned out the light.
Edgar got up with a lurch that threw his shoulder into the wall,
dislodging the picture which fell with the sound of glass cracking.
Edgar smiled sardonically. His shoulder knew exactly where the
picture was. "Damn it," shouted Camilla, furious, but she didn't
turn on the light. By not turning on the light, Camilla signaled how

tired she was of the whole scene tonight. Neither the loopy reordering of time by cannabis nor the cynical joy alcohol provided allowed Edgar to accept Camilla's erotic blandishments.

She had slapped his cheeks with the punching bags of her big breasts, played his member like a harmonica, put a dirty movie on her Betamax and masturbated for him to no effect.

"Don't you still love me?" she asked.

"I do. I just have too much on my mind."

Edgar felt his way to the door, closed it and popped on the light. His useless organ hung exhausted as a dead chicken's neck, red from friction. The hard, slick bathroom light revealed him in laboratory detail. A handful came easily when he tested the consistency of his belly. Coils of the doughy python that would eat him alive looped in his hand. His shanks were gone bald and shiny. The face in the mirror was haggard, drawn and ruined. The freckles of old age were focusing stronger every year on the backs of his hands. Ash-gray hairs were left by the forest fire sweeping away his youth. His mother was dead. Sobs he refused to allow rose anyway. He winced and let them out. They, too, were dry and impotent. How can you lose something you long ago threw away?

Impotent, drunk, depressed, alone, orphaned and insomniac, Edgar wrapped the horror of himself in the commercial splendor of a towel emblazoned hugely with the name of the most expensive place to buy such things, and went out into the kitchen that adjoined the bathroom in an arrangement determined not by the natural order of gracious living, but by the cost of pipe.

There was no more ice. He had used up everything here to no avail.

He drank at room temperature. Maybe this brown, sweet poison would relieve him of the pilot's toil and let him land, or crash, he didn't much care which.

His hopes were mockeries now. A wet sob racked through him. He raised his glass to his dead maternal embarrassment. "Stop it," he said aloud, gagging on another sob. Couldn't he look on the bright side? Now he was free. He'd never be found out. All the circumstances were still right for him to act and save himself. Now he had to do it: the damn horse was in New York visited daily by Betty at Belmont Park where he was training perfectly for the Belmont Stakes. When he wins the Belmont, gauged Edgar as cognac smoothed through his brain, she'll get back to the subject of divorce. This calculation gave him about two more weeks to save his life.

*   *

Edgar's idea of Little Italy as the place to meet Bernie Zilber for lunch to discuss fixing the Belmont Stakes quickly turned out to be a huge mistake.

"I don't wanna go to some dump like that," Bernie had candidly replied when Edgar mentioned the name of a place he had read was the scene of a Mafia slaying.

"Whattya wanna go down there for, all that SoHo crap and Chinks—what's wrong with '21'?"

Of course Edgar's idea of where to go to discuss crime was naive. Undoubtedly more crime had been plotted at "21" than the obscure and sordid clam bars of New York's thinning Italian population. The suggestion had probably already made Zilber think Edgar too much of a fool to do business with. Fixing a horse race required all the elaborate timing and planning of a bank robbery. No one wanted amateurs along on such an escapade. Edgar's hot wet palms, twitching scalp, pounding eyeballs and clenching sinus tract were only the sharpest focuses of the general pain the morning had brought him after his horrid evening with Camilla. It was in this state he had reasoned criminals probably lunched in criminal hangouts just as gentlemen ate at the Brook Club. That's it, Edgar realized. To recoup his gaffe, he suggested.

"What about the Brook?"

"What's that?"

"My club."

"The Brook Club?"

"Yes."

"Hey, I like that. Hey, that's great. The Brooks Brothers Club. That would be great."

A brilliant move, Edgar complimented himself. The granite dignity of the Establishment filled in the gap through which his whole plan had just nearly fallen.

All the way to the Brook Club, Edgar was thinking about what to have for his first drink of the day. A revulsion for Bloody Marys, Betty's usual morning concoction, had become so violent even seeing one started him imagining things like the taste of a peppered glass of dust from a vacuum cleaner bag. He reviewed other options. White wine appeared as a cruel acidic horror related to the worst noises cats make. Screwdrivers, his mainstay through the binge the horse had forced him on, suddenly struck him as bleakly alcoholic jokes, combining the healthy beginnings of a child's day, orange juice, with the bleak end of a failure's day, vodka. Maybe he should simply order the cab to the Bowery and get right down to the inevitable pavement of his eventual repose, clutching a bottle of hypersweet fortified wine, watching the writhing apparitions of delirium tremens.

He stopped at a vegetable stand and bought a bag of oranges from a Korean. "*Kan ta hami-da,*" he said to the expressionless fruiterer, causing surprise. "Whose side were you on?" he added. The Korean laughed nervously. Edgar picked up his bag. If he were going to drink a cocktail, the juice would be fresh.

At the Brook Club bar, as Edgar set down his bag of oranges and gave instructions for his drink: orange juice, champagne, rum and a dash of bitters. Lawrence Morris came over palms-out, starry-eyed, happy to see him.

"In January you were a nobody, now you're a poster," he said with a great grin. He gave Edgar a friendly hug. "You son of a bitch —I can't believe you. Fifteen lengths and a world's record and you make a face that gives you equal billing—let me buy you a drink."

"He's making me one," said Edgar.

"What's this?" asked Morris. "You're bringing your own oranges?"

"I don't like frozen orange juice," replied Edgar.

Lawrence Morris was delighted. "You got real class, Edgar," he said, only partly facetiously.

Edgar reached for his drink, and immediately realized he wasn't going to be able to pick it up.

"Two-hand it," laughed Lawrence. "What've you been doing to yourself?"

"Late night."

"I know, you were in Boston, right?"

"Boston?"

"Betty was at the Walpoles last night. She said you were in Boston."

"I guess I was."

"Boston with the big tits, right?"

"What do you mean?"

"C'mon, pal, how was it?"

"Lawrence, what do you think you know?"

"Well, what did you do in Boston, go sailing in the swan boats, eat those big, luscious Parker House buns?"

Lawrence laughed tears into his eyes. Edgar couldn't help smiling, too. This Edgar Barnes that Lawrence Morris was kidding him about was a randy, rowdy fellow. Edgar liked him too. He wasn't that pathetic middle-aged nude grabbing a handful of belly, boohooing above a useless pecker. But not to be able to hold a glass! Lawrence held his wine by the stem, sure as a surgeon holding an artery. Thank God it was the bar and the glass wide as a birdbath. Edgar bent as low as one could in the Brook Club. He got some down, a great hot draft, in fact, like a chimney fire. By the fourth flash he was ready for another and he could hold a glass single-handed.

Lawrence Morris was a funny fellow, stuffy only when the subject of horse racing inspired him to expand on the antiquity of his family in the sport. The Brook Club is a rich, discreet, American-male, Anglo-Saxon retreat. Men with the confidence of lots of money, of achievement, of Wall Street WASP power, or even just nannied babyhoods got away from office and home here to banter in the well-presented Georgian calm that has delineated the American ideal of rich respectability ever since the farmers and shopkeepers decided King George's take was unnecessary in the surprising and generous prosperity available in the New World.

Lawrence Morris, even though his name had been remodeled by an ancestor along palladian lines, was Jewish, a rarity at the Brook Club. Maybe this difference is what attracted him and Edgar Barnes to one another. After all, even though Lawrence didn't know it, under the Bulfinch bricks, Morris plasterwork and Christopher Wren columns of the name Edgar Barnes huddled the dingy Central European masses of Sonny Turchik. Perhaps this instinctively attracted Lawrence, whose own family name had often changed in travels over thousands of years, to Edgar. Lawrence Morris had befriended Edgar at first for the base reason of getting in on the syndication of Shanghai Pagoda; but when Lawrence found the surprising comic side of Edgar, as rare among this type of unemployed, well-bred WASP pretty boy as the membership of Jews in the Brook, his interest in Betty Bishop's husband came closer to real friendship. That bag of oranges Edgar had brought here for his screwdriver had delighted Morris. And Edgar's astonishing action at the Preakness went even further. It endeared him.

Edgar himself had long since felt Edgar Barnes' ancestry to be more actual than Sonny Turchik's. The story he'd concocted and embellished for the last twenty-two years stretched far back into American history. Sonny Turchik's past stopped right at its beginning in Multanomah, Oregon. All his mother ever told him about her homeland was, "The soldiers come and kill everybody."

"What soldiers?"

"With a red stripe."

"Where?"

"The old country."

"What old country?"

"Over there," she said, pointing past the old black bachelor Huggins Mayfield's shack and the railroad tracks. That was as detailed as she could get. Why couldn't Edgar's recollection of her drop away as easily as her own past had vanished?

Lawrence Morris's roots went deeper into a more luxurious

American past. His great-grandfather had changed his name, got very rich and kept a racing stable at the turn of the century. He had founded a family tradition not only of racing, but of doggedly pressing his way into the Anglo-Saxon Establishment of this profitable New World. With money and eagerness, accepting rebukes that would have driven some men to duels, the ancestor patiently, shamelessly and quite profitably ran alongside until he, nearly, and his son more certainly, became one of the pack.

Lawrence was born and raised to the purple his great-grandfather had bought. Even though it had stood up for four generations now, this purple was different from similarly purchased purples because Lawrence was Jewish. None of his predecessors, despite their courtship of the Christian Establishment, had married outside Jewry. That was difference enough to provoke the uncomfortably pleading-sounding renditions of his family's antique American racing connections Lawrence gave whenever he felt insecure.

That's why it was so awful for Lawrence Morris when Bernie Zilber appeared in the bar with a grin, a hair implant and a wave that glinted from a pinky ring against the staid paneling around him. Seeing Zilber cornering him, Lawrence felt as trapped as an asthmatic in the throes of an attack.

"Great place," enthused Zilber, patting his added hair, moving in on Edgar and Lawrence.

"Lawrence Morris, Bernie Zilber," introduced Edgar.

"Sure, see you at the races," said Zilber, shaking Lawrence's forced hand with not one, but both of his own, one of them carrying that sparkler on the little finger.

This introduction meant, of course, at the racetrack Zilber could now claim access to Lawrence Morris anytime he felt like it, a depressing prospect.

"Jews—how can they be such Hebes?" Morris had often complained to his wife, who was, like him, an upper-class Jewish woman. Here was Hebey the Hebey Jebee physically attached to Lawrence by this diamond-decorated appendage of flesh like a goddamn Siamese twin right in the Brook Club, the one place

Lawrence didn't have to contemplate the less attractive implications of his attachment to the Jewish race.

"What would you like?" offered Edgar.

"I don't know, what do Jews drink in a place like this?" asked
Zilber with a fraternal wink and pat and guffaw for the miserable
Lawrence Morris.

"I have a fresh screwdriver—Valencia oranges," suggested Edgar.

"I really just want a Coke," said Zilber to the bartender, making
himself casually at home with a handful of cheese crackers and
darting predatory glances around the place. Portraits, paneling and
tall goy financiers is what he saw. Lawrence Morris wanted to bolt
away. He and Zilber were exactly the same height, which somehow
made matters worse. Together he felt they constituted a ghetto.

"Excuse me, fellas," said Lawrence with a weak squeeze of
Edgar's arm. He headed for the bathroom livid and startled as a
man who has seen a ghost.

At a table in a corner formed of coffin-dark walnut paneling,
Edgar was startled by his guest's table manners. Bernie Zilber
avidly sucked and savored the stuff brought to them by discreet,
well-trained waiters. His use of silverware and frequent violent,
rapid napkin wiping were all the more apparent to Edgar Barnes
because they reminded him of Sonny Turchik. The self-made man
had made his own manners, too. Edgar remembered how he had
so carefully copied what the Groton Mystics did with their place
settings in mess halls and restaurants.

"So what's up, you got a deal for me or what?" asked Zilber,
licking off his fork.

"I've been thinking about fixing the Belmont," replied Edgar,
beginning not to hurt as badly now that he'd got halfway through
a bottle of wine. Zilber did a take, and then chuckled, showing he
realized this was a joke. Edgar took another sip and smiled at Bernie
Zilber.

"What are you, the funny man?" asked Bernie when Edgar's
pause continued.

"I'm serious."

"What the fuck you wanna do that for? You got the horse of the year. You got once in a lifetime."

"I won't go into my reasons. How much could we make?"

"You're putting me on, Edgar."

Edgar just kept smiling sardonically and sipping as he felt Zilber take him more seriously.

"What, you want to set me up like those schmuck congressmen?"

Edgar shook his head.

"It doesn't figure, Edgar."

"My wife wants a divorce. I don't have any money."

Bernie Zilber changed both his expression and his posture. He had been glancing at Edgar between bites, like a bird being careful of hawks. In fact he'd kept his eyes on every movement in this dining room. He was ready to get out of there first one through the door if anything funny happened. He didn't feel comfortable at the Brook Club, but he was interested and amused by the place. When Edgar sprang his proposition, the something funny Bernie was worrying about was obviously on the way, but suddenly Zilber got the feeling Edgar was absolutely serious. The motivation made sense.

This consideration changed Bernie from his wary feeding mode to his business one. He leaned back in his chair and seemed physically to have expanded. His eyes narrowed and his tongue made bulges as it worked his teeth.

"Fix the Belmont when you got the champ. This is a very, very far-out-type thing."

"How much money could I make?"

"That's what makes it so far out. You couldn't never make what you gonna get by winning. Money in this game is at the sales. It's like a fucking chain letter. Everybody's dipping in and out until it goes poo. Now the Arabs are in too. Two million for this colt, four million for that one. But you can't make those bucks back at tracks, only at the sales. There is no way purses are going to catch up with prices. Soon as a colt wins half a dozen races, he retires to stud.

Never even races as a horse. The whole fucking thing could collapse next auction because there just ain't the prize money to justify
the breeding prices. Horse racing ain't like buttons. You don't need
it. There's nothing to this game but the international fear of funny
money."

While Zilber thus editorialized to Edgar, he was calculating how
much money he could lay off, where and how. Bernie Zilber's own
entry of Napa Valley and Uncle Alex was the only one of the eight
entries who even belonged in a field with Shanghai Pagoda—and
they only belonged there as some equine background scenery for
the Chinaman. This proposition of Edgar's meant Bernie Zilber
would very likely win the Belmont, adding enormously to the
worth of Napa Valley or Uncle Alex at stud, besides whatever
betting coups Bernie could arrange. No longer an uncomfortable
tourist in the paneled and portrait-hung jaws of the Christian Establishment, Bernie relaxed. It was the Christian swimming into his
own maw now, not the other way around.

"You could come out with a dollar."

"How much?"

"You fix it so Shanghai Pagoda doesn't win?"

Edgar nodded.

"Maybe even a half million. How you gonna do it?"

"That's what I wanted your advice about."

"This is a very far-out type of thing," remarked Bernie contem-
platively.

Lawrence Morris turned his back their way when Edgar and
Bernie walked back through the bar after their lunch.

"What a putz," said Zilber on the stairs.

Nineteen

rom daybreak, horses train on the main track at Belmont Park under the scrutiny of their trainers and other interested parties, including an occasional early-rising owner. There's a behind-the-scenes, rehearsal quality to this spectacle as observers blow steam off containers of coffee with tactical expressions on their faces, and binoculars and stopwatches hanging around their necks. For a big race like the Belmont Stakes, the regular jockeys often do work normally left to exercise riders because they want to get or keep their feel for an animal that might win them ten or twenty thousand dollars for the right two minutes' work. (Showing up to ride the morning works also shows the trainer and the owner, if such is there, a jockey's sincere devotion to a particular mount.)

"Breakfast at Belmont," a ballyhoo devised by the track management to expand public interest in racing, invites fans to join the professionals at the workouts. A woman with a bullhorn narrates things for interested spectators masticating bagels and frowning at their racing forms.

When she said, "And here comes Shanghai Pagoda to breeze five furlongs," everyone went to the rail. Betty, graciously thanking people who caved away like cars pulling over to let them siren by, approached the rail with a retinue that included dear Tommy Smithers, a terribly attractive man from the British Bloodstock Agency (whose name she was kicking herself for having forgotten) and a fun man who introduced horse people to each other.

Betty had a lousy night, but at least for the moment she felt super. She wrinkled her nose at the nice smell of her new binoculars as she pulled them from their leather case. In the periphery of her vision, she noticed the glances and whispers of the public identifying her to one another. They nodded. They smiled and looked back at the track not to embarrass her. Was the queen of England's life any different?

Betty was especially aware of the terribly attractive British Bloodstock man. Well-dressed Englishmen look different from well-dressed Americans, even well-dressed Americans well-dressed in English clothes. Englishmen carry themselves differently. They shut their mouths differently, respire and open their eyes differently, button different buttons, choose different combinations and seek different angles. So attractive! Had his manhood been buggered bent in those notorious English schools? What would it be like to have him for a husband?

"Do you know how to work these?" she asked the British Bloodstock man, cocking her binoculars his way.

"Oh, yes, of course. Please, let me show you," he said fooling with them. He had attractive hands. His signet ring reminded her of what a ridiculous figure she had married.

"Better?"

"Much. Thank you."

In his fifties, no mention of any wife, wonderful manners and so attentive! What an improvement on Edgar, now getting jowly from drink and hiding most of the time. Where was Edgar living these days, under the furniture? Would they pull back a sofa and find him there, like something under a rock: moist, poisonous, groping in the unaccustomed light? Betty shuddered and returned to the more pleasant place where she actually was, getting a binocular lesson from handsome Mr. Bloodstock as Shanghai Pagoda turned to begin his morning run.

"Just give that one a twist till it's right," said British Bloodstock with a tap at the knob between the black thighs of the binoculars. What fun. Betty gave him a diamond tiara smile. He smiled back, his eyes staying on hers a tick.

"Would you like to come down to Bothwell?" asked Betty almost before thinking about it.

"I'd truly love that. Isn't Night and Day standing there?"

"Yes. And Prince Quick and Enigmatic," she elaborated. "Do come down—and bring your wife."

"No wife, I'm afraid. I'm a widower," said Bloodstock.

How romantic, thought Betty, a widower! Not just another randy old divorce misfit, but a noble widower, all brave and alone and grieving. Maybe they could be married in one of those adorable stone churches with knights incised in stone on the floor over their crypts, looking up your dress. Betty laughed at her fancy. Her breakfast of champagne with rum and a dash of bitters, one of Edgar's few good ideas, made her gay and randy. The Englishman laughed right back, as if he'd read her mind.

What fun it would be to have some real company in life. Edgar wasn't with her anymore. He never laughed with her like this. He worked against her now, a thorn in her side. She thought of all the fun she might have with this strong, gallant Knight of the Round Table.

The crowd got quiet suddenly and those who had them raised their binoculars in a mass salute to the dark hero who jumped into his run. Even with Montezuma in a black pullover and jeans instead of racing silks, with no number and no other horses alongside, Shanghai Pagoda got the kind of attention the appearance of a meteor causes.

Montezuma had a wrap on the reins to keep the Chinaman from running full out. The horse's head was up, reaching for more at every big stride. It must have been the sight of just such a horse at just such a run that made man think up horse racing.

Betty felt British Bloodstock squeeze suddenly next to her in the tight quarters next to the rail. She considered how pleasant life was at this bubbly, golden instant: her champion moving beautifully in her binoculars, a new man electrifying her entire right side, from ankle to elbow—yes! She shoved her flank into his thigh and slowly swiveled. Ostensibly to get a better view, but really to make Bloodstock feel her circumference all the way around to the front where she cocked her thighs, pushing into him. He didn't retreat.

How exciting and perfect! Betty had so many friends in England. How happy they could be there in the ancient homeland of her race with its wool and weather and roses and horses and smoky tea and smoky whiskey and handsome men in well-cut jackets. Hollyhocks grew up around Betty's door as she pushed into this new fun man, pretending it had to do with following marvelous Shang Shang's progress as he came down the stretch, tearing a rip of cheering all the way down the rail.

She kept her glasses on the horse even after Montezuma had pulled him up, standing in the irons, bouncing into the turn. Betty was using her binoculars like a mask at an eighteenth-century Venetian ball. It was such fun; neither she nor Bloodstock was doing anything noticeably indecorous in the crush at the rail, but between them, despite looking elsewhere through their black masks, their communion had become frank and intimate. Betty dropped down her binoculars and turned toward him, bearing her most dazzling smile. How awful, it wasn't British Bloodstock pushing into her, it was Edgar.

"Wasn't he great?" enthused this unpleasant surprise. Betty's smile dropped like the trapdoor of a gallows. She backed away.

"What on earth are you doing here?" she asked petulantly.

For an answer, Edgar gestured toward the horse. Shanghai Pagoda was jogging back with his gorgeous head sideways, chewing on his bit. Edgar looked through his binoculars. Betty looked puzzled at Edgar, demanding an explanation. He only smiled and patted her back.

"Perfect," gloated Tommy Smithers, holding his stopwatch with the glee of a little boy who's caught a frog.

Edgar was introducing himself to Betty's retinue. His patting hand came to rest on the small of Betty's back in a proprietary gesture. Betty stepped away from this domestic insinuation. She did so partly because it annoyed her and partly because she didn't want British Bloodstock to think she was happily married. Why was Edgar acting this way? she wondered. Was he trying to be the model husband because she'd mentioned divorce?

"How's that groom been about the drinking?" Edgar asked Tommy Smithers as they walked to Shanghai Pagoda's barn. Tommy crossed his fingers for an answer.

Harold, hosing down Shanghai Pagoda with the morning sun behind them lighting up the sprays of water like silver sparks, had gotten lots better with people since this horse had vaulted him into celebrity. He had no trouble at all greeting and joking with these swells gathered to view the champ.

Shanghai Pagoda reared, and Harold brought him right back down as Tommy Smithers' heart raced with a fright. Please let me get through the Belmont with him, prayed Tommy to God Almighty as they stood staring at the glistening colt (when the airliner had bounced scarily in an updraft coming back from Kentucky, Tommy had prayed for death to wait for him until after the Belmont).

Betty had invited everybody to lunch in town at The Four Seasons. First she would pop home for a nap and a change of clothes. The television people were all set to film her leaving the building and lunching with these horse people. She smiled, considering how her life now was busy fun. She wasn't disappointed when Edgar said he wanted to stay at the track. Was he really getting interested? Good, maybe he could get a job mucking stalls when she gave him the gate.

"Please go on ahead," enthused Edgar. They left him chatting away with Bernie Zilber's trainer.

*   *

Betty laughed at how the handbag and the binoculars had got all tangled together. When she tried to pull these wrestlers apart, they fell on the tiles of her bathroom floor. The binoculars struck with a muffled clink. It was a breaking clink, an expensive, pathetic sound that annoyed Betty so much she directed a kick at this failed object. The kick missed and Betty stubbed her toe.

"Damn you little bastard!" she shouted at the binoculars. Betty limped toward her bed.

Four hours' sleep had caught up with her. She dropped her jacket.

"A little napette," she said to her big bully of a bed, which had kept her up all night, clumsily dancing cheek to cheek after waking her up in the deepest part of night's entombment and refusing to let her get back in.

"Yes, it's Betty Bishop. May I speak to the doctor? Tim. I need a big fat squdgy shot of everything you've got because I just feel absolutely rotten and I have to be on TV in three hours." Betty suddenly began to cry. Her doctor said he would be over in an hour and a half. Perfect. It gave Betty time to have a drink and try to sleep a little before he got there.

"Why am I in this mess again?" Betty asked through her tears. After the Preakness she'd got completely drunk and ever since she'd been medicating the aftereffects of that night. She was back on everything.

Was it just a few hours ago the bright prospects of the world were all she could see? Shanghai Pagoda and British Bloodstock and the fans smiling and nodding in recognition wherever she walked? The awful waves and troughs of emotion in which she had nearly drowned had returned. Why? It had seemed so solid and sound before the Preakness. If only she could sleep. "It's not my fault I can't sleep," Betty said hoarsely, wagging her head back and forth on the front row of plumped pillows filing in front of her headboard like a foreshortened photo of tombstones. In her mind, she was apologizing directly to her horse.

"I didn't know how you make it, madame, so I brought everything," said agreeable Pilar as she set down the chemistry set from which Betty could produce a Bloody Mary. Betty sat up and concocted her cocktail.

"Just a minute," she said to Pilar, "I want you to take this all away." Betty didn't want the doctor to see she was being bad.

Glad as a girl with a rag doll, she tucked up with cute little Bloody Mary in her hands as Pilar scooted out with the evidence.

The doctor appeared with the scarifying suddenness that waking from such a flimsy sleep as Betty had managed can produce. She jumped, she felt, a clear foot above her bed.

"Sorry, Betty, how are you?" said the doctor, taking her slim, ring rocky hand in his big soft mitt. He looked at her with grave concern. He felt glands and thumped around her abdomen. She offered herself to him like a puppy to a big dog.

"You're exhausted," he said. "I've told you how dangerous it is for you to get run down like this." He loaded a needle.

"I'm going to give you some vitamin B and things."

The scary intrusion of the needle reprimanded Betty for letting herself go even as it unleashed the angelic forces of good against the seedy criminals hiding in her bloodstream.

"You've got to sleep better," said the doctor.

"Those last pills only work four hours now," answered Betty. "I just wake up feeling horrible and I can't go back to sleep."

The good doctor wrote in his Arabic script a pass to a thousand and one nights for Betty to present to her pharmacist.

"I hope when this is over you're planning on taking yourself somewhere for a good rest," he said in his fatherly timbre. He glanced at the exhausted Bloody Mary on Betty's nightstand and gave her an admonitory wince. "Betty you can't do this anymore," he said, picking up the drained drink, ugly as a bruise, "you just haven't got enough liver left. I told you what's going to happen if you don't stop."

"It's just been so hectic," Betty said ashamed. But why should she feel ashamed before her doctor? He was someone she paid to come by. The doctor left. Betty's arm hurt from the shot. Were the good goblins chasing through her bloodstream getting the pain and fatigue out of there?

"Oh, Shang Shang," she pleaded as she fell into a hot red sleep.

The TV crew called upstairs when Betty failed to appear.

"Madame?" asked anxious Pilar, big-eyed in the gloom of the curtained bedroom. Betty's eyes fluttered.

"They want to know if you is ready."

Betty pulled herself sitting. She felt horrible again. But perhaps, she hoped, not so utterly horrible as she had felt earlier. No one gives you any credit for being brave, she considered as she pulled herself together.

Betty had to call a limousine herself. Edgar had all but disappeared from life with her. He only popped up as an unpleasant surprise now and then. What was he doing out there at the track this morning? Where was he right now when he could be of some use? Couldn't he even perform his accompanying function anymore? In the elevator she imagined herself doddering alone down the sidewalk in her costly suit, glinting with jewels, feeble from fatigue. Black bucks might spring suddenly on her from city crannies, beating her, stripping and raping her and disappearing. Damn Edgar! But maybe Sir Bloodstock would fall in love with her at lunch and guard her through these unsafe modern times. Let Edgar keep disappearing. Let him disappear entirely. She could have the locks changed while he was away.

The television crew was waiting on the street to film Betty Bishop Barnes emerging from her classy building. The brilliant light on light their lamps made in the midday glare might have felled someone feeling as delicate as Betty, but she breathed a notch deeper and smiled beautifully for them. The way her champion had lengthened his stride in the stretch was running through her mind like music. Betty's infirmities and delicacies could not be entertained when she felt her tremendous responsibility as patron of a champion, recipient of a miracle, mother of Shanghai Pagoda.

The adrenaline that exalts an actress through an evening as Saint Joan despite a temperature of 102 and the disappearance of the love of her life carried Betty into the Four Seasons in triumph. As they had at the racetrack, the public whispered to one another under glances in her direction. At her table handsome men rose and smiled. She alighted among these tweed trees like a pretty bird. "Please sit down," she complained insincerely to the looming gentlemen.

"A Bloody Mary," she said to the wine waiter.

The irrelevancy of Edgar to Betty's life was reinforced by this large masculine presence at her lunch. She was the only girl. David Small-Granger, the rueful but gallantly sporting Englishman who had sold Betty her Apollonian colt, Ethelred Wimpole, as British Bloodstock's name turned out to be (would she call him Ethel or Red if they were married?). Tommy Smithers and the agreeable Carey Carlyle who functioned in the horse world as a kind of flux among owners with urges to buy, sell and syndicate were all single men, attractive enough to please any woman.

Why get stuck with one when there are many? mused Betty, feeling like her ancient royal namesake who, according to history, kept a string of lookers writing sonnets and shooting off cannons for her. Here was Betty's Essex. There was her Raleigh and Drake. Once again Betty was a queen and the crown prince in her court was Shanghai Pagoda. The chemistry of pleasing surroundings, alcohol, food and vitamin B (or whatever Dr. Bedside Manners had shot into her) brought Betty to a state of exalted confidence and happiness.

Men, like flowers, decorating every room, she considered: handsome, aromatic (wool, after-shave, tobacco and whiskey) blooms sprouting from shiny leather shoes—and a big nude one bundling her in bed!

One of them was trying to get through to her that lunch was over. Betty could write clearly always, even when her thinking and walking didn't precisely match the way everybody else did them. She added twenty percent for service and put the pencil down.

Laughing on a strong arm, Betty threw her head back, causing herself a giddy spin. Sweet little Pilar helped her get enough tack off to feel the sheets' coolness a moment before she fell into a dark sleep.

*   *

Through a crack in the stall door Edgar watched a man holding a jar on a forked stick under a sweaty colt. The man was warbling a whistle and staring at the animal's groin.

"They's trained to urinate on that there whistling," explained a track veterinarian to Edgar.

"We do urinalysis on your winner, place and show, any badly beaten favorite, bleeders, and any animal that breaks down or acts weird or anything."

In the rank darkness of the stall the vet's assistant kept whistling as he stared at the lump above his jar with the determination of a hypnotist. At last the organ flexed, the horse spread his legs and piss flashing like a drill bit in that gloom spun into the glass.

"Your urinalysis is usually enough but sometimes we do your blood too," said the freckled old vet as his assistant emerged with a lambent jar, shaking his fingers.

Edgar bought the vet a seven and seven at the grandstand bar and listened to stories of drugs, batteries and other mental and physical surprises provided for racing horses by men anxious to have an effect on the order of finish.

"They's a new one called Acupan we caught the other day. Stimulant. Goes through a horse in half an hour and don't leave a trace."

How would the public feel about their champ if they discovered he'd been pharmaceutically stimulated? Edgar smiled sardonically as a pleasant little wave of chemical mutation rose behind his own brow from the acrid screwdriver he sipped in accompaniment to the veterinarian's highball.

Switching a jar of urine that had passed through the digestive system of a horse that had a shot of Acupan for Shanghai Pagoda's own sample after the Belmont would end the dangerous nonsense of adulation that was stimulating Betty to divorce Edgar. The analogy between the glass he held at the grandstand bar and the one he would bring to the Belmont Stakes gave Edgar a chuckle.

Could it be done? A bribe to the vet's assistant should do it. Edgar reasoned a man who made the minimum wage whistling in the dark as he held a jar under horses' private parts praying for piss could probably be bought.

*   *

Like wild animals still living in a food chain, businessmen instinctively dress in colors and patterns to match the surfaces of the sidewalks, streets and skyscrapers they prowl. Among them, Edgar, in poured concrete gray, bore the proud grin of a business success as he swam into a modern elevator with a school of sharks, exiting on Bernie Zilber's floor.

"Acupan in his urine," was Edgar's mantra as he entered the Oriental jungle decor of Zilber's outer office. A handsome Filipino woman in a slit skirt dropped Edgar's name into a receiver as delicately as a camellia on the surface of a forest pool.

"He will be with you in a moment," she told Edgar in a carved ivory voice. Then she giggled and looked down.

Edgar understood why she giggled when he saw behind her, framed under glass, the poster of himself grimacing at the Preakness.

Additionally miffed to still be only of heel-cooling rank, Edgar lowered himself on an orange leather waiting room seat next to a spiky leaf and a modernistic blotch framed in brass or gold. He heard Muzak playing faintly, as if a morons' ball were under way in the next room. Edgar looked at the brown doors to Ali Baba's cave, not without a sense of recognition. Like the self-made man within, Edgar himself had come a long way. If only they knew! And yet his principal purpose in life was to make sure no one would ever even guess.

"Sorry, Edgar, how are you?" trumpeted emergent Zilber, coming through the doors in a bull elephant rush, with his arms outstretched. A two-handed handshake contained a subtle clink as their rings collided. The natty financial success gestured to the poster, hung for the occasion behind his secretary, and patted Edgar on the back, laughing in wheezes.

Zilber's office was big and, to Edgar's mind, amusingly ridiculous. Bulbous chocolate leather furniture sprung on chromium stalks from a thick carpet of the same edible-looking color. The walls were covered in bamboo grass. Some of Zilber's art was abstract and some wasn't. The representational pictures were mainly of doe-eyed Asian girls against Hong Kong harbors. Abstract expressionist mysteries, predominantly orange, formed the rest of the collection.

Bernie gestured Edgar to a brown leather bonbon and enshrined himself on a throne behind his big desk. A milk chocolate leather slab rose to the back of Zilber's skull.

The phone blinked and Bernie raised a finger to excuse himself.

"Yeah?" he said. He wrote down a tiny figure on a neat little pad with a gold pencil and hung up with no farewell.

"So, you really want to do business? You want something to drink? What would you like to drink, Edgar, maybe a screwdriver?"

Edgar noticed the specificity of Zilber's offer. He remembered those appraising eyes taking in everything at the Brook Club. Well, he wasn't about to appear alcoholic to a possible partner.

"Coffee, please—just black."

"Lana, bring us a black coffee, darling—and a Tab for me, please, sweetheart," said Zilber to a desk device.

When these beverages arrived, Edgar decided Lana's slit skirt might very well be another of Bernie Zilber's decorating ideas. Zilber's fantasy, this Oriental jungle in which he was king of beasts, was comic book clear to Edgar. Zilber's business acumen might have sharpened enough to cut his way into the big money, but his self-view still looked to Edgar like the romantic, hopeful vision of a teenage masturbator.

What had been a giggle outside from Lana now became a warm smile. She was an attractive woman. Soon, the whole world might be open to Edgar. As she departed, Edgar looked over his cup at her handsome hams seesawing the silk. The masterful feeling he got from actually beginning the enterprise that would save and enrich him flared his nostrils. He started talking as soon as she closed the door.

"I spent yesterday going through an entire day out there at the racetrack and what interested me most was that urine test they do after a race." Edgar smiled winningly at his shrewd-looking listener. He felt like Edison presenting his lamp to the capitalists.

"What struck me was the possibility of doctoring a sample and switching it with Shanghai Pagoda's—if he wins, of course—to disqualify him. There's a drug called Acupan that's going around now, a stimulant. My idea was—couldn't we run a dose of it through some horse, take a sample and switch it? The vet's assistants are absolutely wretched creatures; I'm sure we could make an arrangement."

Edgar was almost out of his seat, gesturing and glistening with his own genius until he noticed the scowl coming at him from Bernie Zilber. Edgar sat deeper into his seat and experienced a thud of doubt.

"That's shit, Edgar," pronounced Zilber in judgment. He swiveled away, leaving Edgar to flush with embarrassment.

Edgar's old fear that he lacked business skills returned. Offices represented arenas in which he had failed. His two years at one in the Bishop Bank, studying prospectuses and balance sheets and making financial decisions lost Betty a nice piece of money (her fortune was so big it was quickly regenerated, like a lizard's lost tail, but it chastened Edgar). Switches in the portfolios he'd managed had only produced similar falls in value ever since he'd first tried the casino called the stock market. At countless lunches, he'd listened to avid propositions and stories of financial triumph.

What did business-clever men have that Edgar lacked?

A man at the Brook Club who was a blatant conversational dimwit, a prosaic and tasteless dresser, married to a shrew and inhabitant of an apartment without a single possession or proportion Edgar could admire apparently couldn't miss. He read the same tarot cards as Edgar, had less capital and less inside dope and yet he bounded ahead without effort as Edgar sank.

Edgar had finally decided there was no point in his competing with these phone jockeys. After he married Betty, his homes, clothes, possessions, entertainments and travels were superior to anything any of them could ever even approximate, so why compete with them in the only area in which they had an edge? That would not only be annoying, but ungenerous, and Edgar, a twenty percent tipper, considered generosity as important an attribute of gentility as the personal bravery he remembered exhibiting in Korea.

Now Bernie Zilber, a man who had "made out like a bandit" in offices, who apparently could use telephones like burglars' tools and balance sheets like treasure maps, a man to whom Edgar's style wasn't apparent, had taken Edgar's measure and snorted his judgment in scatological derision.

Edgar blinked at the slab facing him, on the horizon of which set Bernie Zilber's implanted hair. How dare this weasel even speak to Edgar Barnes that way! Edgar had bought him lunch in a place no one else would ever take him. Edgar had shown him friendliness and a fabulous opportunity. A vulgar thug! That poster outside!

Edgar decided the thing to do was to steam majestically out, leaving this tugboat bobbing in his wake. Edgar clenched his knees and his teeth, preparing to do just this when Zilber slid back around facing him. Zilber's face was a lens of concentration.

"Can you get to him the night before the race?"

"You mean to dope him or something?"

Zilber got out of his chair and set to pacing.

"All you gotta do, Edgar, is let him out the night before the race."

"What do you mean?"

"If he runs around the night before the race, he ain't gonna run his race. We done it at Bay Meadows with some ringer, a shipper from Hollywood Park. We let him out for a little exercise the middle of the night and he come in dead last."

Now Bernie had gone from cold to warm. Edgar was getting Bernie's version of charm. The entrepreneur was at Edgar's chair, a bristly, manicured hand on Edgar's sleeve.

"Whattyou say? Can you do it?"

"Just let him loose the night before? Well, I suppose we could bribe the groom . . ."

The hand sprang off Edgar's sleeve with the speed of a fly.

"No," shouted Bernie in a sudden rage, "you don't bribe nobody —you go in and you let that black bastard out of that stall and you slap him on the butt."

Bernie changed his tone when he saw Edgar's lower lip had poked out pink with petulance.

"Look. You don't bribe people if you don't have to, get it? It's dumb if you don't have to. Other people lower your chances. The fewer the better, get it? Look, I did Bay Meadows myself, after dinner, there was nothing to it. I says to my trainer, 'I'm here, right? I never left this office'—then I left the office and went over and opened the door and that Hollywood Park horse ran his big race up and down the shedrows."

"The groom is a drunk," offered Edgar.

"Then get him drunk or something. Let the horse loose with him drunk and he takes the blame."

Now Bernie was enthusiastic and hopeful again.

"A hundred thousand and a piece of your horse," said Edgar with smooth conviction. Bernie was surprised. He chuckled and his hand landed on Edgar's sleeve again.

"I'll put some down for you. We can bet my entry from London to Mexico."

"Cash," said Edgar with bright eyes and a boyish smile. He suddenly felt tough as a tire iron himself. In fact he felt as if two bulls of some muscular species had stepped into the clearing of Bernie Zilber's jungle office.

* *

Betty made a Bronx cheer, as if she could pooh-pooh how awful everything had gotten again. She held her legs up and let them fall. The big bed gave them a refreshing bounce. She had to laugh—all those nice TV people hadn't been able to keep up with her. What the hell, they had plenty of footage. This bed was the only thing that seemed to keep up with her. Betty was bound to be all right by Friday. Saturday was Shang Shang's coronation, the Belmont Stakes. She was having a dinner party Friday night.

Even David Small-Granger was coming. That was a sporting gesture, coming to dine with the woman who'd bought a miracle from him for peanuts. Ethelred Wimpole, silly and infuriating Edgar, Jack and Nancy, Cousin Mimi and her authentic Barnes husband, Tommy Smithers with some girl and the Lawrence Morrises would all be there.

Betty raised her legs and dropped them again in the lacy, celestial gloom of her bedroom. She switched on her TV to see which four o'clock her clock was referring to. A movie could be either A.M. or P.M., and so could the cartoons on the next channel, but evangelists, vibrating tweed blanks and a national anthem, indicated Betty was awake at the bad four again. That meant it already was Friday. She repeated her earlier Bronx cheer. Could she pull herself together for a dinner party tonight and Saturday's great event? Betty was pleased to find although she was depressed, she could walk. She slipped on a beautiful, trailing gown. Now she was glad it was so late because it meant no one else was up. There was no one to cast a doubtful glance at her. "Yes, I'm the poor little rich girl," she would say if someone opened a door for a look at her. Actually, in one way, it would be handy if someone were up: sometimes those champagne corks were too hard to undo.

Luckily, two half-full bottles with stoppers in the refrigerator still bubbled. Trailing silk like an empress, or maybe more accurately like the ghost of an empress, Betty passed through her pretty rooms with a lily of fizzy gold in her long fingers. The giggling Chinese on her eighteenth-century lacquer made her laugh with them. The river on a sunny day running through her Monet made her feel the pleasant prospects of a nineteenth-century bourgeois heading out for a delicious picnic, maybe that very boat ride Edgar had denied her in London. What an elegant room this was! Betty sat in a stiff chair at a Georgian gaming table and felt fine. If only she could feel like this at dinner tomorrow. No, it wasn't tomorrow, it was tonight!

A desert requiring terrible endurance stretched between now and the arrival of her differently adjusted guests. Lucky them! They slept at night and rose yawning and brushing teeth as the bright, cheery morning shows twittered on their TVs. They worked all morning, lunched and worked again in the afternoons, or went shopping or something. Then they took baths and put on scent and evening's more luxurious clothes and had some entertainment until they started yawning again and snuggled up for enriching bundles of deep, undrugged sleep. Betty sighed. Like lace, her life was a fragile web of delicate holes. Fewer and fewer threads kept the pattern of her existence on the void.

A salty tear, warm as blood, tumbled over her knuckles. What happened to that resolve, that clarity she had entertained? If only she could go away and get everything cleared out and healthy! But there was no away between now and this evening. In fact Betty knew there wasn't any away anywhere. Even when you went there, when you went "away," you just wound up in another here.

Betty arose to recharge her glass. There was an aesthetic, sentimental pleasure in touring her beautiful rooms in her beautiful, cascading peignoir barefoot. She had assembled all this beauty.

This was her apartment, her idea. Much as Betty loved Bothwell —much as she liked all her houses—she preferred this apartment. Apartments didn't stick out for motorists to stare at the way houses did. They were magically suspended interiors you could only see out of. Nobody knew Betty Bishop was in that building when they drove down Park Avenue, the way they did passing her driveways in Maine and Virginia and Florida. The apartment was Betty's secret garden.

Betty bought everything around her here. She let inherited pieces pile up in inherited houses, but her New York apartment had been her own fun, a girl's shopping spree. Betty frowned. Really good eighteenth-century things, like the ones around her—culled and ferreted out by the best decorators—really weren't anybody's. You found them with little tags hanging off them and when you died, little tags would hang off them again. In India when maharajahs died, their possessions and servants and wives were cremated with them. When they ended, everything they possessed did too. And when people with bad taste died, the same thing happened, because nobody wanted their stuff.

But these things—for instance, this very desk had had the last laugh on all its owners, starting with its first one, Madame de Pompadour. Betty glowered at her brilliantly selected, fabulously expensive possessions. When you were really rich, nothing was yours anymore, everything was wealth's. Maybe that's why Betty loved flowers and horses best, because they died.

With her thumbnail Betty decapitated the wilting blooms on a great antenna of cymbidia sprouting out of a tuft of moss mounted on a Georgian chinoiserie tripod.

The original idea of this library, reflected Betty as she turned on its lights, was to dignify Edgar. Betty dropped on the plump, shiny, chintz cheek of a love seat and threw her head back. This old paneling was to present Edgar in a kind of grand, old-fashioned masculine dignity, like a cigar. Betty blew through a loose gasket formed by her lips around her tongue and took a drink. She'd changed her mind about this room for Edgar when she decided she needed a destination in the apartment outside her bedroom.

He was always out anyway. The estate office sent her his bills to review. He traveled and bought clothes, but as husbands went, he really wasn't very expensive.

Sitting in the library, Betty liked Edgar for a couple of minutes. With everything around her so expensively real, a cheap fake for a husband was something of a tonic. She loved the way he tried so hard to be what he wasn't.

Vain of her hands, she believed at first Edgar worshiped them because he stared at them when they dined together. Then it began to occur to her he was studying her table manners to copy. To test her theory, she started placing her soup spoon on her butter plate before the first course. Betty laughed in the library remembering how Edgar still put his soup spoon on his butter plate to sometimes quizzical looks. Maybe when she did die he'd marry again and have a son who would grow up to be a president of the United States whose self-assured custom of placing his soup spoon on his butter plate at state dinners would make it a custom throughout the Western world in the twenty-first century.

But of course there were no babies for Betty, only tags for all her valuable furniture and soon, one for her big toe in the morgue. Sorrow for her lot began its familiar course through Betty's contemplations until her considerations of parenthood brought her to remember Shanghai Pagoda. Immediately Betty sat up and thought

about her dinner party; the responsibilities of the privilege of own-
ing Shanghai Pagoda left no time for self-pity.

A fugue of time had passed with no moments. As shocked by
blanching night as Cinderella at the twelfth stroke of the clock,
Betty made for her bedroom. She caulked her curtains and entered
that pervasive bed. She set her clock for the next four and took a
sleeping pill.

She mustn't let Shang Shang down. She had promised to see him
through the Belmont Stakes. Hadn't he tried to rescue her? Of
course he was an angel—she'd seen him fly. He'd taken her up for
a look, too. He'd shown her her country and her life from the
champion's perspective. Betty felt as if she herself had beaten all
comers, as if she were her horse.

In that pure, heady air of glory everything came clear again. Get
rid of Edgar, remarry. Campaign her horse in the grand style he
deserved.

Betty made another Bronx cheer. Why should she feel so noble?
She couldn't even sleep. People with no money at all slept like
stones. Pill didn't seem to work. Day was appearing in dazzling
strings no matter how tightly she'd pulled her draperies together.

Angrily Betty marched back out of her suite and threw open
Edgar's door. Surprise! He was there. This time *she* dropped on
his feet. Edgar awakened with a guilty start. Because the crime he
had plotted with Bernie Zilber had actually begun, furtiveness had
entered his subconscious.

"What time is it?" was his first question. Betty would have
answered him if the connections between her brain and her tongue
were in working order. Apparently they weren't, so she only shook
her head, glowered and blinked at him.

"What is it?" he asked, hiking up and looking her over.

Betty's pill was making her weavy drowsy now. She wished she
hadn't come in here. One little reserve of energy popped open. She
sat up and glowered at Edgar again.

"I wanted to remind you to be thinking about divorce," she said,
pleasantly surprised by her own agility as she exited.

She felt much better retiring now. At least she'd done something.

Twenty

hat afternoon, Edgar arrived at the apartment to find the flower boys at work for Betty's dinner party before the Belmont. In fact, one of them was getting water from what Edgar thought of in this effete presence as *his* bar. He grunted at the boyish hi's and avoided snorting contemptuously at the insectile intensity with which they frittered busy as bees among the blooms. Other unfamiliar dinner party subcontractors moved about the place in white jackets. Edgar should have spent this hour at the Brook Club. He still would have had time to change quickly for the party and he wouldn't have been underfoot as the exquisites plucked up fallen petals and wired their lilies.

The sauna provided a bunker for Edgar's retreat as the party advanced upon his position on the eve of the Belmont Stakes, the eve of Edgar's great crime. Edgar looked over the familiar pink geography of his body with less dismay than he usually did recently. His figure, he decided, was robust, the right one for fifty-two. Let corporate masochists jog themselves hollow-eyed so they could slide about in their suits like poles. The true figure of fifty-two was this Edgar one, a handsome, full trunk attended by slim and muscular limbs and ruled by an admired head.

Edgar had been grinning and snorting ever since he'd hand-shaken a genuine crime into effect with Bernie Zilber. No longer an ornament, pleasing and presumed among the bibelots and Staffordshire dogs, the Chippendale and ormolu, Edgar could now consider himself another big snake gliding through the real rough-and-tumble jungle behind the chintz-thin scenery of polite society.

He'd been honest too long. After all, he'd once seen Betty herself pluck somebody else's party favor, a fifty-dollar bottle of perfume, off a place setting at a heart disease dance. Ashtray and towel thieves with the means to buy potteries and cotton mills had sat around him for twenty years. And of course the real thieves, the big ones, coursing with adrenaline as they hacked and jimmied fortunes out of others, were the popular new blood of high society.

A real-estate magnate who had lied and bribed and bluffed his way into a hundred million had explained endlessly to Edgar at dinner in Palm Springs how he supported law and order and a free market. It was a performance of self-righteousness worthy of a medieval priest hawking indulgences. How had the hundred million slipped his way if everything was in order? "Welcome, brother," said Edgar to him now as he stood up slithery with sweat in his sauna, "I'm with you."

The cold shower shattered hot Edgar. He whinnied and returned to the redwood stall for more heat.

If the horse's failure didn't fell Betty, let her divorce him. After his work tonight he would have at least half a million of his own with which to wait it out while his lawyers pried loose more. The husband of a wealthy wife must be recompensed for his time and effort. By God, he would be, too. He'd get plenty, and he'd receive it not on his knees looking up over the rim of a begging bowl, but on his feet with half a million he'd made himself in his pocket.

He flexed his hand, which he could imagine striking smoothly the latch of Shanghai Pagoda's dark stall. Would a black glove be a good idea?

Edgar showered, shampooed, shaved and hummed happy snatches of songs.

"Not many men have real linen underwear anymore," said Edgar under his breath, as he touched his monogram on this garment. Would this cloud-white shirt betray him in the dark among the barns at Belmont? The dark silk turtleneck he'd never worn would crush down to pocket size as he left after dinner. What a good idea. How remarkable the human brain is: Everything there when you need it. Of course, you have to be truly inspired.

He'd rented a car with cash so no minion might report his trip to Betty. He'd timed the last change in guards at the gates to the backstretch so the one passing him in, about to go home himself, wouldn't be able to say how long he'd been in there, even if he did happen to remember Edgar Barnes, which was unlikely. Once inside the barn area, Edgar would wait an hour, do it and drive back to town, maybe to Camilla's for an exultant celebratory thrust of his pirate sword!

The look and feel of a new blue tie with white polka dots of just the right size (amazing how easy it is to spoil such a simple formula as the polka dot) pleased Edgar to a chuckle. The new black suit was stunning. Here it was, the suit he bought for Betty's funeral, on its first outing to a different event, but one not entirely unconnected to that earlier projected debut. The work of a good London tailor doesn't look new on its first wearing. It looks like it's been there as long and magnificently as a castle.

There was a vestibule joining Betty's bathroom, her dressing room and her bedroom. Edgar tapped on its door. He opened the door when there was no response.

Betty lay on her bed, in her party clothes, emitting small, dry snores. The black prince approached the sleeping beauty.

"It's eight, dear," said Edgar kindly. He felt protective toward his own victim. He picked up her hand as she opened her eyes, startled. She twisted her body into an ungainly pose and blinked at Edgar. She pulled back her hand from his and sat up, her legs straight out like the artificial ones a beggar presents across a sidewalk next to his alms can.

"Would you like something?"

Betty nodded and jerked theatrically to her feet.

When Edgar left to prepare her drink, Betty was disappointed to find herself tottery and depressed, even though she'd had one of her doctor's "big fat squdgy shots of everything" at six. People were headed toward her. She must shine for them. Hers was earth's champion.

Her hairdresser had prepared a little takeout kit of cocaine which Betty hoped would pick her up. She closed her door and laid out vial, single-edged razor blade, and the campy cute little cerise Mexican hand mirror from the Smiler's takeout bag the stylist had provided. She rolled a twenty from her handbag and inhaled a couple of scaly little white worms. After putting all this back among the cashmere masonry of stacked sweaters in her dresser drawer, she adjusted her makeup and minced down the hall to join Edgar.

"Champagne," she commanded. She plucked a glass he had filled from his hand and went into the big room where she had passed the night.

"Pretty, pretty," she said to the flowers. A big, overblown Victorian bouquet sprawled over a lacquer table covered with eighteenth-century Chinese comic strips. She squeezed a peony like a child's happy cheek and sat rather abruptly next to this pink globe, staring at it like a fortune-teller.

A clatter announced the arrival of the first guests. The butler fronted them into the great room where the smiling couple Edgar and Betty presented a handsome spectacle of domestic grandeur. The big room was entirely lit by candles except for the little pools of light illuminating a dozen impressionist masterpieces. Among beautiful furnishings, flowers and fabrics, Betty and Edgar looked like the parents of paradise. Edgar, unusually vivid and manic, rose and bowed and handshook and kissed as the ladies and gentlemen populated the furniture.

Betty found the command of gravity was unusually stern. It threw her into chairs and tried to pull her over when she walked. People laughed and chatted as impersonally as the faces on her television. She laughed and interjected platitudes with similar disconnectedness. Form would carry her through she vowed. Only the chemicals she'd employed to help her carry off this evening weren't doing their job. How much longer could Betty bear it?

She'd got to her chair at the beautifully laid table as laboriously painfully and agonized as if the grand oval of plates and flowers and silver were a station of the cross. And there were more stations to go! Dishes came and went, Betty touched them so people would eat. Her wine was all that made any sense. At least it was wine.

An Englishman Betty didn't quite remember was David Small-Granger sat on Betty's right and came more and more into individual focus as he patiently and insistently drew Betty into an authentic communication. His identity uncovered itself slowly.

"We called him the Black Python, you know," he said, for instance. Betty laughed at this not because she understood what he meant, but because she knew most remarks at dinner parties were meant to be laughed at.

"How did you decide on Shanghai Pagoda? It's very good," he continued.

"I didn't pick him—he just picked me," was Betty's stock answer to questions about her colt's origins.

"I remember," replied the Englishman insistently. Betty smiled quizzically at this conundrum. Her pulse caused her to sway rhythmically as she stared at this man who seemed so determined to talk to her.

"He kicked down my door and ran into your arms. It was absolutely predestined."

Of course! This was the nice Englishman who sold her Shanghai Pagoda. "It's so nice to see you," offered Betty, really seeing him at last. She laid a hand on his, flexing her fingers to give her rings little carnival rides. "David," she added triumphantly as his name was handed her by a brain otherwise as quizzical as a cubist picture.

"Will I ever forgive myself?" he joked.

"He's the best," smiled Betty.

"He's probably the best of the century," enthused David Small-Granger. "I do hope you race him next year."

"Oh, yes," agreed Betty. Some sense had formed up, coupled and begun to move logically through her mind. This train was pulled, of course, by the only engine that could get through Betty's fuddle, Shanghai Pagoda.

"I do want to race him at four. I might even race him at five. What the hell, I can afford it!" she chirped. Now her posture had steadied. She even pushed a string bean through the mahogany-colored sauce and put it in her mouth. Very nice. She ate more.

"It's really a pity not to race him in England," said Small-Granger. "You know, your racing here is so bleak—just right round matching turns on the flat dirt. You Americans just want the speed don't you think? I do think our racing shows the heart a bit more."

"We'll race in England at five," piped Betty. Her fancy of an English future had recurred. Where was Ethelred Wimpole of the British Bloodstock Agency? Betty squinted around her table. He evidently hadn't been invited. Damn. Edgar was certainly animated, glittering like a little campfire down at his end of the table, keeping both Cousin Mimi and some girl goggle-eyed and laughing.

Edgar in England was a consideration Betty entertained a moment. She watched him laughing too loud for an English dinner table. He didn't seem to notice whatever joke he'd told the ladies had perished. Betty watched Edgar waving the corpse of it in his jaws like a pup wishing its victim would come back to life to provide more fun. What a fool Edgar was.

*   *

Edgar noticed Betty staring at him, swaying like a cobra. At drinks, she'd collided around the parlor like a bumper car. Edgar smiled. Pull the horse out from under her and surely she'd collapse.

The girl Tommy Smithers had brought to dinner was so cute Edgar made plans to call her as soon as he was a widower. By now he had decided Camilla's voice betrayed her whorishness. She was so materialistic. Clothes and coke and champagne and clubs—that's what she lived for. Edgar decided as a widower he would live with a beautiful young woman like this one who read novels and wanted children.

"Do you like to read?" he asked the cute girl. Dimples went on like lights when she smiled. She named all sorts of authors Edgar had never heard of. She was just the sort of thing he had in mind: adorable, but thoughtful. Yes, a touch of the intellectual was in order during one's senior period of life. They could have real conversations. He decided to investigate the possibility of courting her. "Tommy's a wonderful trainer," said Edgar.

"He certainly is," she said dutifully. Loyalty was another thing Edgar had in mind for his next girlfriend.

"Do you ride?"

"To tell you the absolute truth, I'm just not absolutely crazy about horses," she said. How wonderful. Edgar considered again how clear and progressive everything had become as soon as he'd begun to act against the forces unleashed against him by Shanghai Pagoda. She didn't even like horses! This was a sign that seemed almost directly approving of Edgar's amazing, heart-stopping plans after dinner. Blinking at his dinner partner, he saw Shanghai Pagoda running out of his stall, leaving Edgar Barnes free at last, free to frolic with the likes of this extremely cute girl in quiet splendor. Fifty-two was an age to stare from into hearth fires, turning with a bittersweet smile to gaze at this beautiful companion, reading a worthwhile novel in a chair as snow fell outside on horseless meadows.

How had he ever cared for Camilla, that coldly designing custodian of those big and inspiring breasts? This darling girl was much more appropriate for Edgar's retirement. Her breasts were small and pert and turned up. Green apples! He would keep a little place in the city, but this girl belonged in the country.

"Edgar, what's your secret?" interrupted Mimi. Edgar turned, startled, away from Tommy Smithers' date to Betty's Cousin Mimi. Did Mimi know everything? She was smiling, starry-eyed. There was no accusation in her expression, only flirtation.

"What do you mean?" asked Edgar.

"I swear you have never looked more handsome and young, you make me green with envy."

Edgar chuckled pleasantly; things were simply superb. He glanced back to Betty. She was listing. Edgar saw Small-Granger physically aiding her. Edgar rose from his chair and went to Betty's end of the table.

"I want to lie down," said Betty. "Would you please excuse me everybody?"

Promenading Betty down the hall to her bedroom, Edgar continued to feel especially well. Poor thing, like a little old lady already. Betty minced in his embrace, studying the passing pattern on the rug like movie credits.

The rest of the dinner party was abbreviated by Betty's departure and Edgar's impatient urgency to have people leave. Mimi shoved a breast into him with drunken insistence, and tried to kiss his mouth. "Good night, darling," he said with a polite implication of lust. Mimi winked and swayed out.

*   *

When he turned off the engine, Edgar's senses leaped like Dobermans at every sight, smell and sound coming from the barns. A loner with a toothpick flicking like a snake's tongue hitched up his pants and sauntered past. Edgar could feel inside himself which way the man was going to turn even before he did: left. Of course! Edgar's vivid sensory system reached around everywhere.

The black and tan colors of "The See" were painted on the shutters of the barn containing Shanghai Pagoda. Edgar stepped into shadows when he saw Harold the groom emerge into the light that hung over the shedrow's door. Harold put a finger alongside his nose and blew a tracer through the lamplight.

Edgar heard a flush and saw another stablehand emerge from another door at the end of the building. Edgar reached this toilet in five long strides when Harold turned his back.

Edgar's heart pounded and a cold sweat ringed his collar and bloomed in his armpits. This was the appropriate anteroom to crime, he considered, shutting the lid and sitting down. It was dark and narrow as a coffin on end, smelling of earth and shit. He listened to the clicks made by expansion and contraction of the lumber forming the stable.

No one would be hurt, nothing would be missing, reasoned

Edgar. It was no more damage than Sonny Turchik had done to Rich's house. He wished he'd brought a bottle in there with him. When would Harold get the hell out of there and go to bed?

Edgar jumped as a thought struck him. Leaving the light of the toilet off with the door locked was an obvious way to create the worst suspicions! He turned the bare bulb on, causing two red circles of pain to pop around his eyes which had got cool and dark as wine bottles in a cellar.

He pulled more slack in his trousers around his knees. No sense losing his crease during the crime. He had to be above all this, impeccable and superior. It was only that pure confidence of his that had buoyed him so high through life. How high? Hiding in an outhouse? How far had he actually come since the rat trap he'd fled? This can smelled as bad as his ancient home one had.

He flicked his signet ring. Would Betty stay revived even if Shanghai Pagoda lost the Belmont? He gritted his teeth and shut his eyes. Maybe he would actually have to kill her. Real things were happening now. He was physically here, sitting on a shut crapper in a new black suit, about to throw open the door enclosing the physical manifestation of his fear, about to be rid of it, the thing itself. This was real, as actual as the hard surface and earthy odors under his butt. Would Betty's demise be equally actual? Would blood flow? Would he murder her?

If he did, reasoned Edgar, balling a fist into a moist palm, it was her own fault. She's the one who decided against living, wilting into her bed with a head full of drugs. Killing her was just like unplugging the life-support system on a vegetable. He'd tried to help her, to hold her up, but she'd slumped through his grip.

Everyone knew how he'd tried, like a rescuer walking sleeping pills off someone who overdosed, to keep Betty having fun. Edgar had made sure people noticed how hard he'd tried.

He took off his jacket. As he laid it across his lap he looked in the inside pocket where Savile Row tailors discreetly place their labels. There was his name, "Edgar Barnes, Esq.," and the date he'd bought the thing.

"Keeping your figure, sir," old Pollifax had complimented him.

Edgar petted the shiny roll of fat-packed shirt above his waist. It felt slick and taut and domed as a light bulb, the fabric stretched over his booze blooming midsection. When this was finally all done he decided he would go to a spa, get lean again.

People really did think he'd tried to help Betty, too. This whole last year he'd seen approving, pitying, understanding faces when he carried crazed Betty away, when he explained he would have to come alone to the party, when he regretted that due to some business Betty couldn't make it. They knew he'd done all he could do for her. If a rich and beautiful woman couldn't face life, that was her decision. She certainly couldn't blame bad luck.

Edgar jumped and just managed not to shout when the toilet door rattled.

"Sorry," said a woman's voice. Didn't these people sleep? He heard her footsteps carry her away.

He'd been in there an hour. His legs were bloodless when he stood on them. Edgar kicked blood down through them and got his jacket back on, an awkward movement in this confinement. He resolved to sail out the door purposefully and find the horse and turn him loose. This was it, at last. The door opened like the door of an LST splashing down in the surf to release the marines. Edgar stepped into the barnyard. Things were going his way. No one was about. Harold was gone.

*   *

Inside the cube of blackness Edgar heard the big piece of life tense and throw his head. The horse butted Edgar, silhouetted against the open door. The enormous rush of power and authority Edgar had felt ever since he plunged out of the crapper continued. He grabbed the colt's halter and pulled him into the light. He read the brass plaque on the halter to make sure:

SHANGHAI PAGODA

Like a deer hit by a puma, Edgar shuddered, goggle-eyed. His neck was caught in the crook of an elbow. Legs bit into his thighs.

The horse whinnied and reared as Edgar went down, smelling Harold's winey bachelorhood, straw and horse. "Son of a bitch!" screamed Harold at Edgar. Shanghai Pagoda jumped right over them and ran out into the night.

A vicious kick from Harold knocked the wind out of Edgar. The groom ran out after the horse. Edgar was briefly unconscious. Doubled over in pain, white from shock, Edgar limped out of the stall, tripping over a sleeping bag. He slept here! The groom was sleeping in the stall! Bad luck. How could Edgar have known? In the distance Edgar could hear more and more voices joining in a spreading communication of English and Spanish. Little posses formed up and ran around corners like keystone cops. Edgar sped from shadow to shadow, crouched panting in pain every time he got cover. Just as he dashed for his car, the horse came thundering straight at him. Shanghai Pagoda knocked Edgar over and hit him with a hoof. Edgar rolled under his car, fainting from a pain in his chest, but stifling his moaning as voices and shoes and flashlight tore past the low iron horizon.

Ripped, scuffed and bleeding, Edgar drove out of the barn area crouched as low as he could get at the wheel. Past the barnyard gate, Edgar sat as high up as pain allowed and speeded up toward the polka dots of car headlights on the black highway. There was escape. Held at the gate to the public road by traffic, Edgar glanced in his rearview mirror. Like a demon bent on Edgar's destruction, Shanghai Pagoda was running toward him again. Edgar lurched onto the highway. Metal bashed and glass broke around him, but his car was untouched. The horse caught up with him. Tires howled and the din of metal on metal clattered on all sides as if Edgar were a knight in a battle of armor. Shanghai Pagoda reared and came down on Edgar's hood, which popped off, bent up like a potato chip.

Men arrived as distant cars honked, ignorant of why the traffic had frozen. Harold got to the horse's halter. Edgar threw an arm in front of his face to hide his identity and drove over his fallen hood, dragging shrieking metal as he floored it down the road shoulder. Before he disappeared down the entrance ramp of the parkway, he looked back. They had the horse, but he was plainly ruined.

*   *

Betty awoke suddenly and utterly. She was on her feet before she considered it. She sat back on the bed that had flung her to the floor and picked up her clock. Of course it was four in the morning. It always was. She slammed the clock down as though time were its fault.

There was nothing she could do about being so relentlessly awake, so she put on a robe and hoped she could find a bottle of champagne with an easy cork.

She was staring at a cloud of puffy white stock in a vase on the piano when she heard the front door being unlocked and entered. Betty stepped behind a drapery, surprisingly calm for someone expecting to see a band of burglarizing black rapists enter her home. Edgar!

He appeared to have been in an accident. Rents in his black suit flashed contusions on the white skin beneath. Blood was spattered on his shirt and matted in his hair. He was doubled over, breathing desperately and white with shock.

Betty ran to him, crying, "Edgar, what happened?" He held up his hand as if he expected a blow and made for his room with the gait of a belly-shot moose. He locked himself in there. Betty was baffled. She knocked.

"Edgar?"

There was no answer.

*   *

Edgar was sure he'd had a heart attack. He had barely made it. The pain he felt was so acute and exhausting he couldn't even consider the implications of Betty having seen him. He could only count each breath as a victory over encroaching oblivion.

*   *

"I think I seen him somewhere but I can't remember," said Harold to horrified and desperate Tommy Smithers as the trainer ran his hands over Shanghai Pagoda.

"It was dead dark and he had on black clothes."

By some miracle, nothing seemed broken. Nothing had swollen much yet. Harold had dressed the cuts and rubbed the colt calm.

"Best he gets some rest now."

Tommy couldn't make up his mind whether Harold was the hero or villain of the horror show just concluded. He wasn't drunk and others had said they saw somebody around the barns. Who did it? Who was it? Who tried to ruin Shanghai Pagoda?

* *

Edgar awoke ill. His limbs were heavy and oversensitive. His chest ached. Bruises rang bells all over his body. He had not expected such suffering. When he opened that stall door, a demon had got loose. At least it was done, all done now.

Edgar decided he had to get to a doctor.

"A gypsy cab ran broadside into us and took off," said Edgar to Betty at breakfast. She looked a little shaky herself.

"Why didn't you go to a hospital?"

"I didn't think it was that bad. I hate hospitals."

"Please don't start suing people," asked Betty.

"What?"

"I hate it when they put people's name in the paper suing people. It's always so cheesy."

"I'm not going to sue anybody."

"Good."

"Maybe I better go see a doctor," said Edgar more casually than he felt.

"Where were you, anyway?"

"We all went out to a nightclub after dinner."

Because Edgar had always been surreptitious, his morning lies didn't arouse Betty's suspicions unduly. She knew if she asked him more questions he'd probably wind up elaborating on his mythical family tree again, something Betty could do without the day Shanghai Pagoda ran the Belmont Stakes. If Edgar was fluffing some little idiot's feathers and falling downstairs or something, Betty didn't want to know about it on a sacred day like this one. Let it come out in lawyers' offices when she cut him loose.

He looked a little ghastly, Betty noticed. Something must have gone wrong for him. She smiled at Edgar, who was staring at his coffee as if it were a scorpion. Isn't it just *too* bad, thought Betty sarcastically. Besides, she didn't feel that great herself.

Twenty-one

hat's the matter?" asked Betty with shock. Shanghai Pagoda was covered with cuts. The strange little groom stared at her like a spectator at an execution. Tommy Smithers' face was wrung by anxiety.

"He got out last night," said Tommy.

"Somebody loosed him on me," piped up Harold. "I jumped him but he had the door open and when I run after the Chinaman he got away. I couldn't see him but he was somebody and I can't exactly remember but I'm trying." Harold had the uncomfortable sense no one believed him. After all, they never had.

"Oh, my God," said Betty. She touched her horse. He rolled back his lips and craned his neck her way.

"Shang Shang," she cooed.

"I think we should scratch," said Tommy Smithers, amazed to have spoken that unspeakable sentence he'd carried in his mind all night. There is only one Shanghai Pagoda in a trainer's career, only one chance like this at a Triple Crown, but how unfair and cruel it would be to watch a champion lose unjustly, perhaps even break down from some undetected injury got dancing with cars on the highway. How could this have happened? Who did it? Tommy wished he could beat whoever did it to pulp, to death, mercilessly with a pipe, or a hammer, or an ax.

"Is he hurt somewhere?" asked Betty.

"He seems sound and his temperature's normal."

"And he ate up a real good breakfast," said Harold, patting the battered horse.

"Let's not scratch him, Tommy. Everybody wants to see him."

"He's not going to win today, Mrs. Barnes, and it's not fair to let him lose. He's the real thing." Tommy had a lump in his throat. Harold kept stroking the horse like a buddy trying to keep a wounded soldier from dying.

"But the president's coming," said Betty. "And the TV—everybody's here to see him."

* *

Edgar decided the Turf and Field Club, a glassed-in preserve at the top of the stands, was the best place for him to watch the Belmont Stakes. A private room that little stablehand would never be allowed to enter, with a bar and upholstered chairs, was the place for a man in pain and danger. Bernie Zilber gave Edgar fifty thousand dollars in cash and fifty thousand dollars' worth of tickets across the board on Zilber's entry from off-track betting parlors and English turf accountants. It was much less exhilarating than Edgar expected.

* *

Even though those who knew what had happened to Shanghai Pagoda the night before tried to keep the news to themselves so they could arrange their own betting coups, rumors began to spread. Reporters appeared at Shanghai Pagoda's barn. They asked:

"Did anything happen to him?"

"Are you going to scratch?"

"Can we see him?"

Tommy ordered them off. No one was allowed near his barn. One of the Chinaman's eyes had a swelling over it. He looked like a kid come home after a schoolyard scrap. When Harold led him on his fateful trip to the saddling paddock, he heard people gasp.

The reporters were working themselves into a news frenzy. Tommy wouldn't answer their questions. Betty Bishop Barnes only said,

"He had a little bump," and turned away when they probed further. A television team followed her like blackamoors holding parasols and fans in an empress's retinue.

"What happened to him?" asked the horsey interview girl, chagrined her documentary might be spoiled by a poor finish.

"Something about a gypsy cab," answered Betty mysteriously. Betty had taken a little refreshment to get through the big day. It had an effect on her logic as well as her spirits, but she needed it. She hadn't had much sleep. Things hurt. She was going to do whatever was necessary to see her black beauty through.

The odds on Shanghai Pagoda went from even to 3–1 as soon as he appeared in the walking ring. Montezuma was shocked when he saw mortality all over his god. Harold put his life's savings on Shanghai Pagoda to win, but even this spurt of five thousand dollars didn't pull the odds back. He was 5–1 when he stepped onto the racing surface.

"Gentleman wants you to have this here champagne," said the bartender to Edgar. Bernie Zilber winked from across the room. Edgar smiled ruefully and asked the bartender to put a little orange juice and bitters and rum with it.

"Are you all right, Edgar?" asked the last sort of person Edgar imagined would inquire after him, a caustic, lecherous old blonde.

"Late night," he winked back. She grinned as if they'd spent it together and returned to a young Mexican at her table. The wads of money and tickets in Edgar's jacket and trousers felt like tumors. It was such little money and so sordid. Edgar felt a big gray-green toad of bills in his pants pocket. No one else in the Turf and Field carried such money. These other people chatting and drinking and perusing racing forms were wealthy. They'd long ago broken through the money barrier of actual cash to float free in the rarefied atmosphere of ownerships so vast they were incalculable abstractions.

Fifty thousand in cash and fifty thousand in tickets might as well be live tenement rats running around in Edgar's clothes. His chest hurt terribly, especially on stairs. Luckily, his bruises and cuts all fit under his clothing so if he could keep his face painless and enthusiastic, no one would know he wasn't feeling as cheerful, rakish and dashing as his checked jacket. Congratulatory greetings clasping at his arms and pressing his back raked across abrasions. He tried to turn his winces to grins and fit gaily in with the excited, eager company drawn toward him by his affiliation with Shanghai Pagoda.

"We're so excited for you." beamed a gigantic mouthwash heiress.

"Good luck, Edgar," grinned an athletic financier with a gouging grip at Edgar's raw shoulder.

Across the room Bernie Zilber chuckled and nodded rapidly when Edgar looked his way.

"Jesus, what happened? He looks terrible!" said a voice behind Edgar. Edgar grinned broadly and turned to show nothing was wrong, but he saw the man, a stranger, was looking not at him, but through a pair of binoculars at the post parade, the first appearance of the entries for the Belmont Stakes on the racing surface.

In the bonhomie rising public excitement can create at sports events, the stranger handed his binoculars to Edgar.

"Look at Shanghai Pagoda. He looks like shit," marveled this stranger.

Edgar got Shanghai Pagoda in focus as if he were an assassin looking through a telescopic sight. The colt's coat was splotchy. His head was misshapen. Knots of bruises speckled him.

"We look about the same," Edgar almost muttered. It was too bad about the cuts and swelling. Had he only run around blowing off energy instead of banging around on the highway, no one would know he wasn't fit and the odds on Zilber's entry would have stayed up. Edgar pulled the glasses down as if he could pull the horse out of existence. He didn't want to have to look at this thing, this nemesis which kept returning to torment him. Why hadn't they simply scratched the wreck?

He raised the glasses again. Edgar couldn't stop watching the beast, now jogging with his dark head turned into the spotted neck of an Apaloosa lead pony as if he were confiding accusations about Edgar to the other animal. Pats perfectly placed over a throbbing bruise on his forearm caused Edgar to cry ouch. It was the stranger wanting his binoculars back.

Without binoculars, the horse was tiny as a fishing fly complete with the silk dab of black and tan behind his mane. Edgar couldn't take his eyes off him. Shanghai Pagoda had him hooked. Edgar felt his fate reeling him taut to his harmed horse. It was hard for Edgar to breathe.

"Won't be long now," grinned another congratulatory acquaintance, patting Edgar on the back right where a cracked rib stabbed him with pain.

The flagellation continued wherever Edgar walked. He was leaving the Turf and Field Club before he realized his destination. As inevitably as Shanghai Pagoda was being led to the starting gate, Edgar entered the elevator that would take him down a couple of stories, across the betting floor, past the guard and down the aisle to Betty's box. It was perfectly safe, of course. The little bastard hadn't really even seen him. Anyway grooms no more sat in owners' boxes than stokers sat at captains' tables. Still, Betty felt like danger to Edgar in another way. An ominous excitement grew in him heading for her, like the thrill felt by a suicide finally walking toward the Golden Gate Bridge.

"My real name is Sonny Turchik and I let out the horse last night because I thought if he lost you might get back to dying. Plus Bernie Zilber gave me fifty grand in cash and another fify in tickets on his entry to do it. It's your fault, Betty—if you hadn't decided to divorce me . . ."

The urge to blurt out this confession made Edgar giddy. His pain vanished and his step lightened. The grin on his face was sincere and radiant as he picked his way through well-wishers' smiles to the Bishop Stables box.

Tommy Smithers had just brought Betty back to the box from the saddling paddock. A professional at blending in and out of groups of horse owners, Carey Carlyle at once left the crowded Bishop box for another to make room for Edgar. Betty was surprised to see him. The level of noise and excitement, the distraction of loading the starting gate and the flare and flash of media lights made Edgar's overwhelming desire to confess like the unbearable frustration of those dreams that hurl the sleeper back into consciousness from insoluble dilemma.

"What? I can't hear," Betty kept signaling like a charade player as Edgar pulled her close.

"I did it!" he shouted at her. She only looked hopelessly confused as he gripped her thin wrists, repeating, "I did it."

She pointed to the horse as his meaning occurred to her. Edgar nodded eagerly, glad she knew. Betty looked astonished at him. Then some calculation visibly took place. Edgar expected fists trotting over him, then the arms of guards, expulsion and Sonny Turchik's return, the traumatic resumption of a life he'd deferred for twenty-five years. Instead of judgment and punishment, Edgar only got postponed. The flag was up for post time, all eyes aligned on the start of the Belmont Stakes.

The big metal contraption from which horses start was spread across the track right below them. With brutal mechanical clumsiness all the doors opened simultaneously with a guillotine clang and the racers jumped out. Shanghai Pagoda went straight to the front, leading the mob into the first turn with Napa Valley for company. These two drew away through the turn, causing Bernie Zilber to curse his rider for letting Napa Valley go too fast too soon. Tommy Smithers wasn't angry his horse was going so fast, he was sad. The one sight he considered worst in all the world would be to see Shanghai Pagoda fade. This was too great a horse to be passed by his lessers on a great racing day. Too fast. When would the awful deceleration begin? Now they were a dozen lengths in front of the rest.

That brutal, jackhammer stride Montezuma remembered in his last two races wasn't happening this time. There was something light and heavenly and even giddy in the way the Chinaman was running. He floated farther ahead, like a bubble coming up through a flute of champagne. Napa Valley had dropped off as Montezuma's angel curved into the turn on the hoofbeats the rider later said he couldn't even feel.

"He's doing it!" shouted Tommy. He and Betty jumped into each other's arms. Shanghai Pagoda's huge, scalloping stride carried him down the stretch all alone, triumphant. When he passed the wire, Montezuma shot straight up in the irons and held his whip up in a salute that was answered with a gorgeous and mysterious roar from the most private and personal part of everyone in the crowd.

*   *

Betty laughed and laughed in the winner's circle. Everyone grinned and glittered in the media light. Then Harold jumped on Edgar.

"It was him!" he shouted, punching. Handicappers to a man, it was clear to the guards who was the criminal in the unseemly and shocking scrap rolling right under the legs of the champion. They hauled off the insane groom and picked up the gentleman, who had gotten astonishingly bruised and beat up for such a brief struggle.

Betty and Edgar stood staring at one another. Betty began to laugh. She went up to her bruised husband and gave him a kiss.

"I get it," she said.

Edgar was astonished into a painless state again. Lights were too bright. Only Betty, of course, could have understood. Betty was the standard against which Edgar measured his whole life. To think he'd almost lost her, and how he'd betrayed her only made her more intensely darling in the nearly unbearable wave of pain that swept through him. He stepped toward her. Her eyes were right on his at the end.

At the funeral, Edgar was in his dark blue pinstripe because his black suit had of course been ruined.

Afterward, at the reception or wake or whatever the strange event could be called (a bar and a pianist playing tunes of the thirties made it not a lighter, but a queerer occasion), people who hadn't seen each other for years took one another's measure and people who had seen one another for years exchanged some remarks about the deceased, but talked mainly of other things.

Lawrence Morris was the only person to cry. Too much of Edgar's champagne and rum and orange juice with a splash of bitters made him sentimental.

"We're older than we think," he said to Tommy Smithers.

"Fifty-two is so young."

Everyone agreed that Betty had carried off the whole thing with dignity and grace. To have it happen right there in the winner's circle must have been a terrible shock for her, but it was in the winner's circle at the Preakness where Edgar had done something funny that other time.

Many people pointed out if you did have to die so young, it was at least a quick death at a happy moment. As Mimi told Betty, "Edgar must have gone to heaven with a smile."